A small

Bare stone floors, graying whitewashed walls and a single narrow cot covered with a drab blanket. Beside the bed, a wooden chair and, on its seat, a new candle, matches and a jam jar filled with fresh daisies.

Sue-Ellen stumbled and took a few steps inside. She struck a match, lighted the candle and jumped when shadows shot, dancing, over the walls and ceiling.

The air smelled of incense, and she saw a small glowing spill upright in a holder that stood in a niche like the one in the next room.

Then she saw the marks, scratched numbers in rows. She made out recorded days from 1922 and 1923. The numbers had been made not with pencil or pen but with something sharp that scratched through the whitewash to the dusty stone beneath. And beside the numbers something . . . red. No, rust, something once red turned to rust, like old bloodstains . . .

ABOUT THE AUTHOR

Stella Cameron is a multitalented author whose decision to write romance and romantic suspense came in 1981 when she went back to school to study creative writing and literature. She is constantly inventing stories about people. And as she herself admits, "I'm an incurable lover of people, of words, but above all, an incurable romantic." Stella makes her home in Bellevue, Washington, with her husband and three children.

Books by Stella Cameron

HARLEQUIN INTRIGUE
50–ALL THAT SPARKLES
83–SOME DIE TELLING

HARLEQUIN SUPERROMANCE
185–MOONTIDE
340–ONCE AND FOR ALWAYS

HARLEQUIN AMERICAN ROMANCE
153–SHADOWS
195–NO STRANGER
226–SECOND TO NONE
243–A PARTY OF TWO
268–THE MESSAGE

A Death in the House

Stella Cameron

Harlequin Books

TORONTO • NEW YORK • LONDON
AMSTERDAM • PARIS • SYDNEY • HAMBURG
STOCKHOLM • ATHENS • TOKYO • MILAN

For my father Peter Lloyd-Worth:
a Dorset gentleman

Harlequin Intrigue edition published February 1989

ISBN 0-373-22107-X

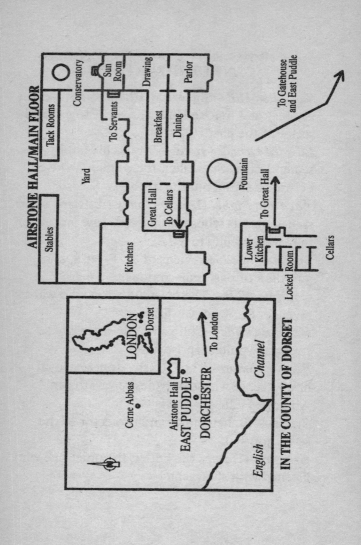

AIRSTONE HALL/MAIN FLOOR

Stables

Tack Rooms

Conservatory

Sun Room

Drawing

To Servants

Breakfast

Dining

Parlor

Yard

Great Hall

To Cellars

Fountain

To Gatehouse and East Puddle

Kitchens

Lower Kitchen

To Great Hall

Locked Room

Cellars

IN THE COUNTY OF DORSET

LONDON

Dorset

Cerne Abbas

Airstone Hall

EAST PUDDLE

DORCHESTER

To London

English

Channel

CAST OF CHARACTERS

Sue-Ellen Hill—She was destined to unravel the mystery at Airstone Hall, and piece together the secret of the past.

Edward Ormsby-Jones—Would his family secret destroy Sue-Ellen, the woman he loved, before he found out the truth?

Alice and Mabel Ormsby-Jones—Edward's two spinster aunts whose catlike eyes saw more than they were willing to tell.

Michael Bastible—Vicar of St. Peter's, and guardian of past indiscretions.

Colin Bastible—The reverend's son who wanted revenge. But who was his victim?

Helen Bastible—Colin's fragile sister whose strength would surprise all.

Bea Smallman—The Ormsby-Joneses' loyal housekeeper whose only desire was to run Airstone Hall.

Sylvia—Kitchen maid, and protector of the secret journal.

Grossby—He was the butler, the quiet one who listened with sharp ears.

Prologue

February 17, 1923

Her breath made beads of moisture that drizzled over the stone walls. Thin running lines, dripping, darting, joining...like blood from a wound.

How long had she been here? Her mind slid back: days, weeks and months. All mixed up now. If she forgot, no one would ever know how long she'd been a prisoner in this cellar room.

The light flickered. A candle, gummed into its base by clots of wax, stood on the ground. *Please don't let the candle go out like it did those other times.*

She should hum. When she hummed she could pretend that she wasn't alone, that a gentle hand brushed back the matted tangles of her hair and smoothed sweat from her brow. The room was cold, so cold, yet she sweated. They must be right, those who had brought her here. She was sick, very sick, and if she wasn't careful she'd have to stay locked away forever.

The shadows shouldn't do that. They shouldn't crawl over the ceiling, such a low ceiling, like giant rising arms, hands twitching. The shadows were part of it. The shadows were sent to watch her, to keep her in the narrow cot with the damp blanket clamped to her neck. If she pulled the blanket over her head the shadows couldn't see her face, but the blanket smelled of mold, like the room. And she made the mold...of her own breath.

There came the footsteps—in the tunnel outside. It was a tunnel, wasn't it? A passageway winding down beneath the earth, darker and darker? She did remember coming here, the grim face of the woman who had brought her, the promise that if she was good she would be allowed to leave at the right time.

She sat up. The scraping came. The handle turned. Maybe today she'd smell fresh air. Maybe today the key wouldn't grind in the lock, shutting her in again. Alone.

The woman entered, a tray in her hands. "Still tired. Such a pity. And I'd thought you were young enough to recover. But perhaps I was mistaken."

No words of reply would come. So much to be said, but no words.

"You should get up. If you don't walk you'll never get strong enough to go home. You do want to be better, don't you? You do want to get away from here? You're too weak to go anywhere yet. Who knows, perhaps you'll always be too weak."

"No!"

But the woman wasn't listening. She cracked the metal tray down on uneven gray flagstones and turned to retreat.

"No! I'm well. I'll be good. Let me go."

Laughter. The woman's laughter, blotted by the thick door thudding shut, jarred every bone.

Her own scream rent the air. And another and another. Her throat closed.

Walk, don't stay still. She pushed to her feet, arms outstretched until she reached a wall. Eight steps to the first corner. Ten steps to the next. Eight. Ten. Eight. Ten. Dizzy, she slipped to the ground behind the door.

Now she knew the truth. They'd lied from the beginning. Walk, they said, but they didn't want her to walk. Don't get weak, they said, but wanted her to get weak.

They wanted her to die.

Footsteps. They were coming back. She pulled up her knees beneath the faded woolen dress, curled over, shrank down. She hadn't died yet and that had made them angry. So they were coming back.

This time they all came: *him* and the woman and the other man; the children. The children of Airstone Hall had come, too, all but the true heir, the one who belonged there more than the rest. They'd come to see what happened when you weren't good.

"You didn't eat," the woman said. "I was right, you don't want to get better."

"She doesn't want to get better," the husband agreed, shaking his head. "She knows she can never be forgiven for wanting what she cannot have. Imagine, she thought she could be mistress of this house."

"Imagine." The woman sighed. "She didn't know that she wasn't good enough to take a lady's place."

"Imagine, imagine," the children said.

And the man stroked his chin, "Perhaps it's time."

The children nodded, and so did the other man.

Kneeling, the woman pushed the tray, clattered it nearer. Candlelight gleamed dully on congealed porridge in a thick white bowl. "You don't want your porridge?" she asked and picked up the bowl, smashed it. Globs of gray mush fouled the woolen dress, splattered the wall. "But," the woman continued, "you do want this," and she held out a piece of broken pottery, jagged as a mutilated knife.

They came close, bowed over her, lifted her until she was stretched on the cot, arms held aloft in unyielding hands.

"Do it. Do it."

And the blade edge came down, again and again.

LIGHTNING, SHATTERING the evening sky beyond the window, jolted her. She stirred and sat more upright in her wing-backed chair. The images from more than sixty years ago had come again, not that she minded, for she was the guardian of the girl's story, the one destined to avenge her death.

Stiff, she got up slowly and arched her back. There were others who knew the evil that once took place in this house.

What they didn't understand was that they were completely in her hands. She controlled their destinies and always would.

Her reluctant ally was late for their meeting. As she thought it, the door opened and a tall figure entered. She saw him grope for the light switch.

"Don't turn that on."

"It's dark."

"Exactly." The man was a fool. "No one must know we're here. Come in. Shut the door."

He did as she asked, moving slowly, feeling his way. "What is all this? Why the summons to appear?"

"Go to the window," she commanded. "Tell me what you see."

"Why—"

"Do it." There could be no holding back. Her plans were threatened and, if necessary, that threat would be removed.

She followed him, stood beside him while he peered down toward what had once been the stable yard.

"I don't see . . . A flashlight? Two flashlights?"

"How observant of you. It's her."

He shifted, put his face closer to the glass. "Sue-Ellen Hill? Who's with her?"

"A contractor. Apparently she never stops working, day or night."

"Ah yes, of course." He laughed and another crackle of lightning slashed, throwing white light over his aloof face. "Our enterprising American is very determined. Nothing stops her, does it? Rain nor sleet and all that. Bit like the post office."

"I assure you this may be no joke. She isn't what I expected. She doesn't understand how the English think. And she's ambitious, controlling."

"And that worries you, doesn't it? You weren't prepared for an efficient interloper."

She ignored the barb. "I blame you for this."

"I beg your pardon?"

"You could have influenced Edward's choice. Persuaded him not to bring a foreigner to England sight unseen. He listens to you. I had no idea he'd employed such a young woman."

"It probably makes no difference."

Her head ached. "But it could. She could. She's the type who goes after what she wants."

"And you're afraid she may decide she wants Edward? And this beautiful Elizabethan house that goes with him, perhaps?"

Yes, she thought. Yes, dammit, she was afraid of that. She said, "A man would have posed no threat."

Treading silently on soft old carpet, he moved around the casement to get a better view of the bobbing lights. "Tearooms," he said and laughed. "Tearooms in the old tack rooms. She's resourceful, I'll give her that. I thought she was supposed to turn part of Airstone into a hotel, nothing more. But our Edward got a bargain. She's positively bubbling over with money-making ideas."

She trembled. Rage made a blackness in her brain. Moving closer to the window, she stood, partly behind a drapery. "Why do you find this amusing? We all stand to lose. Only I won't allow it."

He moved restlessly and asked, "Why should we lose? What are you really afraid of?"

Practice had taught her the questions to ignore. Pretending not to hear, she concentrated on the yard below. Behind one of those moving flashlights was Sue-Ellen Hill, aged twenty-seven, of Augusta, Georgia. She would be gesturing excessively, her voice rising and falling with that appalling enthusiasm and that awful drawling accent. She had a pleasant face. The pale blue eyes were arresting, the collar-length hair vibrant, if unremarkably tow-colored, but she was common, completely unsuited to an administrative position on this estate.

"She isn't pretty, not really pretty," she said, thinking aloud.

The man cleared his throat. "Many would find her appealing. Wholesome. Beautiful skin . . . and figure."

"Too heavy," she responded and folded her hands behind her back, wound them tightly together. "Not Edward's type. He prefers diminutive, quiet women. And he'd never get involved with an American. Not that he's spending much time on his private life lately. His law practice is all that really interests him since Lenore. That and making sure this place operates successfully with as little effort as possible on his part." She closed her mouth firmly. Enough had been said to get her message across. No need to show all her hand.

"Diminutive and quiet, hmm?" Amusement was in his words again. "Did you have someone in mind?"

"Interpret what I say in any way you please," she told him. "But for Miss Hill's sake, pray Edward isn't fool enough to notice her as more than an employee."

"Edward's romantic inclinations don't concern me. But I suggest he's not a fool at all. He wanted someone who could turn part of this architectural albatross into a successful commercial enterprise, and he appears to have chosen well."

Why couldn't men see the obvious? Edward might not be interested in the Hill woman, yet, but that could change. "He should have been making enough money from the house being open twice a week in the summer. That and the sale of the Yorkshire estate would have carried him for years. How could he make half of his family home into an obscene boardinghouse?" She paused, selecting her next words. "Who does she remind you of?"

His head turned but she couldn't see his eyes. "I don't follow you."

"She reminds me of . . . She's like Lenore." There, now it was in the open.

"No." His elbow caught a drapery and brass rings clattered on their rod. "She's nothing like Lenore."

"Are you sure? There's no physical similarity, but there is something familiar. Lenore was a controller, too. She knew what she wanted and she almost got it."

The sound of his indrawn breath came, then slowly a hissing through his teeth. "I think Edward's engagement is something we'd better not discuss."

"Oh, but I disagree. It's quite appropriate."

He passed her, brushed against the chair. "It may be six years since it happened, but I haven't forgotten the horror, and I doubt if Edward has. Good night."

"Go," she told him, "but remember what I expect of you."

"I owe you nothing."

"You owe me whatever I say you owe me. Unless you're ready to give up more than I think you are."

He stood still. "Are you threatening me?"

"Lenore didn't get what she wanted, did she?" The words, the memory, gave her pleasure. "Or that silly little Jenny before her."

"Finish what you have to say."

"In good time," she said. "When I'm sure you fully understand. Why didn't Lenore become Edward's wife?"

"What are you saying?" He gripped the chair. His fingernails scratched coarse damask.

She let silence slip in before she said, "Lenore died. Sad, wasn't it? Dangerous animals, horses."

"It was an accident," he said, but his voice faltered.

"Of course it was an accident. I was merely remarking on what a shame it was that Edward's fiancée didn't live long enough to take her place at his side."

"Are you suggesting . . . ? I can't believe you would—"

Her timing was perfect. "Just do your part to make sure my plans aren't interfered with."

"And if I—"

"No." She would always win. "No, there will be no if. I deal in certainties."

"What are you asking of me?"

He knew, but he would pretend to the last. "Sue-Ellen Hill won't be here long. Her project will fail and she'll leave. We will both work toward that end."

"We can't be sure she won't succeed regardless."

"Listen to me—really listen," she said. "With or without her decision to do so, Sue-Ellen Hill will leave."

Chapter One

"Now?"

"Yes, miss. They want to see you at once. They're waiting. Oh, dear, I couldn't find you anywhere." Connie Butters, upstairs maid, spoke in breathy bursts as she urged Sue-Ellen through the front door and up the broad sweep of staircase leading to the second floor of Airstone Hall. "Miss Mabel and Miss Alice won't be pleased. They won't be pleased at all."

"Why?" The Misses Ormsby-Jones were her new employer's aunts. In the ten days since Sue-Ellen had arrived in Dorset, one of England's southern counties, she hadn't seen either of the ladies . . . or her boss for that matter.

Connie stopped a few steps above her and turned around. Her brown eyes were bright with anxiety. "Oh, miss, they do expect their wishes carried out. If they aren't, the fur flies, I can tell you that. Take my advice and don't cross them." She'd come outside to find Sue-Ellen just as driving rain joined fierce lightning. Now, backed by a row of gloomy oils—portraits of men in satins and plumed hats, pale women with rosebud mouths and rounded bosoms— the maid, her limp brown hair plastered to her head, appeared pathetic and out of place.

Sue-Ellen smiled. Saying she didn't give a damn what the old women thought would only spook the frazzled Connie more. "Thanks for the tip. And don't you worry, Connie.

I'll explain that I was talking to a contractor and you had a hard time tracking me down."

That mollified Connie. She returned the smile with a slight one of her own and hurried on. At the top of the stairs she turned first right, then left. Her metal-tipped heels clacked on bare and warped wood that sent up a strong odor of lavender wax and the dust it attracted. Another left turn and up three more steps to a broader corridor.

The paintings stretched endlessly beside them, and various heavy chests, curio cabinets and stiff couches covered in needlepoint scenes faded into obscurity. Dim light from high wall sconces spread dull circles only slightly paler than the shadows that lurked between. Sue-Ellen shivered and crossed her arms as she walked. A hot bath, even in the antiquated bathroom that was part of her otherwise charming suite, would have been her first choice after leaving the bone-chilling storm. With that thought, another crack sounded and a spear of brilliance pierced a high leaded window, sending eerie prisms over the opposite wall.

A gruesome night. But, Sue-Ellen reassured herself, just the kind of night to fascinate any history-hounding American tourist who chose to stay here. If she had her way, Airstone would become the most celebrated bed and breakfast in England. The raw material was certainly here—and it was certainly very raw at the moment.

Connie stopped outside a door and waited for Sue-Ellen to join her. Rising to her toes, she turned the handle and waved Sue-Ellen into the most overwhelmingly oppressive room she'd ever seen.

"Wait here," Connie hissed, and went through another door covered by a plum-and-green brocade curtain.

Sue-Ellen looked around, wrinkling her nose at the cloying scent of some stale floral perfume. Carved wood, more expanses of the terrible brocade, tall marble-topped tables on spindly legs, rows of shelves fronted with glass and lighted inside, chairs with wooden legs and embroidered seats, a chaise of some slippery-looking puce material—all crammed closely together and every available surface cluttered with what appeared to Sue-Ellen's uneducated eye to be gaudy bric-a-brac.

Connie reappeared, still on tiptoe with her head craned forward on its thin neck. "They'll see you now." Again she whispered.

"Right." Sue-Ellen realized she'd also whispered and repeated more assertively, "Right. I'll go in." She passed Connie and entered a room of larger proportions than the first, with windows where the other had none, but exuding the same atmosphere of expensive hodgepodge.

"You are late, Miss Hill."

A dry nasal voice jarred Sue-Ellen, and she peered in the direction from which it had come. Two women, so still they seemed part of the inanimate scene, sat, one on each side of a round table draped to the floor with a lace cloth.

"I'm sorry. I was busy with a contractor, and Connie had difficulty finding me. What can I do for you?" She wouldn't antagonize, but neither would she be intimidated.

"We are not accustomed to being inconvenienced by staff members."

We? We are not amused. Sue-Ellen smothered a smile and said, "It wasn't my intention to inconvenience you. I didn't know you wanted to see me until a few minutes ago." And if necessary she was going to have to remind these people that she worked not for them, but for their nephew.

"Kindly come closer." The taller woman spoke again. She sat erect, her thin, jewel-encrusted hands resting one atop the other on the table. "Sit there." A finger, imperiously raised, indicated a spindle-backed chair placed where the two sisters could observe its occupant closely.

Sue-Ellen sat down, keeping her damp and scruffy Reeboks close together. She still wore her yellow rain slicker but had pushed down the hood. Hardly the outfit for what felt like a royal audience.

"I'm Miss Mabel Ormsby-Jones," the tall woman informed Sue-Ellen. "This is my younger sister, Miss Alice Ormsby-Jones."

And neither of them was likely to remember too well what it felt like to be eighty, Sue-Ellen decided. She smiled and nodded . . . and waited.

"I see no reason for this to be a long interview, Miss Hill. You will, of course, pay close attention to what you are told and then we should have no trouble."

Irritation, mixed with a trace of apprehension, made Sue-Ellen shift to the edge of the chair. "Your nephew has made his wishes pretty clear. I'll be carrying out his instructions and reporting to him when he gets back from, er . . ."

"Dorchester," Alice supplied, speaking for the first time. She raised her face from a small needlepoint sampler that rested on her lap and Sue-Ellen recoiled. That Alice wore no glasses, even for close work at such an advanced age hadn't registered until now. Small eyes, catlike and oddly young, gleamed an almost yellow color.

Sue-Ellen took a moment to recover beneath the unblinking stare. "Yes, Dorchester. I haven't seen him since I arrived, so we'll have a lot to talk over when he gets back. Bea Smallman said that should be late tonight or tomorrow morning."

Bea, the housekeeper, was a middle-aged powerhouse who had been a treasure since Sue-Ellen arrived. Supportive and always available to answer questions, she'd done her best to help.

"We wouldn't know when Edward intends to return," Mabel commented, her chin lifting. "We wouldn't know anything about his comings and goings. But it is our duty to make sure this house isn't compromised. That is why we've called this interview."

How did a house get compromised? "As I told you, your nephew made his wishes clear before I came."

"Our nephew is young. Only thirty-five. He's made a mistake that must be rectified. If he'd consulted us we'd have made sure you didn't waste your time."

"Waste my time?"

Alice looked up again as if taking a silent cue. Her narrow nostrils flared. "By coming here. There can be no

question of Airstone being turned into a...a—'' she waved
a hand ''—a place for foreigners to stay.''

Sue-Ellen stared, then realized her mouth was open and
closed it. Hooded lids lowered over those feline eyes, and the
woman returned her attention to her needlepoint. There was
a suggestion of a tremor, palsy perhaps, that shook Alice's
gray-haired head.

''So, Miss Hill. Do we make ourselves clear?'' Mabel
asked. A satin-shaded wall light shone through the sparse
white hair she wore piled into a plaited crown, and glinted
on diamonds about her stringy neck. In rustling black silk
she resembled an ancient dowager duchess.

Sue-Ellen moved restlessly. ''No, you don't make yourselves clear. I'm sure I must misunderstand what you've just
said. But when I talk to your nephew I'm certain everything will be set straight.''

''You will not speak to Edward about this interview.''

This was unbelievable. ''I most certainly shall. In three
months Airstone Hall will open for business. That's my job,
to make sure it happens and as successfully as possible.''

''Miss Hill.'' Mabel stood, her body cadaverously thin in
its black shroud. She supported herself with a silver-handled
ebony cane. ''There are things you don't understand about
our kind of life—how could you? We have certain stan-
dards. There is an order to things. Edward has made a mistake in trying to interfere with what has been a tradition for
hundreds of years—Airstone Hall inhabited by our family
and only our family. But there will be no change in that. Do
you understand?''

''No, I—''

''But I think you do. To continue with this foolishness
would be a mistake, Miss Hill, a bad mistake.''

The tiny hairs on Sue-Ellen's neck crawled. In some bi-
zarre and obscure way this woman was threatening her.

''Listen to my sister,'' Alice said, fixing her unwavering
stare on some point in the distance. ''Our home will never
become a hotel.''

SUE-ELLEN MADE HER WAY along the corridor from her suite. "Sir," she said aloud. No she couldn't call him that. "Mr. Ormsby-Jones."

Her tennis shoes squeaked with each step. A gray morning. Gray inside and gray outside. From her window, through a thick and swirling fog that had crept in on the heels of the storm, she'd been scarcely able to see even nearby trees.

"Edward." She tried the name aloud. He'd signed his correspondence: Edward Ormsby-Jones, never Edward. So what was she supposed to call him? These people were so formal.

She felt sluggish. After leaving Alice and Mabel Ormsby-Jones the night before, she'd taken the long-awaited bath and tried to relax. But the old women's ultimatums revolved in her brain and she'd gradually felt herself wind up like an abused clock. Finally in bed, she'd tossed, settled, resettled and tossed again, but sleep had been elusive until it was almost time to get up.

At least she was starting to find her way around the house without too many wrong turns. She reached the last two doors at the end of the passage. These were Bea Smallman's rooms, but Sue-Ellen had yet to be invited into them.

Should she tell Edward about his aunts or not? She'd just have to play her cards as seemed best.

What *was* the right form here, the pecking order? She was to oversee necessary work to make part of Airstone Hall ready to operate as a hotel specializing in bed and breakfast. When that phase was accomplished she would become the hotel manager. Edward Ormsby-Jones had hired her by mail after she answered a newspaper ad in the States, and she'd been excited by the challenge, was still excited by it ... as long as she didn't dwell on last night's unexpected opposition.

That her employer remained no more than a name didn't help her confidence. All instructions since her arrival in England had been relayed by Bea Smallman, because the

master of the house had chosen at this time to stay in a town
a few miles away, where he had a law practice.

Bea was wonderful, but Sue-Ellen needed to clear a stack
of queries, and today was the day she'd make sure that
happened.

Ancient carpet worn to indistinct blue-beige hues bisected the broad and magnificent main staircase. She sped
downward past glistening banisters, each post upheld by
grinning mahogany cherubs. There would be no trouble
advertising this place to Americans hungry for glimpses of
the past. She had already started drafting rate scales for
various vacation packages, as well as standard nightly bed-
and-breakfast costs. But she had a way to go with preparations and she dared not proceed with some of the more expensive items without Edward Ormsby-Jones's approval.
And then there were her other ideas she was certain he'd
welcome.

"Good morning, Miss Hill."

Bea Smallman approached the foot of the stairs carrying
an armload of linens. As always the housekeeper wore a
tailored suit, a silk blouse adorned with a simple gold locket,
and exuded refined efficiency.

"Good morning," Sue-Ellen responded. She'd been invited to call Miss Smallman by her first name, but the
woman had yet to use hers. All so complex. "You did say
Mr. Ormsby-Jones was to return home by this morning?"
Sue-Ellen paused in the entry with its impressive stone
screens that gave some illusion of privacy in what had been
the original Great Hall, the heart of the house. Now the hall
was a showcase for family portraits and precious antique
furniture, and was rarely used, from what Sue-Ellen could
gather. She intended to change that.

"Edward got back late last night. He may not be ready for
visitors."

Sue-Ellen glanced from the intricate open-worked screens
to Bea's dark eyes. The woman looked uncharacteristically
flustered. She patted short dark curls that were already in

perfect order, planted and replanted her feet in their low-heeled pumps.

"You mean he sleeps in on Saturdays?" Sue-Ellen checked her watch. Nine seemed a perfectly reasonable hour to expect an interview with the boss who wanted her to perform miracles in three months.

"Edward likes his privacy. That's why he..." Bea hesitated, coloring faintly. Her complexion bore the healthy glow of hours spent outdoors. A pleasant-looking woman, Sue-Ellen had already decided, sturdy and without artifice and entirely at home in surroundings that fitted her perfectly.

Sue-Ellen waited politely for the housekeeper to continue. She didn't.

"Well, don't worry. I'll just run down to the gate house and ask if he can see me. If it isn't convenient he can always say so, can't he?" she finished brightly and didn't wait for a response. From the corner of her eye she saw Grossby, the butler, approach smoothly from the direction of the kitchens. So far they'd only exchanged a few words, but Sue-Ellen wasn't entirely comfortable with him, or the way he seemed to weigh her with his eyes.

With a nod to the tall, saturninely good-looking man and a smile at Bea, she slipped through double glass-paneled doors to the vestibule and then outside into the still fog.

The biting January cold, purported to be typical in the south of England, continued to shock her every time she left the house. That Airstone Hall had been updated enough to have central heating was a daily relief.

Sue-Ellen pulled a blue woolen hat from the pocket of her parka and crammed the shapeless concoction down over her ears and eyebrows. She knew her thick blunt-cut hair would stick out unprepossessingly, but she was a woman with a mission, a lot of work to accomplish in too few weeks, not a beauty-pageant contestant. Already the time limit she had to work with caused a panicky feeling.

The gate house, at the end of a long curving drive on the west side of the house, was an unlikely piece of architecture that appeared to have been built in someone's fit of whimsy. Undoubtedly old, though not as old as the early seventeenth-century house, its green-tiled roof resembled that of a pagoda and sat incongruously atop golden stone walls edged with turrets. Bow windows sported diamond panes, and a doorway apparently designed to admit only pygmies had an unlikely Norman-shaped stone arch.

The blurred outline of the structure emerged through the shifting damp blanket that filled the air. This was where the elusive Edward Ormsby-Jones made his home. Odd that he didn't choose to live in Airstone Hall.

Sue-Ellen saw a vehicle. She slowed her pace as she drew level with an olive-green Jeep. Somehow a Rolls-Royce, or at least a Jag, would have better fitted her image of the invisible man.

Uncertainty brought her to a complete halt. She was thousands of miles from Georgia and her family. The promising job she'd held as assistant manager of a luxury hotel in Augusta was a memory. Ten days on this estate, which was to have been her ticket to adventure in a foreign country, had produced her worst qualms ever over the reliability of her judgment. Now she was about to confront the man who had hired her, a man about whom she now realized she knew little. Not his marital status—although there had been no mention of a Mrs. Ormsby-Jones—and certainly not whether he would be likable or would like her. Her immediate future depended upon this man. Perhaps more than her immediate future, since she wasn't about to crawl home and admit that her family and friends were right to have reservations about her leaving a good job and a bright secure future. She must be mad!

A desire to flee hit with force. But the gate-house door, swinging open, made it unthinkable to do anything but confront the unknown.

A man backed through the door, talking to someone inside the house. As he turned he walked into her. "Whoops. Hello there," he said and laughed, showing very white teeth. "And who are you, little lady?"

Hate at first sight. Second to "babe," nothing infuriated her more than being called "little" anything. "I'm Sue-Ellen Hill, Mr., er . . ."

His smile stayed in place, but cool blue eyes made a slow descent to her sneakers, flickering at points on the way: her ugly hat, the bulky army anorak, her well-worn jeans. She made herself breathe evenly and make her own inventory.

Thirties, about five foot ten, well built, black curly hair a shade long, handsome in a too smooth, almost prettily perfect way—and cocky in his expensive tweeds with a heavy tan trench coat slung carelessly over his shoulders.

His hand, shooting out to clasp and pump hers, made Sue-Ellen flinch.

"Colin Bastible," he announced. "You must be Edward's latest venture. Pretty good one this time, I'd say."

Sue-Ellen was rarely speechless. This was one of those rare times. Colin Bastible, whoever he was, didn't seem to notice.

"Edward and I are old friends. My father's the local vicar—St. Peter's, in the village. I expect you've seen it. Edward's pater and ours have been friends forever and our grandfathers before that."

"Ours?" It was the only word that jumped out. She'd met the Reverend Michael Bastible, both at Airstone and on the day she'd walked the three miles to the village of East Puddle.

Colin frowned, then his expression cleared. "Ours—I mean my sister, Helen, and I. We're twins, although you'd never guess it. Come and meet her—and Edward. I was leaving, but I can't miss out on a happening." He put an arm around her shoulders and leaned over her. "You, Sue-Ellen, are definitely a happening. Things can get remarkably dull around here."

Did that mean that in a dull place like this even someone as uninteresting as Sue-Ellen Hill was noteworthy? With effort, she managed not to shrug away from him as he bent his head and walked her through the door.

"Edward. Helen. Look what I've found."

These people were different, Sue-Ellen reminded herself. They spoke differently, thought differently. But it didn't matter, this inane chatterer frosted her.

Packing boxes lined a narrow hall, but she saw little else before she was led by Colin into a small sitting room furnished with surprisingly modern gray leather interspersed with rosewood pieces—and more packing boxes. Was he moving out? Sue-Ellen wondered the instant before she saw a pretty, exceptionally pale woman and the bespectacled blond man who looked up from a sheaf of papers on a table by French windows.

"This," Colin announced with a flourish of one hand, "is Sue-Ellen Hill, the Yankee wizard who will turn Edward's money-eating ancestral home into a money-spitting gold mine. Sue-Ellen, this is my sister, Helen Bastible, and Edward Ormsby-Jones."

"I'm from Georgia, Mr. Bastible," Sue-Ellen said. Strain had overtaken caution.

He frowned. "I think someone told me that."

"In Georgia we aren't Yankees."

The frown was replaced by a blank stare.

"Don't take any notice of Colin. He can be remarkably thick."

Edward Ormsby-Jones's voice was a complete surprise. Rather than nasal or pinched as she'd come to anticipate, it was husky, gravelly, warm—and very soft. The accent was as expected, but fascinating.

"I really must apologize for not being here when you arrived." He rose, loomed over her in rustling green oilskins atop a dark sweater and tan pants. The pants were tucked inside heavy green rubber boots. "I intended to telephone, but I've got a sticky case on at the moment."

"Edward's always got a sticky case on," Colin Bastible remarked, his tone suggesting he took his friend's occupation lightly. "Sometimes I wonder if he looks for them. Thwarted need for adventure and all that."

"Do shut up, Colin." Helen Bastible spoke for the first time. Her brother had been accurate when he'd said there

was no resemblance between the twins. Helen was as frag-
ile-looking as Colin was husky and vibrant. Her voice was
a genteel echo, and the beautifully manicured hand she extended appeared so delicate that Sue-Ellen held it with care.
"Colin doesn't appreciate Edward," Helen said, tucking
strands of short blond hair behind an ear. Her doelike gray
eyes, trained unwaveringly on Edward Ormsby-Jones's face,
suggested she very much appreciated him.

The eyes of a woman in love, Sue-Ellen thought, and immediately put the lid on her natural curiosity. The private
lives of these people were none of her business, and she
didn't have time to speculate about them. She spoke directly to the master of Airstone Hall. "Miss Smallman has
been great. She passed on all your notes and answered any
questions I asked. But we do need to touch base on a number of things."

"That's fantastic," Colin Bastible said, coming closer.
Beside Edward Ormsby-Jones in his gentleman-farmer garb,
Colin appeared almost foppish.

"Fantastic?" She wished he'd take his sister and go away
so that some constructive discussion could take place.

"Fantastic," he repeated. "I don't think I've ever talked
to someone with exactly your accent before."

His apparently infatuated smile left Sue-Ellen unmoved.
This was a seducer in seducer's clothing and he wasn't her
type. "I hope you like it," she said. "Where I come from I
hear this accent every day." He continued to smile as if she
hadn't been even a little rude.

Sue-Ellen turned her attention to Edward. "I've made
some progress and some discoveries. Not all of the discoveries have been pleasant."

"You mean you're having problems?" he asked.

"Potential problems." She hadn't meant to start out this
way. Complaining about the man's relatives was unlikely to
endear her to him. "Nothing that can't be handled."

"Good. We can't afford delays." He smiled and she
started to relax.

The wire-rimmed glasses had been the focal point of her impression, these and well-cut wavy blond hair, together with his height and bulk in the oilskins. Now Sue-Ellen noted the most interesting feature in Edward's slender face: light brown, almost amber eyes that were alternately lambent and piercing. If his lenses hadn't had noticeable thickness she might have speculated on their usefulness as a defense against showing too much of what he felt.

Helen put a hand on his arm and he absently patted her fingers before removing them. "We'd better put off our walk," he told her, still looking at Sue-Ellen. "Forgive me, Helen. You probably wouldn't enjoy it in the fog anyway. But I'll meet you both at the Arms tonight."

He dispatched his friends, firmly turning aside Colin's plea not to "miss any fun" and dropping a kiss on Helen's cheek. Sue-Ellen noted that kiss. No passion on Ormsby-Jones's side if she had to guess. The old curiosity must definitely be packed away.

"I won't take up a lot of your time this morning," Sue-Ellen said, determined to establish a good rapport as soon as possible, "but we do need to talk."

"My time is yours. The hotel is my first priority, at least until it gets off the ground. I really am sorry I couldn't be here when you arrived. Rotten timing on my client's part. Why don't you tell me what snags you've hit?"

He pushed back his coat and sank both hands in his pants pockets. Marked grooves beside his serious mouth suggested he knew how to laugh; so did lines at the corners of his eyes. Those between his brows probably meant he could frown equally successfully. He was frowning slightly now.

"As I said," she responded, "there's nothing I can't cope with."

Edward allowed himself a moment before answering Sue-Ellen Hill. She'd attempted to brush aside her first comment about potential problems, but his well-developed intuition told him she was troubled and trying to cover up. He should have made time to talk to her before now.

She unzipped her parka. Getting hot, no doubt.

"But you have hit a few rough spots?" That sounded as if he was taking her lightly. He wasn't. "Why don't you sit down. Let me take your coat." Damn. He thought he knew what was coming and he didn't know what he'd do about it.

"From what you wrote I assumed the idea of Airstone Hall becoming part-hotel wasn't new," Sue-Ellen said.

She'd made no attempt to give up her coat or sit down, and he was becoming unbearably warm in his oilskins. "Why don't we kill two birds with one stone?" He smiled at her.

"Um . . . I'm not sure what you mean."

The hat was a fright, but he liked the thick shiny hair that protruded below. She gave a sturdy businesslike impression and he liked that, too.

Edward looked directly into her clear blue eyes. "We need to talk and Max needs a walk . . . and so do I. We can do both. I was going to check a section of the wall that my gardener tells me needs repair."

"Max?" Her glance took in the room that was still a mess.

"My dog. Here, boy! He's sulking because he expected to go home—" That was something he hadn't intended to discuss with her, not now. The truth would come out, but today was definitely not the right time.

"I don't understand—"

"Max! Good boy!" The old codger came through sometimes. He'd decided to unfold his mostly golden Labrador body from his hiding spot behind the couch and slink, stomach close to the rug, and pass Edward. "Come here, boy!"

"He's wonderful," Sue-Ellen said, dropping to her knees. Max had literally swathed his ungrateful self around her legs while he raised mournful brown eyes to her face.

"Let's walk," Edward said, "if you don't mind walking in this miserable weather, that is." The sooner he jumped in with both feet and confronted whatever she had to say, the better.

"I don't mind. It's different from what I'm used to, though." She grinned, a straightforward grin that increased the impression that she was the type of woman he'd find easy to work with.

"I can imagine," he told her. "People don't come to Dorset to get a tan—not even in summer." That brought a full laugh from her.

He didn't bother to lock the front door as they left. The crumbling section of wall his gardener, Massing, had mentioned was about two miles across an uncultivated section of the estate. That should be long enough for them to become comfortable with each other and discuss business at the same time.

The route was uphill, and as they climbed the fog thinned to fine mist. Edward breathed appreciatively and peered up into dancing particles of damp. He loved this place. But he loved his practice, and there wasn't time in his daily routine to play the landed gentleman on an estate the size of Airstone. He looked down on the bowed head of Sue-Ellen Hill. She was to be his salvation, the answer to his dilemma.

"What do you think of Airstone?" She looked up, squinting, and he took off his moisture-coated glasses to see her face.

"It's a beautiful house, absolutely fantastic. I tried counting rooms, but I gave up at about a hundred and twenty."

"Most of them are closed now. Have been for years."

"All the more reason to find a use for them again. Your hotel idea is going to be a smash."

Her enthusiasm made him smile. She exuded energy, even her walk was loaded with purpose. He'd chosen well, he was sure of it. "You're making progress, then."

"Uh-huh. By the way, what was that big room on the third floor used for?"

He sidestepped a rock outcropping. "That's the Long Room." They were getting higher and higher. Soon they'd reach a point where there should be at least a hazy view of

East Puddle to the south and the several hundred acres of parkland that surrounded Airstone. "It was a gallery in my grandfather's time. But the original purpose was very practical. Back when clothing wasn't too substantial, or shoes, the people who lived here would take their winter strolls back and forth there. You noticed it stretches the whole width of the house?"

She nodded.

"Children would play games while their parents chatted. And, of course, they probably held dances as well."

"Like a social club."

He paused, considering. "I suppose. Yes, that would have been it." She was nice to talk to, interested in everything, and she genuinely approved of Airstone. If she didn't she wouldn't be the kind good at pretending otherwise.

Her tennis shoe slipped on mud, and he took her arm until she was beside him again. He tucked her hand through his elbow and she showed no sign of awkwardness at leaving it there.

They walked on. His earlier tension had faded. Whatever was troubling her couldn't be that bad.

Sue-Ellen's mind seethed. He wasn't what she'd expected. There was nothing stuffy about him. He was, in fact, exactly the confidence booster she'd needed after last night's setback. He made her feel he trusted her judgment and that he'd support her efforts.

They'd risen completely above the fog, and a pallid sun struggled through the mist. Ahead lay another gentle hill topped by a spinney. Max ran in circles, his long tail waving like a triumphant battle flag.

"He hates being cooped up in Dorchester," Edward remarked.

She still wasn't sure what she should call him. "Do you have an apartment there?"

"Yes. I've got three partners, and one of them lets me use rooms in his basement when I don't have time to come back here for a day or so."

He removed his glasses to wipe the lenses. She could tell he was shortsighted by the fractional lowering of his lids.

Their feet sank into a carpet of fallen leaves and twigs as they entered the trees of the spinney and passed into filtered light. There was no point in waiting any longer to get into their discussion. And, much as she'd rather not, she'd better at least mention his aunts' attitude...gently if possible.

"I already told you how helpful Miss Smallman's been."

"Bea's marvelous. A godsend. Always has been."

"Yes. And I thought things were going fairly smoothly until yesterday."

Edward stood still, jolting her to a halt. "What does that mean?"

Sue-Ellen removed her hand from his arm. Suddenly he seemed very big and quite formidable. "I told you there had been...minor problems." His expression became closed. She wondered how difficult this was going to be.

"What we're undertaking is completely new. There are bound to be some growing pains," he said.

She drew up as tall as she could at five foot five and pulled off her hat. She should have dressed in something businesslike and insisted on conducting a formal interview in formal surroundings.

"What I'm talking about has nothing to do with growing pains." While she talked she tried to straighten her hair. "With respect, your aunts' attitude toward my project—and toward me—came as a shock."

The abrupt bowing of his head, a cough and his hand clamped over his mouth confused her.

"Are you all right?"

"Er, yes, yes, quite all right. A tickle in the throat, that's all."

Max returned to deposit a stick at Edward's feet, providing the diversion she had an uncanny sensation the man welcomed. He bent to wrestle the stick free, threw it and watched Max bound away through the trees.

"Mr. Ormsby-Jones."

"Edward."

That answered that question. "Edward. Your aunts requested a . . . an audience would be more accurate. They informed me that under no circumstances would any part of Airstone become a hotel."

He stood up slowly. A flush had risen in his cheeks. "My aunts are old ladies. They find change hard to accept."

"I realize that." She felt like a heel for embarrassing him, which she clearly had. "But they wield considerable power over at least some of the household staff members, and I need all the support I can get in that area. The staff is too small as it is."

Edward folded his arms and she felt him drawing away. Her charming adventure was rapidly losing some of its charm.

He seemed to consider how to answer before he said, "Bea will make sure there's no resistance from the staff. I'm sorry the number isn't adequate, but there's nothing I can do about that until we start making money from the hotel."

And that was evidently as far as she would get on the subject . . . for now. At least she'd made sure he knew about the undercurrents in his own house. Spreading her feet she took a deep breath and began, "My main purpose in talking to you today is to get your okay for expenditures and clear a few additional ideas I think would help make Airstone more attractive to visitors."

He threw another stick for Max who was now thoroughly wet and coated in mud and leaves. Sue-Ellen waited until Edward gave her his full attention. "What you gave me was a basic plan. Get a portion of the house ready to operate as a hotel and do it within three months, because my salary can't be afforded if it isn't productive fairly soon."

"Correct. And you sound as if you're on your way."

"I think I am. I've worked through a lot of the details and now I want to discuss them with you. I see this as a multi-step undertaking with a large part of the success depending on how we market. To market successfully we must be able to compete for business with the many other similar establishments I've learned are springing up in England. In short, we must come up with some attractions that other country houses aren't offering.''

He watched her face intently and no longer seemed aware of Max who had returned yet again to fuss in the brush at their feet. ''You're talking about alterations to rooms we'll be using for guests.''

She shook her head. He probably had little idea of exactly what he'd started. ''That's the easiest part. When I start shooting out ads to travel magazines all over the States and loading every travel agency in the book with brochures, and quoting the kind of prices you need to charge if you're going to make this worthwhile, we must have more to offer than a pleasant room, and bacon and eggs for breakfast. Joe Tourist can get that at any old boarding-house across this country.''

She paused, excitement pumping the blood through her veins. ''I know what we need. All you have to do is give me the go-ahead to proceed. In my rooms I've got sheets of figures and projected expenditures and income for the various packages and options I've worked out. I didn't bring them all with me today, but I can give you a quick run-down.''

He crossed his arms and rested his chin on a fist. ''Shoot.''

Sue-Ellen paced, aware that Max trotted back and forth behind her. ''The rooms are beautiful, but they're old.''

''I thought that was the point. People like old things.''

She flipped a hand back and forth. ''Yes and no. There's old and *old*. They want to *feel* the old, but they want to be comfortable.

''We need new mattresses?''

If she laughed he'd clam up and she'd get nowhere. ''Yes, but that's minor. We need to renovate the bathrooms. At least they have hot water, but that's about all. They're small and unappealing. I've got contractors ready to go to work the minute I give the word. I'd like them to start on Monday.'' The main problem was that they'd made their preliminary arrangements at long distance. She'd had no idea just how extensive the necessary renovations would be.

''What exactly did you have in mind?'' He sank to sit on a mossy log. ''We can't go overboard until we start bringing in money.''

''You knew there would be work to be done. We discussed that by mail.''

''Yes, but I hadn't envisioned the kind of massive outlays you're suggesting.''

''Money makes money,'' she told him with more patience than she felt. ''You *have* to put out to take in. We can do a lot with mirrors. Not cheap, but long-lasting if we vent the rooms—no windows is one of the problems. Makes you feel closed in. Mirrors create a feeling of space and airiness.''

''There already are mirrors in the bathrooms.''

Her back was to him now, and she raised her eyes heavenward before facing him. ''I mean that I want to cover the bathrooms with mirrors. Walls and ceilings. And have a lot of green plants. The old fixtures can stay if the plumbing's redone. They add atmosphere and—''

''Mirrored walls and *ceilings*?''

''Yes. And we'll need showers—''

''*Ceilings?* Why? So people can see themselves in the bath?''

She smothered a laugh. ''That hadn't been my thought, but it has merit, I guess. Particularly for the honeymoon suite.'' The look in his eyes made her wish she'd censored her last comment.

Was it her imagination or had he paled?

''What honeymoon suite?''

She was going too fast for him. ''We can get a fortune for something I've got in mind. You know the Scarlet Chamber?''

''I know it.'' A vaguely threatening note had entered his voice.

"Well, it would make a fantastic honeymoon suite. It's got the cutest little anteroom where the lovebirds could have cozy breakfasts, and I was even thinking that when we get the restaurant under way we could start room service and then we could do dinners for two, very discreet, very expensive. And for the bathroom off that suite I'd like to see an oversized tub..." She paused. Now he was red. "For two, you see," she finished lamely.

He mumbled something that sounded like "I don't believe this."

There could be no turning back. His reaction was a surprise, but she'd bring them both through this awkwardness.

"The tack rooms and the old stables..." she continued.

He nodded mechanically. "What about them?"

"Tearooms. Have afternoon tea available for the people who come twice a week in spring and summer to tour the house, and offer daily service for hotel guests who want to spend a few hours wandering around the grounds. These afternoon teas—the ones with scones and jam and so on—are all the rage, I understand."

Edward sucked in his cheeks and made no response.

"But that brings me to a potential problem. Massing, the head gardener, is most unhelpful. All he talks about is keeping people off the grass and out of the conservatory. He seems to think Americans won't know a weed from a camellia." She didn't add that she fell into that category. "Massing said he wouldn't have foreigners tromping all over his prize specimens, as he put it."

"He said that." It was a flat statement, and her stomach sank a little lower.

"And the conservatory is a definite pull. We could charge separate admission for that. We could sell seeds in ready-to-mail packets like picture postcards. 'The Blooms of Airstone,' or something like that."

"Um..."

"Please, I don't expect to do everything at once. I'm just running over my entire plan—as it is now, of course. There will be more as I go along."

"I'm sure there will."

She stopped pacing and peered at him suspiciously. He sounded distant. His averted face made it impossible to be sure how he felt.

"I'd like your permission to go ahead with the tearooms at the same time as the guest rooms are being converted. It'll save money to consolidate the work. I already have estimates. And then there's the Great Hall."

"The Great Hall?"

The way he echoed her began to grate. "The Great Hall. Eventually I'd like to see it used for large functions. Wedding receptions, parties . . . but that will come later."

"Later."

"Yes. What I'd like to offer in our first brochures are evenings in the Great Hall with the lord of the manor. You know the kind of thing I mean."

He showed a renewed spark of life. "No." His voice was very soft and very clear. "Why don't you tell me what you mean?"

"Well." Gaining confidence again, she went to sit beside him on the log and placed her hands over his arm. "You probably don't understand this, but Americans have a thing about British aristocracy, royalty, because we don't have them."

He nodded and she couldn't read his expression.

"So, I thought we'd offer getting-acquainted sessions when people arrive . . . with you presiding. I don't suppose the Ormsby-Joneses have a tartan."

"No. We don't have a tartan."

"Too bad. You'd have looked terrific in a kilt." She closed her mouth, felt herself color. "I mean, there's nothing more mysterious than a British man in a kilt." That was even worse. "But it doesn't matter. I'm sure you'll do just as good a job in a dinner jacket. I did kind of toss around the idea of having your aunts present, too. They're very re-gal in an old-fashioned way."

Edward made a strangled noise. "Did you suggest this to them?" He was definitely pale.

If only he knew the tenor of her only discussion with the old ladies. "No, not yet."

"I suggest you don't." His eyes were wide behind his glasses.

"Perhaps not," which was an understatement.

He stood up slowly and waited for her to join him. "Sue-Ellen, we're going to have to finish this conversation later. for now I feel a need to take a very long walk and check my walls, probably miles and miles of walls. Can you find your own way back?"

"Of course." She was being dismissed and it rankled, but there was no point in antagonizing him, and she had pre-sented him with ideas he couldn't have considered before. "You will give some thought to my ideas so that I can put in orders soon? And we will need more employees, defi-nitely by the time we're ready to open."

"I certainly will think about everything you've sug-gested," he said, backing away. "I'm amazed at your inge-nuity." Then he hesitated, ran his fingers through damp hair and came close to her, toe to toe. "One or two decisions come to me immediately." There was a quiet calm about him now. "No extra staff—at least for now. No honeymoon suite. No oversized bath for two. No restaurant. And, fi-nally, no soirees with me playing jackass lord of the manor."

"But—"

"No buts, Sue-Ellen. You've given me a lot to think about, and I need time to do that."

"But—"

"I'll see you at the gate house tonight. At seven, if that's okay. And you'd better bring all those figures of yours with you."

"Don't you have plans for this evening?" The fair Helen who'd probably never had an original thought would be waiting with her fresh brother.

Edward was already walking away. Over his shoulder he said, "I'm used to keeping my own social schedule straight. Tonight you and I have business to settle. I've already told you that business comes first with me. I'll expect you at seven." With that he strode away through the trees.

SUE-ELLEN MUTTERED all the way back to the house. If all he wanted was a second-rate boardinghouse he didn't need a first-rate hotel manager, and she wasn't going to waste her time on him.

In the hall she passed Sylvia, the voluptuous blond kitchen maid. She appeared to be in her mid-twenties. Too much makeup detracted from a pretty, if petulant face, and the apron she wore cinched around a small waist accentuated large breasts, overly exposed beneath a thin blouse, and shapely hips.

"Sylvia," Sue-Ellen called, a second before the woman was about to enter the kitchen wing. "I've just talked to Mr. Ormsby-Jones, and I'll need a meeting with you and the rest of the staff on Monday morning. Will you make sure everyone's available at ten? In the kitchen will do."

"Some of us are busy at ten," Sylvia said, posing with her weight on one foot.

"Then you'll just have to get unbusy, won't you?" Sue-Ellen responded and got a wonderful surge of satisfaction at the truculent downturn of Sylvia's mouth. "Be there. all of you." Edward Ormsby-Jones be damned. He'd hired her to do a job and she was going to do it. She'd find a way to handle him. The time had come to show these people she meant business. The sooner she started turning Airstone Hall into what Colin Bastible had called a money-spitting gold mine, the better.

She stomped upstairs, located the corridor leading to her rooms and broke into a run to reach her door.

The quarters she'd been given were wonderful. She entered the sitting room with its beautiful sixteenth- and seventeenth-century pieces and went immediately into the bedroom. That she might be allotted a place like this to live while she was here had never entered her imagination.

After hanging the anorak in a tall freestanding wardrobe and pulling off her tennis shoes, she gave her hair a quick brush, captured it in a rubber band at her nape and headed back to the sitting room, giving the sumptuous Jacobean four-poster a longing glance as she went. This evening's interview with Edward promised to be grueling, and she expected to be more than ready for bed when it was over.

A large writing table, its wood almost black, was proving the perfect place to work on her calculations. For the rest of the afternoon she intended to check and recheck everything she'd done. This morning Edward had been unprepared for some of her more inventive ideas. By this evening he'd have had time to think them through and realize that at least some of them had merit. She could work on the rest later.

The sitting room was long and narrow with the writing table set between two windows that overlooked the now unused stables. She'd left her papers spread out and she pushed up the sleeves of her sweater as she approached.

Something smelled funny.

Sue-Ellen stood still and sniffed. Cleaning fluid—or acetone. She shrugged. Painters were already at work in several rooms, and although they were on the other side of the house, those smells were pervasive.

Sinking into a chair by the table, she switched on a lamp. The narrow windows admitted little light, and heavy draperies that didn't open very far made the problem worse.

She rested her left hand on the desk and looked down. Her fingers slid on something slimy.

Oh, my God.

The papers were as she'd left them . . . except for splattered crimson globs, which drizzled to the edge of the table and dripped down one leg.

Chapter Two

The message was clear. The aunts were letting her know they'd meant what they said. She was supposed to leave Airstone and run back where she'd come from. Wrong. It would take more than a little creative stage setting with nail polish to break her spirit. No doubt the pair had decided she was likely to report their original warning to Edward, and they'd arranged this sickening piece of nastiness hoping she'd hotfoot it back to him and complain. Then he'd say that his aged relatives couldn't possibly have done such a thing and that she had no means of proving the spilled polish hadn't been her own, and what credibility she had with him would be shot. Even though she never wore polish on her short nails.

The room was so still . . . as if an unseen presence held its breath. Sue-Ellen stood up slowly, turned, holding her own breath. The polish was still gummy. It must have been spread only minutes ago. She searched shadows behind chairs, beneath tables. Nothing. But someone had been here, must have left the room a matter of seconds before she came in. Someone had crept through what was now her private place, touched the things that were personal. Her skin crawled. In the future she'd lock the door when she came and went.

Clearly the old women couldn't have pulled this off alone. Someone else's help had been enlisted. But whose? Connie's? Sue-Ellen didn't want to believe the pleasant little maid would stoop to this. Regardless, she must be alert. She didn't know exactly who in the house was friend and who foe. One thing she did know was that whoever her enemies were would be very disappointed when she didn't react. And regardless of the effort and frustration it cost her, she wouldn't react.

She had a few hours before her scheduled meeting with Edward, and she'd use the time to reconstruct her ruined papers. The first step was to clean up the mess.

Quickly she spread out the sheets to keep them from sticking together. The photograph of her family, one of the few personal treasures she'd brought with her, had been tipped over. She righted its simple wooden frame and her teeth clamped together. Her forehead tightened.

The glass had been removed from the frame and a single blob of red, stippled to produce a fine spray like blood from a puncture wound, obliterated one face from the smiling group.

With trembling fingers, Sue-Ellen picked up the picture. The mutilated face had been hers.

PROMPTLY AT SEVEN the knocker sounded on the gate-house door. Miss Sue-Ellen Hill was certainly prompt. Edward left the box of books he was unpacking and went to let her in.

Tonight was for mending bridges, he reminded himself as he ushered her from a night that felt as if snow was in the air, to the warm sitting room. She might be overenthusiastic and brash, but she was definitely competent, and he couldn't afford to waste the outlay he'd already made in bringing her here. Besides, he liked her, and if she had a few ideas that caught him off guard he had to be big enough to at least look at them before he threw them out.

"I brought the figures," she told him, and set a folder on the table. "I'll leave them with you to study, but we can't let any more time go by without taking some action."

She was single-minded and more than a little overbearing, but he'd chosen her because she showed initiative, hadn't he?

Determined to set the right tone for their discussion, he insisted she sit down and have some sherry. Then he picked up his own coffee mug and the folder and stood near the fireplace. "I owe you an apology for being abrupt this morning." He smiled, knowing that the usual effect was to soften his subject.

Sue-Ellen appeared not to notice his effort. "That's all right. I tend to come on a bit strong, and I'll try to do something about that."

So they were both contrite. A good start. "Look, we had an understanding of my expectations before you came. And you've performed well. It was understood that your responsibilities included assessing necessary renovations to those areas slated for hotel use."

The wave of her hand was a little impatient. "Yes, yes. And that I was to get contract bids, oversee work, deal with advertising, reservations . . . and eventually manage the hotel. I understood perfectly. But I also understand that I overwhelmed you this morning."

Her straightforwardness was disarming. "Not your fault. Obviously I hadn't calculated how much damage could be done by years of disuse. I do now. But remember, we do have to start out somewhat carefully and work up."

"I realize there are limitations."

He glanced from her serious face to the folder. He opened it. "You do think we'll be able to meet our original goal of having the place open for business within three months?"

"Absolutely. Only I've used up more than a week of that already. I'm adamant that we must reach agreement in some areas that weren't covered in our correspondence."

She was strong, self-assured, the kind of woman who had always appealed to him. "I should have been prepared for some unforeseen elements. In a way I was, just not to the extent you've put forward." He frowned at the figures, recalling for the first time in a long while, another woman who'd known what she wanted and acted on her instincts. The memory brought regret, and it always would, but surprisingly, not the pain it once had.

Sue-Ellen talked on, using her hands and frequently tugging her hair back. Tonight the jeans and sweater had been replaced by a simple blue woolen dress that flattered a full figure while it made her appear sophisticated. Good shape, he noted absently.

"So," she said, her wide mouth set, "May I at least do that much?"

"Perhaps we should run over everything just once more," he said, without meeting those pale blue eyes, which disconcerted him with their direct contact.

Her sigh let him know she was also holding tight to her temper, being very sure not to show how frustrated she must be.

"We go ahead with all the room renovations as I've outlined, paring down some of the modifications I'd hoped to employ, putting the honeymoon suite on hold—for now—" at this she crossed her arms "—but leaving the possibility for adding one later on. We agree that the tearooms are a good idea and should be implemented, and with your head gardener's assistance, the gardens will be made available to visitors. By that I mean that rather than the very confined area normally shown to people touring the house, guests staying here will be allowed to go where they please."

If he was honest with himself he'd admit that her imagination and the potential for the huge success he'd started to see through her eyes excited him. He only said, "I suppose I see no reason why not. On all counts. You will keep me closely informed on expenditures, though?"

"Of course. We'll put the restaurant and banquet facilities on the back burner, but I do think we should tackle the conservatory—"

"Excuse me," he interrupted her at the sound of the front door opening. Must be old Bastible. He had his own key and never hesitated to use it.

"I say, Edward—" the Reverend marched in with his typical obdurate vigor "—haven't seen that no-good son of mine, have you? He's been kicked out of another job y'know, and— Miss Hill! Sorry, Edward. Didn't know you

had company." He held a battered felt hat in one hand, and
his thatch of thick gray hair bore the imprint of the crown.

"Colin gone astray?" Michael wouldn't want to discuss
Colin's latest escapade, whatever it was, in front of Sue-
Ellen, but to drop the subject abruptly would look suspi-
cious.

Michael cleared his throat and fiddled with a button on
the old sheepskin jacket he wore incongruously over cleri-
cal garb. "Don't suppose so. Not really. Just wanted a few
words with the chap. Haven't really talked to him since he
got back. Like to know, well, you know." He invariably
spoke in jerky phrases that matched his always-in-a-hurry
persona. He was husky and energetic, and Edward often
marveled that the man's spirituality was unshakable enough
to keep him in a largely passive occupation.

The poor old reverend. Colin led him quite a dance, and
Helen, in her quiet way, must be a worry, and an irritation
sometimes. A thirty-two-year-old daughter content with a
life as her father's housekeeper must concern him, as far as
her future went.

"Colin and Helen walked up from the village this morning," Edward said. "I gathered Colin, er, needs a rest for a
while." That was a polite way of saying that he had got
himself in trouble again. Colin's "troubles" tended to take
similar courses: boredom with whatever job he was doing—
he was an unenthusiastic architect—lack of funds because
he lived beyond his means, and finally, involvement with the
wife or daughter of someone in a position to sack him.

Michael was helping himself to a sherry, a very small
sherry that he was unlikely to finish. He gave his bushy gray
mustache a tug. "Well, I'm glad he came to see you. I've
hardly set eyes on him. Wouldn't have known he'd arrived
if his bags hadn't been in the hall. Give him a few helping
words when you can, will you, Edward?" Dark brows raised
significantly over brown eyes that looked much younger
than his seventy-three years.

"I'll do that," Edward said, aware of Sue-Ellen's still
watchfulness. "You and Sue-Ellen have met?"

"Yes, indeed. Bea introduced us." Michael turned to her. "Bea tells me you're very industrious, Miss Hill. 'Bursting with ideas' was the phrase she used. I'd better get on. You and Edward must have business to discuss." But even as he made leave-taking noises, he took off his coat.

Edward smiled a little. Michael wasn't one to miss anything going on at Airstone. He was almost as involved with the estate as Edward himself. "Sit down, Michael," he said. "Sue-Ellen was about to talk about the conservatory, and that's your bailiwick." Michael tended the conservatory— as his father, the previous vicar of St. Peter's had before him—with ferocious tenderness bordering on obsession.

"The conservatory?" Michael's heavy brows shot up again. "What about it?" His normally serene expression tightened.

Sue-Ellen didn't appear to notice she was on sensitive ground. "It's absolutely marvelous," she said, waving one of her capable hands with the enthusiasm Edward was coming to expect. "Too good not to be shared with as many people as possible."

Edward winced. If only he'd warned her to tread lightly. "Michael slaves over the place," he told her, praying she'd catch on. "Took over from his father years—"

Michael interrupted. "What do you mean, Miss Hill? As many people as possible?"

She smiled at him, still oblivious to the change in the atmosphere. "Please call me Sue-Ellen. Everyone does. I was going to explain more to Edward about how we should exploit an existing resource. People would pay well to see some of the specimens you've got in that place. Not that I know a hollyhock from a petunia."

Edward felt weak. He sat heavily on the edge of an armchair. She was on her own now, and the going was likely to get tough.

"Miss Hill...Sue-Ellen—" Michael drew himself up very straight "—one does not grow hollyhocks or petunias in a conservatory, not in *my* conservatory. I have an orchid collection that's famous throughout the horticultural community in this country. I hardly think—''

"Michael." Edward passed a hand over his hair. "Michael, Sue-Ellen hasn't had enough time to find out the kind of work you do in the conservatory. I'm sure she'd be delighted to have you explain more." He gave her a meaningful stare. She'd colored, and for the first time he saw an uncertain light in her eyes.

"Yes," she said faintly, "yes, I'd just love to have you show me around. I was telling Edward that in the States there are some famous gardens, like Butchart in Victoria—that's British Columbia, but I expect you know that—but anyway, it's quite common to package seeds in mailable form with a space on the outside for the address. They'd go like hotcakes here. I know they would. We could have some fantastic T-shirts made with an Airstone logo and flowers and so on. Maybe mugs and caps—stickers for car windows. The possibilities are endless."

The desire to laugh almost undid Edward. She was wonderful, irrepressible. And the look on Michael Bastible's face, open horror, was priceless. With a struggle, he kept a serious expression. "Do sit down, Michael. Sue-Ellen, this is all very new to the reverend. We've lived a pretty quiet life here, and much as I admire your energy you must remember that I said we'd have to go slowly."

"It's out of the question," Michael announced as if he hadn't heard a word Edward said. "Out of the question."

Edward stared from Michael to Sue-Ellen, who was also staring. Diplomacy was everything here. "Don't worry, Michael. Nothing will happen in the conservatory without your okay."

If Michael was mollified he showed no sign. He sat on the couch, as far from Sue-Ellen as possible, and eyed her with suspicion.

Sue-Ellen had been toying with the stem of her sherry glass. She took a sip and returned her attention to Edward.

"We'll come back to the gardens," she said. "We have plenty to get on with. But before I leave you for tonight there's something important we need to talk over. At least, I think it's very important. Bea doesn't seem too enthusiastic, but she said the decision is yours, which it is in all things around here, of course.'' With this she gave poor beleaguered Michael a sidelong look.

"I think everything will work out better if you try to go along with Bea as much as possible," Edward said. "She's got a good nose for what works on an estate like this."

"She isn't infallible," Sue-Ellen announced. "We have to capitalize on the things about Airstone that are fascinating."

"I thought you'd already agreed that there's little that isn't fascinating about the place."

"Yes. But we're probably missing some wonderful bets."

He couldn't think what she'd come up with next. "Such as?"

"There are parts of the house that haven't been used for years."

"I can't imagine—"

"No. That's what you're paying me for."

He was tempted to ask if she had an extra supply of humble pills. Her self-assurance was enviable...and magnetic. "Go on."

"People are fascinated by mystery. The sense that they're treading where people trod ages ago but where no one has been since. They love to wonder what might have happened in an old room in times no one really remembers. Do you know what I mean?"

"I'm sure you know what you're talking about," he told her, "but I can't guess what you have in mind." His chair was close to the couch and she shifted toward him until he could smell her subtle perfume.

"Parts of Airstone are more or less closed off," she said with earnest intensity. "I'm not talking just about the wings we've already discussed as usable for the hotel. I've spent some time poking around—you don't mind?"

He shook his head, amused, visualizing her making a purposeful inventory of every nook and cranny at the Hall.

"Good. There are all kinds of interesting possibilities. But what I'm really fascinated by are the cellars. Bea showed me some of them herself, and I admit they'll be a challenge, but worthwhile, I think. But there was something I wanted to ask you about."

He glanced at Michael who watched Sue-Ellen with what appeared to be bemused fascination. "I'll tell you whatever I can."

She leaned closer. "Well, I was in the Great Hall. It's fantastic, crammed with things people love to look at. Anyway, I was looking at that big tapestry beside the fireplace, trying to figure out how they made a thing like that. I lifted it away from the wall to look at the back. Did you know there's a door behind it?"

He'd forgotten all about it. "I used to know when I was a boy. Haven't given it a thought for years."

"There's a rusty padlock above the handle. I got the creepiest feeling just thinking of what might be in there. It was wonderful."

Again Edward couldn't contain a smile. "Probably nothing but musty old passageways and the occasional rat."

"Your father might not approve of any of the closed-off sections of the house being disturbed," Michael said, getting up to peer through the window into a moonless night. "You know how he can be sometimes."

"Well, yes, but if this were an issue, and I doubt if it is, I don't think he'd care one way or the other. You know how he is—" He stopped, not looking at Sue-Ellen but feeling her eyes on him. He was jumping into areas best avoided.

"If you mean he doesn't know what's going on anymore, you'd better think again, Edward. Arthur knows when and what he chooses to know. He wouldn't want strangers snooping about those old passages. Better left alone, he'd say."

"Who's going to tell him?" Edward asked.

"I shall certainly tell him, my boy. Your father and I have been friends since many years before you were born. I'm his only link with the world he knew and I don't intend to keep information from him...not when it relates to his own house.''

"Excuse me.'' Sue-Ellen touched Edward's arm and he reluctantly switched his attention to her. "Perhaps I'm misinterpreting something here. I'd assumed your father was dead. In fact I'd assumed both your parents were dead.''

"I'm sorry. How foolish of me. It just never came up. My mother's been dead for some years. My father is, er, selectively, er—''

"Don't beat about the bush, Edward,'' Michael broke in with some asperity. "Sue-Ellen, Edward administrates Airstone for his father, Sir Arthur Ormsby-Jones. Arthur hasn't been too well in recent years. The pressure of running a place like this, the mounting debts, taxes, all that, became too much, and it seemed advisable for him to, um, be...for him to remove himself. He lives at The Lawns on the other side of East Puddle.''

"A nursing home?''

Edward sighed. She was so blunt. "Yes, it's a kind of nursing home. More a retreat.'' He preferred to think of the place that way. "Father does come home occasionally if the mood hits him, but that isn't very often. Almost never.'' She would draw the conclusion, accurately, that his father was mentally feeble. Edward hated the thought.

She considered quietly for a moment before saying, "I can't see why your father would object to making use of parts of the house that are wasted space at the moment. I'd like your permission to at least open that door and see what's there.''

"Why bother,'' Michael said, sounding bored. "I remember it from years ago. All you'll find is a bunch of musty passages and queer little rooms that used to be occupied by servants. That and a second kitchen that must be a horror by now.''

"Wonderful!'' Sue-Ellen unconsciously clasped Edward's hand. "That's exactly what I hoped for. We can even hint at a little haunting. They'll eat it up.''

Edward only half heard what she said. Her touch had surprised him. Women who touched naturally, laughed and moved without artifice, were outside his experience.

Michael wasn't preoccupied by anything but the subject under discussion. "This isn't my house," he was saying, "but I strongly advise against doing anything Bea doesn't consider a good idea. Her instincts are good. She's undoubtedly decided the staff won't like all the fuss and that it wouldn't be worth it in the end. And Arthur would be most unhappy. He doesn't like change."

"I'm afraid I don't understand why," Sue-Ellen said, unmoved. "And while we're on the subject of places that could be better utilized—why is the library locked? Bea didn't want to discuss that, either, although she was nice enough about it."

"Edward?" Michael's nostrils flared.

"The library is off-limits," Edward told her simply. He'd been remiss all the way around, he decided. If he had thought things out he could have headed off her questions and ensured this discussion never took place in front of Michael.

"Why? I'm not suggesting we allow people to handle the books, but at least the doors could be opened and the entrance roped off so they could see without going in. I bet it's beautiful."

"It is," Edward said. Probably the most beautiful room in the house, as far as he was concerned.

"Most hotels have a reading room for guests," Sue-Ellen continued.

Now she was going too far, had already gone too far. "We won't discuss the library again."

"I should think not," Michael muttered. "No one goes in that room but your father and myself...and you of course, Edward," he added hastily.

Sue-Ellen withdrew her hand and Edward closed his with an unwelcome sense of loss. This evening had not gone as planned. Michael had effectively scuttled any hope of going forward without rancor. But at least some progress had been made.

"I'd better get back," Sue-Ellen said, getting up. "You've given me a lot to think about."

Edward murmured an indistinct response, not sure he liked her implication. In the hall he helped with her coat and reached one for himself.

"No, please," she said. "I know my way. It isn't necessary for you to come out."

"I'd rather see you to the house. Michael can entertain himself for a few minutes."

At that moment Michael joined them. "I'll walk with her," he told Edward, who found himself wishing even more fervently that Michael hadn't shown up. "I could use the exercise before I head back to the vicarage."

There was no point in arguing. He watched them leave before slowly closing the door. Why did he feel uptight? Why did he feel the comfortable, if tedious, order of things at Airstone was in jeopardy?

HE WAS INTERESTING. Irritating, preoccupied, possibly deliberately obtuse when it suited him, but interesting ... and attractive.

Sue-Ellen raised her shoulders and peered guiltily up at the silent clergyman who walked beside her. What would the Reverend Michael Bastible think if he knew she was analyzing Edward Ormsby-Jones, the man? She wasn't sure she cared.

"We can cut through the shrubbery and skirt the fountains," Michael said suddenly, holding her elbow and steering her from the path without waiting for a response.

"It's very dark," she said when the silence began to grate. At every step she expected to turn an ankle.

"We're a long way from civilized things like streetlights. I'm sure where you come from there aren't any places like this."

She bristled. "Georgia has some beautiful estates. Different from this, but lovely in their own way."

"Hmm. Watch where you tread. I can hear the fountains, and it wouldn't be hard to walk into the pond around it without realizing what you'd done until you were down in the cold weeds."

"Is it deep?" So far she'd hardly had time to do more than notice the ornamental fountains and pool that dominated the approach to the house.

"Very, I'm told. There's a story that some lovelorn young woman attending a party here—in the dim and distant past, of course—rushed from the house after being jilted and was assumed to have disappeared."

"Did she ever show up?"

"So they say. This is only a tale, mind you. They say her bloated body was found when the pool was drained for cleaning weeks later. The weeds had snared her and held her out of sight."

Sue-Ellen shuddered. "That's disgusting." She was grateful to see the cascading water and the lights of the house beyond.

At the foot of the steps Michael Bastible stopped and stared at the sky. "Sometimes it's a good idea not to go farther than we have to go to accomplish a given task."

Message time. She'd have sworn before tonight that he liked her. Now she wasn't sure. "What does that mean?"

"This hasn't always been a happy house."

Her skin turned icy. "Most houses have their unhappy stories."

"True. I just thought I should mention that this house has a thing or two better forgotten."

"Edward didn't say anything—"

"Edward doesn't know much more than you do. If you like him, which I sense you might, you'll do him the greatest service by never telling him we had this conversation. Can I trust you in that?"

The still air had a texture of its own, which pressed in on her. Yet again she was being told that her project was unpopular and that it would be appreciated if she would back off without telling Edward why. "I'm not sure I should say yes. If I can't turn to him, who can I turn to?"

"Me. If you have a problem come to me. You only have my word for this, but I can be trusted. Will you trust me? I assure you that all I'm concerned with is protecting the feelings of some old friends."

What else could she say but, "Yes. Thank you," and wonder if she was talking to someone who felt as strongly negative about her as the Ormsby-Jones sisters. Or was he only concerned with his precious conservatory?

"Good," he said. "Go on in. I'll watch."

He'd watch, Sue-Ellen thought as she closed the front door behind her. Exactly how many people were watching her, and waiting for her to fail . . . ?

The house felt heavy about her. Usually she spent part of the evening in the parlor with Bea, but the housekeeper would have retired by now. Sue-Ellen started upstairs, tiptoeing, although no one was likely to hear her.

A noise. Snuffling.

She paused, looking toward the Great Hall, a dark cavern beyond its cold stone screens.

Her imagination must be on high.

The sound came again, and a muffled word . . . a moan? Sue-Ellen set her teeth and turned sideways to stare into the gloom. She leaned over the banisters, straining to see. And her eyes caught something, something at floor level that barely extended from one of the two openings in the screens.

A foot.

Chapter Three

The huge thud of her heart was like a blow. For a second she didn't move. The only light came from a small amber-glassed fixture in the vestibule and, faintly, from upstairs. Blackness in the narrow passage leading away from the entrance hall was something she felt...and its solid quality, as if it were full and waiting.

She took a slow downward step, her hands slippery on the banister. There had been a moan, hadn't there? Stumbling in her hurry, she sped to the hall. She stopped. A shoe. An old-fashioned black shoe with a pointed toe and a strap that buttoned at one side. The ankle, in a heavy brown stocking, was swollen.

Taking in a breath, Sue-Ellen approached until she could grip the edge of the archway through the screen and look around the corner.

She dropped to her knees. Again she'd been caught, frightened sickeningly, by a deliberate and childish prank. The ankle wasn't an ankle but a roll of newspaper stuffed into an old stocking and shoved inside the shoe.

But the moan had been real. She stood and peered toward the back of the house. That was where the brilliant perpetrator of this latest effort had stood, she was sure of it. There were dozens of rooms there, dozens of doors into which someone familiar with the layout could slip and escape without needing to turn on a light.

Had they assumed she'd run for help without investigating? Would they then have removed the shoe and tried to make her appear paranoid? Whatever their design, it had backfired. And it had made her not frightened, but fearless. She knew exactly what she was going to do next.

With the shoe in hand she ran upstairs to her rooms. Once inside she locked the door, stashed her latest exhibit in the bottom of the vast mahogany wardrobe and changed into a black sweat suit and tennis shoes.

She couldn't leave yet, not until she was sure everyone assumed she'd gone to bed.

Waiting was hard. Sitting at the writing table, the smell of the acetone she'd used to clean up earlier still strong enough to make her eyes sting, Sue-Ellen worked on a journal entry, the first since she'd arrived. The small lamp with its blue brocade shade, cast an oval puddle of yellow light on the pages. Recording the events of recent days would help her remain objective, and one day she'd want to remember everything that happened on her English odyssey.

Now and again she checked her watch and listened to the sounds of the house. Eleven-thirty, and she heard nothing but the creaking and settling she'd become accustomed to hearing and the slapping of tree limbs against the windows.

She should write to her parents. They'd be watching the mail every day. Her mother's face came to her, an older copy of her own, but still wonderfully young for her fifty-six years. Sue-Ellen smiled, imagining her mother's reaction to what her daughter intended to do tonight.

She could probably leave now. Until tonight, she'd spent every evening since her arrival in the coldly elegant parlor with Bea. The live-in staff retired to their quarters on the third floor around eight-thirty, and at nine-thirty, as if a small silent alarm sounded in the housekeeper's head, the woman would yawn, say, "Well, tomorrow's another day," and go to her rooms.

Bea should be asleep by now, and the aunts, whose suite was in a parallel corridor. The women didn't seem to set foot outside their domain anyway. They took all meals there and monopolized Connie's time.

Sue-Ellen considered Connie Butters—the most convenient hands available to the old women. Sue-Ellen had learned that Connie didn't live at the Hall but walked in from the village early every morning. Bea had mentioned a "feckless" husband and "gangling" teenage son. Connie was potentially likable, or had been until today.

Waiting any longer would be pointless. Leaving on the desk lamp, she used both hands to turn the door handle and slipped into the corridor. Tiny lights in high sconces still shone outside each room.

Swiftly, scuttling close to the wall, she made it past Bea's rooms and around the corner where she stopped to catch her breath. Sleuthing was a course she'd missed on her way to a degree in hotel management.

Humor didn't help. Her heart thudded unpleasantly.

Down another corridor, a pause to peer in the direction of the aunts' suite, around another corner, and the main stairs were ahead. These were easy. Although only a suggestion of light slid from above to wash the gloom, she was surefooted, and the carpet helped her tread noiselessly.

The Great Hall offered a bigger challenge. Moving with extreme care, more afraid of making a sound than of bodily harm, she felt around her before taking each step to avoid walking into furniture. Slowly her eyes adjusted, and she could make out the bulky shapes crowding the hall.

Pale stone glimmered where the floor-to-ceiling fireplace divided the farthest wall. Earlier she'd spoken of the fascination of going where people had gone long ago. Right now she'd have sworn a throng of oldies and deadies seethed on every side. Swapping this outing for a stint pushing a shopping cart through a brightly lit supermarket might be a real treat.

A muffled snap came from behind.

Sue-Ellen let out a breath, took in another and vowed to stay calm while she turned, making sure she did nothing suddenly. What would she say if confronted? She'd been so certain that the person who pulled the shoe stunt would wait until she went upstairs, check, find the shoe gone and go his or her way to worry about what she might do with the evidence.

But there was no movement. No stealthy figure slithering, wraithlike, from couch to chair to harpsichord. She looked upward, toward the minstrel's gallery above the stone screens. For a second she'd thought a flicker of light showed. Only darkness. Her nerves of steel must be bending a little.

Suppressing the panic that threatened, she carried on, lifted an edge of the vast tapestry hanging by the fireplace, and edged behind its weight. The dark and dust were suffocating. She closed her eyes, fighting down the one weakness she refused to name, the one she had never overcome. Shaking, ordering her mind to think only of the task, she took a small flashlight from her pocket and switched on its minuscule beam. From another pocket she removed a Swiss army knife and flipped out a blade.

The first time she'd found the door, an artful effort made to match the wall paneling, she hadn't studied the padlock closely. Now she knelt, training the flashlight up close. The original handle was of brass, an elegant affair that wouldn't offend any eye. Above this, a hasp had been attached with heavy screws, and Sue-Ellen frowned at the cavalier marring of something beautiful.

After what felt like hours, she stopped digging at the padlock and sat back on her heels. If she dared, she'd poke her head from behind the hanging, but it was her shield and she'd have to cope, at least a little longer.

When the lock snapped open, it was with a report like a rifle being fired in a small cupboard. Sue-Ellen leaned a sweating brow on her fists and struggled for breath. She couldn't take this much longer. She could go back, should go back. There was nothing that said she had to do this. Immediately she buried the thought. Nothing was going to stop her from finding out if the best parts of this house were going to waste. And no one was going to stop her from doing the job she'd come to do and making a success of the whole project.

The door opened inward. A shoulder, applied with her whole weight behind it, gradually forced a black and widening hole leading to... She swallowed, swallowed again. A passage, she reminded herself firmly, and servant rooms and a "horror" of a kitchen. She also reminded herself that she'd made up her mind to do no more than get the lock undone tonight. Lingering too long at one time could be risky. She must do her research in secret and then present her findings to Edward if they were worthwhile. If they weren't, he need never know she'd come here. No one need know. And she mustn't forget that, regardless of what happened, she hadn't been forbidden to explore.

She wouldn't think about rats.

Her flashlight beam, swept in an arc, picked up graying whitewashed walls, the top of a flight of steps leading downward... and a light switch. That there might be electricity here had never crossed her mind. Sue-Ellen pushed the switch down and screwed up her eyes against the yellow glare from a single naked bulb suspended on a long wire.

The flight of steps was short, leading to a square stone area on the far side of which she could see another door, this one Norman in shape, of black wood and standing open. Beyond lay a dim passageway.

She should go back. Tomorrow night would be soon enough to do this.

Slowly she descended to the next level and crossed to the door.

Perhaps, if she could cajole Edward a little, he'd agree to come with her. But Edward and cajoling didn't go together, did they?

There was weak light in the passage, and a few steps to the left brought Sue-Ellen to yet another door. It was locked. The house of locked doors. The air reeked of mold and disuse. Maybe she should have listened to Michael Bastible. Was that a voice she heard, muted, distant and moaning?

No. That ploy had been used already. She was only losing her mind.

The next room she reached wasn't locked. Just as Michael had warned, it was strange, a windowless cubicle with a niche in one wall as if for a statue. The place reminded her of a monk's cell. But it would make a great gimmick: for the traveler who's experienced everything but a night in an Elizabethan dungeon—alone. Dungeon was a slight exaggeration, but some appropriate props could always be added.

The lights went out.

Sue-Ellen bottled the scream that rushed to her throat, and willed herself to stay still, to think, to listen. No one could move through those narrow passageways without so much as a rustle, could they? She held her breath.

With arms outstretched, ranging around, she groped until her fingers touched what had to be the wall just inside the door. Then she found the edge of the jamb and gripped it with one hand while she flattened her back against cold stone. Now she'd keep her mind very, very clear. If someone came into the room she'd feel the presence, even see the denser form, and then she'd slip out and run. Until then she mustn't turn on the flashlight. She palmed the light, holding it against her thigh.

No sound. No one came.

Minutes passed. She closed her eyes and prayed. Don't let fear paralyze her or make her scream or run wildly.

The electricity could have failed. The wiring down here must be old. But once she moved she was committed...to whatever...or whomever.... She hadn't been seen coming here; couldn't have been. Or could she? Evidently there were people around who were adept at watching her movements. No. Old wiring was the answer this time. Another minute or two and she'd get out.

When she finally slid the button on the flashlight, sweat had turned cold on her back and she shivered. The ridiculous little spear of brilliance touched only where pointed.

But it picked out no staring eyes, no hovering murderous villain ... not even a lone rat.

Weakness had seeped into her muscles. Wanting to leap and dash but unable to do more than creep along, Sue-Ellen reached the little stone anteroom to the lower region and stared ahead, convinced the door to the Great Hall would be closed. She saw the colored threads at the back of the hanging.

A great sobbing breath escaped her. Reaching out, she covered the light switch and clicked the button. Instantly the bulb just behind her glowed its weak old light. Fear ebbed, replaced by determination and anger. Grown-ups playing silly games weren't part of her experience, and they certainly wouldn't be allowed to intimidate *this* woman.

Sue-Ellen squeezed behind the hanging again, turned off the light and shut the door. These people were determined, she'd give them that. Someone knew what she'd done tonight. And then they'd tried to make sure she wouldn't take any more unscheduled house tours. Could the Reverend Bastible have spent several hours waiting to see if she would defy his advice? Seemed unlikely. But someone had seen her progress through the house and had waited long enough to have a chance to give her a good scare. The biggest puzzle was who. Surely Connie had gone home hours ago. Right now Sue-Ellen would like to make a tour to see who was and wasn't safely tucked up for the night.

Finding her way back across the Great Hall was easier this time. She knew roughly where each piece of furniture was.

Someone was watching.

Sue-Ellen stopped walking. Her skin felt shrunken. She looked up quickly, toward the gallery...and saw an immobile shape. Automatically she clicked on the flashlight, but even had the beam been able to reach far enough, she was too slow. The form dropped from sight.

But whoever it was had made a mistake. Running as fast as she dared, Sue-Ellen dodged past the screens and leaped the stairs, two at a time. She'd never been onto the gallery, but she knew exactly where it was.

The first corridor to the left on the second floor ran outside the library, and another turn brought her in front of the door leading to the gallery.

Brazening this out was the only approach now. She threw open the door, walked in and found herself in a room behind the gallery. Why had it never occurred to her that there might have been such a room in which the musicians could prepare before a performance?

Her courage waned a little. But she crossed the narrow chamber...and stopped. Increased draft, the indistinct but rapid thud of feet, let her know her mistake. Her follower had done exactly as she had planned to do in the cellars— waited behind the door for her to pass, then made an escape.

Sue-Ellen sank to the floor. She rested her head on her knees, more tired than she ever remembered being. Okay, if nothing else, she'd learned that her enemies probably outnumbered her allies and that Edward Ormsby-Jones's wishes were not automatically taken as law in this house. So, she'd just have to help him out. He might never know how much she'd helped him, but she'd have the satisfaction of outmaneuvering the opposition.

Using protesting muscles, she pushed to her feet and proceeded to the door.

That was as far as she went. Rather than going into the passage she pulled back, easing the door almost shut until she'd left herself a narrow peephole of a crack.

Outside the library, indistinct but unmistakable by the light of a sconce, stood Sylvia. Clad in a loosely belted, almost transparent robe, she glanced nervously and repeatedly left and right...until she was joined by a man who slipped from the library.

He locked the door, pocketed the key and turned. Sue-Ellen held her breath. Colin Bastible, a single book under one arm, looked as furtive as Sylvia.

Could one of them have turned the lights off in the cellar, then gone to hide in the library? If so, who had been in the gallery? The idea didn't work, because it would mean they knew where she was at this moment. Clearly they didn't. Sue-Ellen gritted her teeth. All she wanted was to go to bed and get ready for another day at the job she was being paid to do. Who was having a clandestine affair with whom around here wasn't her concern. But she couldn't simply walk past Colin and Sylvia and wish them a pleasant goodnight.

Seconds later she wished she had done just that. The clinch that started was instantly torrid. Sue-Ellen didn't regard herself as a prude, but Sylvia, naked but for the robe, which soon dangled from her elbows, was an embarrassment. Sue-Ellen looked away, closed her eyes, opened them to see Colin making a meal of Sylvia's overwhelming breasts. The book had slipped to the floor. These two clearly had similar interests in life.

Just when Sue-Ellen feared she was about to hear the muffled sounds of lovemaking on the carpet, the stifled moaning ceased. She risked another peek. Sylvia, a glazed smile on her face, leaned against the wall while Colin wrapped her robe around her and refastened the tie. He straightened his own clothes, holding Sylvia off when she tried to wind her arms around his neck again. She gave a small sexy giggle, and he covered her mouth, shaking his head sharply before he whispered in her ear. Sylvia's broad smile gave Sue-Ellen a good idea of the gist of Colin's comment.

He picked up the book an oversized, leather-bound volume, and gave it to Sylvia. Her smile widened even more and she nodded. An instant later Colin sped downstairs and disappeared toward the back of the house. That must be the route he took to come and go for visits with Sylvia.

Sylvia waited another moment, smoothing the red fabric luxuriously over her breasts and thighs before she, also, went downstairs. She would have to cross the house to a distant staircase leading to the servants' rooms. How often, Sue-Ellen wondered, did Colin creep into Airstone in the dead of night? Did he and Sylvia always use the so-called off-limits library for their trysts? He probably wouldn't find it too difficult to lift the key from his father, and once inside the room, he and his lover could be ensured of privacy. The book was a puzzle, but there was no reason not to suppose that even nymphomaniacs liked to read.

Finally she could escape back to her room. She looked at her watch and shuddered to find it showed one-thirty. Seven-thirty in the morning would seem early.

The instant she stepped into the passageway again the sconces flickered and died. Sue-Ellen groaned aloud. She couldn't help it.

At least she knew her way from here.

Afraid the silly flashlight would catch the attention of some insomniac who might see it pass at the crack of a door, she set out with the certainty that she'd had quite enough of things that went bang in the night, and creeping around like a cat burglar.

Halfway along the passage to her room she got that sensation again—that someone was watching.... She squared her shoulders. This night had been entirely too much and mustn't be repeated. Her psyche wouldn't take the pressure and she didn't have time to crack up.

Oh, God. She did hear breathing, and a swishing sound. But only an instant before she smacked into something sharp and an arm shot around her.

Chapter Four

"What—"

A large hand covered her mouth. "Keep still."

All she could do was mumble and struggle. The sharp object was between her and the man who held her with one strong arm.

"Sue-Ellen...oh, this is ridiculous."

Edward! She mumbled again, starting to lose her temper.

The next thing she felt was his hair brushing her cheek and his mouth close to her ear. "Sue-Ellen, I want to get out of this house without being seen or heard, do you understand?"

She nodded but didn't understand at all. Why would he be afraid to do as he pleased in his own house?

His grip didn't slacken and she held still. He smelled nice, woodsy, appropriate. His jaw grazed hers. The roughness of what must be a day's growth of beard prickled. She closed her eyes. He smelled and felt nice, and she was a madwoman held captive in a dark passageway, but still reacting to primitive stimuli.

"I'm going to take my hand from your mouth. If I do that, will you keep quiet?"

She nodded again and he freed her.

"How...?" She leaned toward him and he lowered his head so that she could whisper into his ear. "How could you tell it was me?"

Again the beard brushed her cheek and the mouth came close enough to touch her skin. "Size," he said.

"Oh." Thinking about that might be interesting. He'd taken enough notice of her to be able to recognize her by touch. Not such a bad thought.

"If we stay here, one of the old...one of my aunts might wander along. They do that at night sometimes. If I'm seen here the balloon will go up."

She smiled into the darkness. The refined Edward sounded as if he might be capable of less-than-genteel language when really pushed. What was she supposed to do? Say good-night and go on her way? No. Something needed explanation. Namely, why Edward needed to creep around the house in the middle of the night behaving like a criminal.

"Would you like to come into my sitting room? There's this awful—there's a hot plate where I can heat water if you'd like tea."

Without replying, he shifted whatever he was carrying into one arm and used the other to guide her to her rooms. Once inside he walked to a couch and set down a cardboard box, then took off his navy woolen jacket and draped it over the back of a chair. Sue-Ellen observed him. He moved around as if he lived here—actually here in this suite of rooms.

"Mind if I wash my hands?" He smiled and, without waiting for an answer, went into the bedroom. The sound of running water came from the bathroom, and shortly he was back and sitting beside his box.

Sue-Ellen crossed her arms, feeling strangely displaced. "Would you like that tea?"

"There's Scotch in the cupboard. I think that's definitely what this occasion calls for." And he got up again and went to a small corner cabinet that had been locked since her arrival. She'd intended to ask Bea about that but had been too busy.

Edward produced a bunch of keys from his pocket and opened the narrow ornately carved door. "How about you?'' He took out a bottle of Chivas Regal and two glasses. "No ice, I'm afraid. I never did take to ice in my drinks."

"That's fine." Hard liquor wasn't her thing, but if there was going to be a night to bend in that area this was definitely it. "Edward, what were you doing creeping around in the dark—and how come you behave as if you live in these rooms?"

He'd poured two generous measures and swung to face her. A flash of color swept over his cheeks and the effect was startling. He looked suddenly very young. "Caught," he said on a long breath. "Bound to happen. I thought the old . . . I thought the aunts would get around to telling you what they thought about it eventually. But not until they'd sulked a bit longer. Bea wouldn't have mentioned it, and the rest of the staff aren't likely to realize you don't know."

Sue-Ellen accepted the glass. "I really don't know what you're trying to say, Edward. You're talking in code."

He waved her to a chair and sat beside his box once more. "Came to get this." He tapped it. "More books. Didn't want to risk running into the aunts and going through another tirade."

If she kept quiet and let him work his way through, this would go faster.

"There's a storage room at the end of this corridor. Up a couple of steps. I expect you noticed it."

"No." Bea had made it clear that no part of the family's wing could be used for guests, and Sue-Ellen had concentrated her exploration efforts elsewhere.

"I used to play in that room when I was a boy. When I decided to move to the gate house I stored a few things there."

She frowned. "You're in the process of moving into the gate house?"

He nodded and swallowed some Scotch.

"That explains it. I thought you were moving out and wondered where you were going. Where did you live before?"

He colored even more brightly and removed his glasses. The ritual polishing took a while, but he eventually looked up at her with his extraordinary amber eyes. The redness had receded from his cheeks, and she thought again how interesting his looks were. His mouth was . . . He had a very nice mouth, very nice.

"You have to be at the center of things," he announced abruptly. "And you also have to be comfortable. You've got a big job to do here, and you deserve to have a place of your own that's good to go back to at the end of each day."

Sue-Ellen couldn't think of a response.

"Anyway, that's why I decided you should have my rooms."

She set down her glass. "You gave me your rooms? Oh, Edward, you shouldn't have done that. I can't drive you from your own home. We'll swap places at once. In the morning. I can work perfectly well from—"

"No! Absolutely not. I won't hear of it. You're settled now."

"But you're not." She stood up and paced. "I'm so embarrassed. No wonder your aunts said I didn't belong here."

"They said that? In those words? I'll—"

"Please. Don't say anything. Now I see how they must feel. I'm an interloper and I've ousted their nephew they must adore. After all, you're their only resident relative."

Edward's groan, the way he propped his forehead on one fist, brought Sue-Ellen swiftly to his side. She sat down and, without thinking, massaged the back of his neck. "Please don't let this get to you. I understand the pressures of trying to run a house like this, or at least I'm beginning to. It was nice of you . . . really sweet to give me your own quarters, but I'll be happy at the gate house."

He turned his face toward her. His glasses dangled from his fingers. "This has gone far enough," he said, pulling the corners of his mouth down. "I've been unmasked. I'm a conniving . . . I used you."

She removed her hand from his neck. "I'm your employee."

"You're also a very convenient reason for me to move away from my two dear aunts. If you knew how long I've been looking for an excuse to put some distance between us. You were it. Finally I can come and go as I please with little or no fear of running into one of the old . . . old bats is what I mean. Sorry if I sound weak, but sometimes it's hard to break habits, much as you may want to."

Sue-Ellen smiled. Then she laughed. "You fraud. And I thought you were being the proverbial English gentleman. Aren't you ashamed? Frightened of a couple of . . . old bats?"

He laughed, too. "Frankly I don't think I am ashamed. What you've experienced so far is probably mild. Try being thirty-five and having to be polite during regular interrogations about your movements, your friends and so on. Then try being expected to show up for one of their revolting teas at least once a week. And when you go they don't actually *say* anything, just watch and drop the occasional 'we' question. 'Have we done anything we want to share with our aunts?' 'Are there new friends we'd like to discuss?' "

Sue-Ellen's grin turned into a yawn. "Why didn't you move before?"

He considered for a moment. "Don't misunderstand this, but cultures can be very different. I was brought up to respect my elders. Evidently the lesson stuck. Then I suppose I feel a bit sorry for two women who never became independent—who knows? They still rely on me, and I have to preserve their funny little dignities. Anyway, please, enjoy this place and I'll enjoy mine. I love that gate house."

She hunched her shoulders. He amused her as he was now, a strong man bound by tradition, the behavior expected of a man in his position. Also, she liked his honesty and the caring side he showed. "You're the boss," she told him.

"And you're tired," he responded, getting up and putting down his glass. He retrieved his coat.

Sue-Ellen rose, also. "Things start early around here."

He grimaced. "I know. Too early. But it's Sunday and you could take things a little easy." About to pick up his box, he hesitated and straightened. "For a lawyer I'm pretty sloppy about some things. What were you doing pussyfooting around at one in the morning?"

She hadn't even noticed his failure to question what she was up to. "Um . . ." Should she tell the truth? All of it? He would want to know and do something about the maliciousness, even if his aunts were responsible. But Edward had been in the house tonight, too, at least at some time after she'd left her room. Surely he wouldn't get involved in the type of thing that had been done to her.

"Sue-Ellen? Why the guilty look?"

Caution was the best approach for now. Complaining could only make her look foolish and jumpy. "I couldn't sleep," she said and looked away. "This was a tough day. I thought I'd take a walk."

"You went walking in the dark?" He sounded incredulous. "You could break your neck out there."

Yeah, or drown in the pond. These people were full of cheerful warnings. "I'm surefooted and I didn't go all that far." She disliked lying.

"Just the same, I don't think it's such a good idea. I'd prefer you not to wander around alone in the night."

Did he also have a reason for preferring her not to explore his cellars? Again she could think of nothing to support such a notion.

"I'll remember what you've said."

He rested his hands on his lean hips and smiled at her. "I'm glad you're here," he announced. "I made a good choice. Someone with guts and imagination was what I needed and you're it."

At first she was too taken aback to respond. After swallowing she said, "Thanks. I'm enjoying it here." Not strictly true, or not all of the time, anyway.

His sudden, bearlike hug was even more of a surprise. So was a quick kiss planted on her cheek before he swept up the box and headed for the door.

"You're a brick," he said. "Thanks for understanding my little subterfuge about the living arrangements. Frankly it does make sense for you to have my rooms, but it's definitely to my advantage."

"Yes, I see that." *A brick*. Not exactly what she'd prefer as a classification. But the hug had been wonderful and the kiss sweet. This Englishman was quickly dissolving her programmed ideas about the cool British.

"Good night, Sue-Ellen."

"Good night." She wished he didn't have to go, and that was absolutely crazy. All he'd done was be nice.

"Listen." He came closer. "I'd love to share my retreat with you."

She stared at him, startled.

"Oh, hell. No, I didn't mean that the way it sounded." He laughed. "You poor old thing. I'm not propositioning you. What I mean is that anytime you need to get away, my house is your house. Here—" he worked the key ring from his jacket pocket and slid off a key "—this is to the back door of the gate house. Use it whenever you like—whether I'm there or not."

He left with a last irresistible smile.

Sue-Ellen flopped onto the couch. Why wasn't he married, or at least significantly involved? Perhaps he was. She pursed her lips, irritated that she disliked the idea of Edward's being involved with a woman. She'd better keep in mind that to him she was *a brick*, nothing more, which was as it should be.

Should she have told him about the events of the past twenty-four hours—in detail?

Dragging with tiredness, she went into the bedroom and kicked off her sneakers.

She opened the wardrobe and reached into the corner where she's stashed the marred papers and photograph. Wrong corner. Dropping to her knees, she moved aside hanging clothes to search. The papers and photo were gone. So was the old black shoe.

Chapter Five

"You look tired, Miss Hill."

"Mmm." Sue-Ellen was beginning to tire of Bea's formality. "I didn't sleep well last night." That was an understatement. After a sluggish Sunday she'd gone through another restless night anticipating the potential problems of today.

"Perhaps you should go back to bed for a while. I'll have Connie bring you some breakfast later."

"Thank you, but no. And, Bea, would you please use my first name?"

The woman's hand went to the gold locket resting against her pink silk blouse. "Of course." But there was a hint of reticence in the voice, and the rhythmic stroking of the locket suggested discomfort.

These people would have to cope with their own complex social system without troubling her. "I have a seven-thirty appointment with one of the contractors. I want the conversion of the tack rooms and stables started at the same time as the repairs and alterations for the guest rooms. That's scheduled to begin on Wednesday."

Sue-Ellen had found Bea where she could always be found around seven in the morning—in the impressive breakfast room where she ate in formal splendor. Silver-domed dishes covered a vast sideboard of some dark and cracking wood, the front panels of which had been heavily carved into the shapes of fruit. Sue-Ellen finally chose a poached egg, a sausage and a croissant. Her appetite was one thing that never failed her. She frequently wished it would.

"The new linens should arrive today," she told Bea, and sat in a chair facing the housekeeper. "I got a call on Friday promising they'd be here. Also the dishes and flatware and glasses."

Bea made a polite noise. The division of authority here could prove a problem.

"The kitchen is more than adequate to cope with the additional volume. Mrs. Leaming can store the dishes wherever she thinks best." Mrs. Leaming was the cook, a florid silent woman who had yet to bestow a smile upon Sue-Ellen. "Did you mention to her that I'd ordered a microwave oven?"

"I thought you might like to discuss that with her yourself." Bea kept her attention on the coffee in her cup. "It might be a good way to establish better rapport . . . if you know what I mean."

Sue-Ellen paused with her fork halfway to her mouth. "No, I don't think I do."

"Well, I just meant that since the, er, accommodations project is your area you might prefer to deal with any questions arising. . . ." She raised a palm.

Sue-Ellen felt guilty. Bea was simply trying to show that she accepted the new situation. "You're right, of course. I'll be talking to Mrs. Leaming later, at ten. I've asked for a meeting with the entire staff, which brings me to a question."

Bea raised her brows.

"Mr. Pitts? What exactly is his position?" The man was ancient. He shuffled from place to place, a green baize apron tied over his worn black suit, and he muttered unceasingly.

"Mr. Pitts is the steward. In the order of things he's second in command to me."

"He is?" Sue-Ellen couldn't hide her amazement. "Is he, um, has he been here long?" Asking if the man was sane might be unwise.

"Forever," Bea said, her expression blank. "And then there's Grossby. He's our butler, but you already know that. Unfortunately, since the staff is rather small, he also has to take on many tasks that wouldn't normally be his. Mrs. Leaming's job is self-explanatory, and you already know what Connie and Sylvia do."

Sue-Ellen hadn't expected a complete rundown of everyone's duties. "Thank you."

But Bea hadn't finished. "Massing's head gardener, and he has several men who come in from the village regularly to do the heavy labor. Then, naturally, there's the cleaning crew. They're here twice a week. There's no way we could keep the house up without extra help."

And that would be at least doubly true before long. "No way," Sue-Ellen agreed. "That's what I want to talk to everyone about this morning. Workloads are likely to get tough until people are hired specifically for the hotel. Edward says that can't happen until we start showing a profit. In the meantime I'm going to have to set some ground rules."

Bea's cup met the saucer with a crack. "Ground rules?"

"Of course I'm not talking about your side of things," Sue-Ellen said hastily. "But there will be some changes once there are paying guests in the house." She nodded to the sideboard. "Breakfast is a good example. I think people will really go for all this old-fashioned ritual, but it'll take some organization to choreograph, particularly on Tuesdays and Thursdays during the months when the house is open."

"Those . . . the guests will eat in here?"

Sue-Ellen frowned. All she needed was opposition from Bea. "I thought that would be appropriate." She glanced significantly at the endless stretch of the dining table where forty people could sit without crowding. "Where else would they eat?"

"Well . . . there are other rooms. Perhaps they could go out to your new tearooms."

Diplomacy was the key here. "Don't you think it would be better to keep the tearooms as just that? I thought formal breakfast in here would be a real draw."

Bea appeared to consider this. Then she smiled. "Of course. Of course, you're absolutely right. And it won't interfere with the tours because those don't start until ten. This room is roped off. They only get to stand outside and look." A slight wrinkling of the nose suggested distaste.

Sue-Ellen took a slow unsatisfactory breath. "Yes, well, perhaps there's a way to route the tours so they don't reach this room until later, because some guests will want to sleep in."

Bea stared. "Until after ten?"

Edward should have prepared her for this. The old habits and routines he'd alluded to were going to be tough to bend. "I just meant that some people might only be finishing their meal by then," she said, trying to mollify. "And this is such a lovely room. People can be forgiven for wanting to hang around. Naturally," she added, suddenly inspired, "we'll make sure they can't start before eight-thirty or so." She smiled at Bea. In other words, the housekeeper's private time in this room she clearly revered would be kept sacrosanct.

"You're very organized," Bea commented, but her thumb had gone to the locket again. "You do know I'm one hundred percent behind you and Edward in this?"

The announcement surprised Sue-Ellen. "Thank you. I'll need your help all the way." She'd taken Bea's support for granted. Evidently too much so. In the future Bea would be involved closely in the decisions Sue-Ellen made.

"If you have problems—any problems—let me know and I'll back you up."

Sue-Ellen's spine stiffened. Bea expected trouble? "I'll remember that." She was being overly sensitive. Saturday night had shaken her up. For an instant she considered mentioning the incident in the cellars. Just as quickly she discarded the idea. Bea would wonder why Sue-Ellen hadn't asked to go in the daytime. She had been wondering the same thing herself.

There was one thing she must ask Bea. "I feel a bit silly about this, but is there another key to my rooms?" She intended to find out exactly who would be able to get through her locked door. "I seem to have lost the one you gave me."

Bea shook her head slowly and frowned. "No, I'm afraid not. That one was mine. I should have had another made."

"Oh, dear." Sue-Ellen sighed. "Perhaps Edward would have one since the rooms were his."

Bea showed no surprise that Sue-Ellen knew about Edward's move. "I doubt it," she said. "I don't think he ever used one. But you could ask him."

She could and would. The extraordinary possibility that he had been the one to remove her stash of exhibits had persisted throughout Sunday and last night. How was she to know exactly what was in his box of "books"? But as much as the evidence seemed to add up, the motive didn't.

There was another question Bea could answer. Sue-Ellen glanced at the grandfather clock ticking loudly in a corner. She didn't have much time before her appointment.

Pushing her scarcely touched plate of food aside, she picked up her coffee cup. "Bea, I know this is none of my business, but you know how curiosity is. Was Edward ever married?"

"Married?"

Sue-Ellen could feel Bea staring at her. She kept her eyes trained on the inch of cold coffee in her cup. "Mmm. He seems like the kind who would be."

"He's never been married."

Now Sue-Ellen looked up. Bea's voice was flat.

"There was someone once. Her name was Lenore."

There was a shifting sensation inside Sue-Ellen. "What happened?" This really was none of her business.

Bea shrugged. Her mouth was a grim line. "It was awful. Happened about three years after I moved here from Yorkshire, so that'd be six years ago, I think." She shook her head and gazed into the distance.

Sue-Ellen leaned forward, waiting.

"They were engaged," Bea said quietly. "Would have been married a few weeks later. The aunts didn't like her, of course." She made a clucking sound. "Threatened and cajoled Edward, they did. Made Lenore's life a misery with their warnings."

"Warnings?" Sue-Ellen's heart began a slow thud.

"Oh, silly old stuff about how women with designs on becoming mistress of this house usually ended up mad. Don't ask me where that kind of story starts. They probably dreamed it up to frighten her off. Only it didn't work."

"So why didn't they get married?" She could hardly bear the suspense.

"She died. Killed. Right here at Airstone. She was riding, and something spooked her horse. It threw her and she hit her head. She was dead when they found her."

AFTER A DECENT INTERVAL while she'd let Bea think old thoughts and while she tried to quiet her own tattered nerves, Sue-Ellen excused herself and dashed for the door that opened into the stable yard. She carried her parka and started to tug it on.

Pitts chose that moment to shamble from the scullery.

Groaning to herself, she skidded to a halt. "Good morning, Pitts. Nice morning, too." Not having looked outside, she had no idea whether or not it was nice.

"Cold," he muttered, taking her parka from her with gnarled fingers. How tall he might once have been was impossible to calculate. He was bent to a degree that forced him to peer up at her.

He held the coat while she turned awkwardly, ducking a little so he could help her put it on. "Thank you very much, Pitts." She waved, and forced a smile as she backed away.

He shook his head. "Changing things. Meddling. No good'll come of it. You mark my words. No good."

Sue-Ellen nodded, then shook her head, still backing away until she could escape. In the fresh air she began to run, and as she did her spirits lifted. Pitts was an old man reacting in his fuddled way to change—just as a few other people around here were doing. Given time and her own determination she'd win them all over.

A cobbled yard separated the stables and tack rooms from the house. When she'd first seen the abandoned areas there had been no doubt they should be put to use, but for what? Clearing the accumulated junk of many years would be a mammoth job in itself. Then the idea for the tearoom had come, and she could see in her mind exactly what should be done.

She opened a sagging door and went inside, stepping over heaps of rotting bridles and reins and other horsey paraphernalia she didn't recognize. There were saddles piled in one corner, and she'd already decided these should be made part of the decor, together with whatever else could be salvaged. The biggest job would be the installation of a kitchen, which must be done since transporting food from the house wasn't feasible.

Sue-Ellen trailed back and forth. Before today it hadn't occurred to her to wonder why there were no horses. Now she thought she might know. After his fiancée's death, Edward could well have decided he didn't want to ride anymore, or to be reminded that these buildings were the last his Lenore had been inside.

Made Lenore's life a misery with their warnings. Sue-Ellen shivered. Now her imagination was really on overload. Next she'd be totting up the odds in favor of the aunts engineering a fatal riding accident. She stopped pacing. How far would the women go to remove people of whom they didn't approve?

This train of thought was becoming outrageous, and destructive to concentration.

By a quarter to eight the contractor still hadn't shown, and she walked outside to fill her lungs with fresh air...and saw Edward, Max trotting peaceably at his heels, walking purposefully from a wooded area to the north.

She hailed him and he strode toward her. "Morning." Less heartily he said, "I hope you're in better shape than I was yesterday morning. I shouldn't have had that Scotch. Or the other two I had when I got home. What are you up to?''

"Waiting for a contractor who's already fifteen minutes late." He looked terrific, if unsuitably attired for a morning tramp in the woods. His voluminous oilskin coat topped an elegant dark gray suit, white shirt and navy silk tie. The pants were tucked into his green rubber boots.

He must have caught her glance. "Workday for me again," he said. "Weekends never last long enough. But poor old Max expects his walk in his favorite sniffing grounds before he has to spend the day under a stuffy desk."

"You take him to Dorchester with you?"

"He goes where I go. Great fellow. Listens to every word I say and never disagrees."

They laughed, and Sue-Ellen remembered what she'd intended to ask him. "Do you happen to have a key to my suite?" She managed to sound casual.

"Good Lord. I never thought about that. Yes, I do." Just like that. No hesitation. No apparent discomfort. Edward hadn't been the stealthy thief in her room on Saturday night. She felt his honesty and openness in her bones.

"Here." A key snapped from the ring he produced and he handed it to her. "Sorry about that." He paused, screwing up his eyes. "You unlocked the door the other night."

"Yes, I know. I had Bea's key, but now I can't find it. I'll get a copy of this one made just in case."

"Fine. Anyway, good luck today. I'll be back this evening and we'll get together then."

"Edward!"

They turned in unison to see Helen Bastible, in high-heeled shoes, trotting carefully over the cobbles. Sue-Ellen was struck afresh by the woman's fragile appearance.

Helen nodded at Sue-Ellen before reaching to hold Edward's hand. "Could I cadge a ride with you? I've got to go into Dorchester for a few things, and it's so much more fun to go...well, you know." She smiled up at Edward who seemed even bigger beside her tiny figure. Today Helen wore heather-colored tweeds, jacket and a gored skirt with a mauve blouse, and the outfit suited her. Sue-Ellen wished she didn't feel she'd prefer it didn't.

"How will you get back?" Edward asked. "I don't expect to be free before late afternoon."

"Oh, I can find plenty to do until you're ready."

I just bet you can. The woman had walked all the way from the village to pull off some time with Edward. Again Sue-Ellen felt too substantially built and too plainly dressed beside Helen. Men usually went for the feminine type.

"Fine then," Edward was saying, and Helen held his arm. "See you later," he told Sue-Ellen, and she caught Helen's hard stare before she walked away, glued to Edward's side.

At eight-fifteen, frustrated and harried, Sue-Ellen returned to the house to call the contractor. The man was from a firm in Poole, a town thirty miles to the south, on the coast. Surely at six or seven in the morning, or whenever the man had supposedly left, the traffic couldn't have been so bad as to make him this late.

She had his card in the notebook she carried in her pocket and used the telephone in the dining room.

Five minutes later she stood, eyes narrowed, ordering herself not to do anything rash.

"Right. That's all I'm taking," she said aloud and marched to the kitchen.

Mary Leaming, buxom, graying, encased in a flowered dress overlaid by a starched white apron, sat at the kitchen table drinking tea. As Sue-Ellen entered the cook raised a sharp nose turned red by the heat and strength of the drink. She pursed her lips but said nothing. Grossby, in black vest and pin-striped pants, but without a jacket over his white shirt and dark tie, lounged against a counter beneath lofty glass-fronted cupboards containing the china used by the family for everyday meals.

Sue-Ellen unzipped her parka and stuffed her hands into the pockets of her jeans. There was time enough to be formally dressed every minute of the day when they had guests in residence. "Who called Chalkers?"

Mary Leaming leaned back in her creaking chair. "Who would Chalkers be, miss?"

The woman knew damn well. Sue-Ellen turned to Grossby. At least he didn't look truculent.

"Is there a problem, Sue-Ellen?"

He would be the one to get fresh. Immediately she was annoyed with herself. In her present mood she was unlikely to be rational. "Yes, there's a problem. Someone here knows what it is and I want to hear them admit as much."

Grossby's lean dark face showed what appeared to be genuine concern and deference. "If I can help you in any way—"

"I'm not interested in platitudes." She sounded like a shrew, but was sick of people offering to help while all the time she was being undermined. At least one member of the staff, probably more, was working against her, and she intended to find out who that was, even if it meant offending the rest in the process. Any rift could be mended later.

"I called a meeting for this morning. Where is everyone?"

Mrs. Leaming lumbered to her feet, the picture of umbrage. "Sylvia said ten. I'm sure I don't know what all this fuss is about. And what's more I don't want to know. We've got enough to do running a house like this with only a handful of full-time staff—"

"We'll get into that." Sue-Ellen cut her off. There was open hostility here . . . everywhere. "I apologize for being abrupt, but not for being angry. Grossby, would you kindly get Connie and Sylvia. I'm getting to the bottom of this right now."

"Well!" Mrs. Leaming's pudgy chapped hands were spread on ample hips. "I've never heard the like. We'll just have to sort out a few things around here."

"Such as?" Sue-Ellen's control returned.

"Miles." Mrs. Leaming addressed Grossby. "We're going to have to insist we know what's what. Mr. Edward wouldn't stand for us being upset any more than Sir Arthur would. Are you going to stand there while she orders you around like a scullery maid? She isn't our boss, nor will she ever be if I have my way."

Grossby moved between Sue-Ellen and the cook. He winked at Sue-Ellen. "Leave things to me, Mary," he said, grinning familiarly. "Best to find out what we're dealing with before getting upset. I'll call up for Connie. Sylvia's in the pantry."

Sue-Ellen felt, forcefully, that she didn't want this man as a confidant. He was tacitly aligning himself with her. The thought inspired no confidence. That he was a user was something she'd sensed from their first meeting.

"Pitts should be here, too," she said, not returning his grin. "When does the cleaning crew arrive?" She knew that the women, a group of housewives from East Puddle, came every Monday and Wednesday.

"Not until ten," Grossby said, still smiling. "Did you want to talk to them, too?"

"No. Not today. But I will soon because we'll need them more often once the hotel's under way."

Mrs. Leaming made a harrumphing noise.

Grossby wound the lever on an antique intercom board, waited and then yelled for Connie to come to the kitchen. "Is there really a need to get Mr. Pitts?" he asked with a meaningful shrug.

"Yes," Sue-Ellen announced. Bea probably wouldn't arrive until the interview was almost over, but that might be just as well, since the housekeeper was bound to be torn in her loyalties at this point.

After what seemed like an interminable interval during which Mrs. Leaming chose to remove an impressive array of copper pots from hooks above the gigantic black stove, the entire staff, with the exception of garden personnel, was assembled. Mrs. Leaming continued heaving the pots through to the scullery with much clanging and banging.

Sue-Ellen waited for her to return for a third time before stepping into her path. "I have other things to do," she said. "Let's get this over with. Who called Chalkers and canceled my morning appointment?"

Silence.

"I repeat. Which one of you called the contractor I was supposed to see at seven-thirty this morning, said you were a staff member here, and told him I'd awarded the work to someone else?"

As she said the words she began to seethe again. Whom could she trust? The contractor had told her the message came in on his service and that the caller left no name. Whether the aunts were involved in this or not, they would not have placed the call personally, and the only fair thing to do was confront all the staff rather than Connie alone.

Sylvia had moved closer to Grossby, her blue eyes wide and innocent and, effectively, a little frightened. "What's she saying, Mr. Grossby? Have we done something wrong?"

Grossby patted her shoulder, and a look passed between them that made Sue-Ellen consider the possibility that Colin Bastible wasn't Sylvia's only sexual diversion.

"All right," Sue-Ellen said, deliberately keeping her voice level. "Let's take this one step at a time. One of you deliberately sabotaged my efforts today. I'm not sure which of you it was and I definitely don't know why, but it had better never happen again, because if it does I won't be the one to discuss it with you. I don't go in for malicious fun and games." She stared hard at one face after another, searching for a reaction, trying to decide if there was so much as a flicker. Her nocturnal follower was undoubtedly among this crew, also.

"Mistake," Pitts said clearly. "They don't listen to me, but they'll find out."

Sue-Ellen looked at him. "What's a mistake, Mr. Pitts? And who are 'they'? Can you tell me?"

He only shook his head.

Connie Butters alone appeared uncomfortable. "My work keeps me upstairs, Miss Hill," she said as if anxious to get this over with and return to work. "I wasn't aware of the contractor coming. Why should I be?" She lifted her chin as she finished.

This would get Sue-Ellen nowhere. "Very well. I'm telling you all that I've rescheduled the appointment for two this afternoon. Now, do whatever you're supposed to be doing. There were other things I wanted to discuss, but they can wait."

"What we do is Miss Smallman's business," Mary Leaming said, venom weighting each word.

"I realize that. But you are also supposed to support me in this phase of my work. And to a certain extent when the hotel's in operation. But we have some weeks before we need worry about that." Weeks in which she intended to make sure Edward okayed the hiring of several new employees who would report solely to her. Sue-Ellen was aware of the difficulty inherent in divided authority, and she had no intention of treading on Bea's toes. So far there had been no problem, but in this kitchen she saw the possibility of an end to peaceful existence with Bea if care wasn't exercised.

"We don't like it." Sylvia spoke suddenly, and when Sue-Ellen turned to her, the calculating glint in formerly guileless eyes was a shock. "This is a quality house," Sylvia continued, "and we don't take kindly to you turning it into a bed and breakfast."

"I—"

"No, we don't," Mrs. Leaming chimed in. "Some of us have been in service a long time. Our job is to look after the family, not a lot of strangers. Not that it'll come off."

Sue-Ellen gaped. "How dare...? I'm not turning anything into anything without having been employed to do so. And what Mr. Ormsby-Jones chooses to do with his house is his affair, isn't it? Not yours?"

Sylvia sniffed. "We'll be laughed at in the village. Used to be a bit of prestige working here, I can tell you. Not anymore, or it won't be if you have your way. I'm not doing a scrap more than I'm already paid for, so there." She flung around and marched into the scullery.

"And do the rest of you feel like that?" Sue-Ellen asked.

Connie shrugged, her eyes downcast. "There's a bit of it. Bound to be, miss. You wouldn't understand the way it is here, but having the house open is bad enough . . . cheapens things. There's talk in the village about how this house is turning into a common tourist attraction, and you can't expect any of us to like that."

Nonplussed, Sue-Ellen sat on the closest chair. "I see." Connie was right. She didn't understand. "Go back to work all of you, please."

Connie left, and Pitts subsided into an old wicker chair near the hearth. Soon he snored gently. Sue-Ellen took off her parka and wrapped it around her arms. Somehow she had to line up some allies, and she might as well start with Mary Leaming. She certainly needed the woman. "Mrs. Leaming, did Bea tell you we're expecting a microwave to be delivered?" By her own admission Bea hadn't, but the entry should work anyway.

Grossby was polishing silver and she saw him pause.

"Microwave?" The cook had lifted a teapot. She put it back on the table. "What would we do with a microwave? Nasty, they are. We've always done things the same way in this house—"

"And you like the way you do things. I understand very well. We all like our own ways. But don't look on this as changing anything. It's going to make it easier when we have a lot of people to feed."

"I'll have you know there's been dinner parties in this house where we served—"

"Yes," Sue-Ellen interrupted again, losing patience. "I'm sure there have been many grand and glorious affairs at Airstone. But I'm talking about situations where people will drizzle down for breakfast all at different times."

"What's wrong with the way we do things now? It's always worked to have people eat in the breakfast room—"

"They'll still eat in the breakfast room and they'll still get the silver and all the trimmings, but you'll need to be able to accommodate the latecomer with something quick and hot, or reheat a cold dish."

"We English don't mind—"

"Cold toast and congealed scrambled eggs. Yes, I know. But some people do, and we want to make sure we build a good reputation for first-class food. Look, don't worry about this now. When the oven arrives I'm sure you'll soon love it." She was tiring of the hassle.

"I'll talk to Miss Smallman about this," was Mrs. Leaming's stiff response, together with the presentation of her broad back. "Newfangled ideas messing up our ways. I won't stand for it. I don't know what Mr. Edward was thinking about. I should talk to him myself. I should talk to Sir Arthur."

Sue-Ellen closed her eyes.

The bang of the kitchen door made her jump. Connie scuttled in, her hands clasped. "Where's Miss Smallman?" Her brown eyes were stretched wide open. "Mr. Grossby, the misses say I've got to find her right now."

Grossby set down a serving spoon. "She went into the village," he said. "She should be back by now. What's up?"

Connie wrung her hands, saw Sue-Ellen and turned bright red. "They had me call Mr. Edward in Dorchester."

"Why did they do that?" Grossby asked with more calm than Sue-Ellen could have managed.

"Because of the theft. Someone broke in and took the jewelry Mr. Edward's grandmother left. They assume it must have happened on Saturday night."

Chapter Six

"We warned you, Edward."

He whistled tunelessly, determined not to lose his temper.

Aunt Mabel sat in her customary spot on the left side of the little round table. "Did you hear what I said?" She puffed up her thin chest like an offended black crane.

"Yes, aunt. I heard. You're suggesting Sue-Ellen Hill crept in here on Saturday night and stole Grandmother's diamonds."

"Exactly. That's exactly what we're suggesting, and we expect you to take appropriate action immediately."

"Immediately," Alice echoed, her head bent over the inevitable piece of needlepoint.

Edward was in a difficult spot. A juggler was what he'd have to become to avoid disaster here. A juggler and a master of deception. Neither appealed.

"I suppose I should call the police in at once."

"Constable Merryfield?" Alice raised her face. "Absolutely not! What would your dear father say? The indignity. That unpleasant little man marching around Airstone pretending to be official? Then he'd go straight to the East Puddle Arms to talk about us. We'll deal with this ourselves."

Edward ran a forefinger down the crease in one pant leg. This would be amusing if it weren't annoying, and difficult to resolve without destroying either pride for some, credibility for others.

Bea had also been summoned to this meeting. She sat in a cretonne-covered chair that matched the one Edward used. "Perhaps," she began tentatively, "you didn't put the box back into the safe?"

"Rubbish," Alice snapped. "We always put it back. We're most careful."

"And when was the last time you had it out?" Bea continued.

Mabel tapped her colorless lips with an arthritic finger. "Last Thursday. I remember exactly because our tea was late." She sniffed. "Anyway, while we waited for tea we took out the diamonds and talked about how Mother used to look at them."

"Last Thursday?" Edward said. "So how do you know they were taken on Saturday night?"

"Because we saw the box in the afternoon."

He counted to ten in his head. "You said you hadn't seen it since last Thursday." He hoped no unsuspecting lawyer ever got his aunts on a witness stand.

"The diamonds," Alice said with asperity. "That's when we last saw the diamonds. We saw the box on Saturday when we put some papers in the safe. Then yesterday we discovered we'd forgotten to close the safe. We shut it without checking inside. Then this morning the diamonds were gone. Oh, dear." She took out a lace-edged handkerchief to dab her eyes. Edward smelled lavender and mothballs.

"So if I'm not to call the police, what is it you want me to do?"

"Get rid of her. Send her packing at once. And forget this silly notion about opening a...a hotel, for goodness' sake."

Bea shifted and caught his eye. Her eyebrows raised a fraction. Thank God for Bea. He needed every level head he could find.

"Aunts. I can hardly sack Sue-Ellen without cause. Am I supposed to accuse her of grand theft?"

"Of course not. Just tell her to leave the diamonds be-hind when she goes and nothing else will be said."

"I see. What if she goes and doesn't leave the diamonds? What then?"

"She'll leave them."

"And if she refuses to go and denies everything, what then?"

Bea had put a hand over her mouth, Edward suspected, to hide a smile.

"She's a foreigner, isn't she? Threaten her with action that'll get her into a lot of trouble. That'll do it." Mabel leaned over her stick, the silver handle gripped in both hands.

"Without evidence you have no right to threaten any-one," Bea said in a low voice. "Are you sure you haven't simply misplaced the diamonds?"

Thank you, Edward wanted to say. "Bea's right," he said. "Why not have another little look around before we do anything?"

"Don't treat us like dull children," Mabel said with hau-teur. "If you want evidence, start searching this house. Search Miss Hill's room first, before she knows we suspect her."

"But why do you suspect her?" Bea asked.

Alice and Mabel exchanged a significant glance. "We just do. Leave it at that, if you please."

"That's not possible," Edward said. "With respect, you'll have to be more specific."

Again the two women looked at each other and, after an instant, nodded. Mabel was the one to speak. "It happens that we know Sue-Ellen Hill left her room in the middle of Saturday night."

"What?" Bea gripped the arms of her chair. "Who told you that?"

Mabel settled back, a satisfied smirk in position. "I can't divulge our sources. Or I won't, unless Miss Hill denies it. I don't think she will."

Edward sank into his own thoughts. It was perfectly possible that he hadn't been the only one to see Sue-Ellen on Saturday night, but he knew there was no question of her committing the crime his aunts suggested she had. In fact he had a pretty airtight notion that no crime had been committed, and the answer lay in going along with this charade and pulling everything back together when it was over.

"We'll search the house," he said abruptly. "All of it, not just Miss Hill's room. We'd better start at once. The sooner we get this over, the better. After all, we wouldn't want to give Miss Hill time to fence her loot, would we? That means get rid of it to someone who'll pay well for it," he added.

"We know what it means," Alice said, drawing in her nostrils. "But I think we should wait until tomorrow. Someone can make sure she's followed if she leaves the estate, and if we don't panic her she's likely to think she's safe."

He considered briefly. "All right. Tomorrow we search. I'll stay here and oversee things."

"We've got to keep this quiet," Alice said, and Edward thought, as he had since he was a child, that her yellow eyes were like those of a spiteful cat.

"Yes," Mabel agreed. "There must be no talk, no scandal. We've always avoided scandal."

Edward stood. "I'll tell the staff in the morning. No point in upsetting them tonight. Coming, Bea?"

She declined. Bea was a wonder, the only one who could smooth the old ladies' feathers, and no doubt that's what she intended to do now.

He left and called Sue-Ellen when he reached the gate house, requesting that she join him as soon as possible. Then he waited, reminding himself over and over that he must be tactful, supportive of her but without undermining his aunts. He prayed they wouldn't do anything too foolish before tomorrow. If they did, there might be no saving them from losing face.

Within minutes Sue-Ellen arrived, and her tension was a palpable thing that instantly put him on guard. Did she already guess she'd been accused of the theft?

She took off her coat and he hung it up.

"Sit down," he suggested. "Let me get you a drink."

"No, thank you."

He hated this. Her eyes, always startling in their clarity, were shadowed with some indefinable emotion. She held her lovely mouth in a hard line, and her tightly crossed arms suggested battle stations. She did feel threatened.

"Cold out?" He couldn't believe he'd asked such an inane question.

"It's always cold out—and damp."

"You don't sound too enamored of England."

"I'm very enamored. Or I could be if things weren't being made so difficult for me."

He ran a hand through his hair. "Of course you know I don't suspect you of this theft, Sue-Ellen." That was the last thing he should have said.

"No." The look she gave him suggested she'd never considered that he might suspect her. As she met his eyes now, he could almost see the idea taking shape. She was remembering how he'd bumped into her in the middle of the night—exactly when his aunts suggested the crime took place.

She went to stand next to the window. Today's weather had become a pervasive mist that slunk about trees, hanging between limbs like the beards of mythical wizards. "Why did you want to talk to me?" she asked.

"I told you before I left this morning that we'd get together when I came home." How would he explain the projected search without alienating her?

"That was before our latest drama. And thanks to some help from a few friends I've accomplished nothing worth reporting."

He loosened his tie and undid his collar button. There'd been no time to change. "I'm not sure I follow you. What's been happening—apart from the obvious? And what does *latest* drama imply? Is there something else I ought to know?" Please let her say no. Enough was enough.

"Oh, I don't know." She left the window, sat on the couch and pulled her feet beneath her. The gesture, an obviously unconscious one, made her seem small and young, and forlorn. Edward quelled an impulsive urge to sit and take her in his arms. But the idea didn't immediately fade. Holding her appealed to him, and dammit, he had the lousiest timing.

Max, who had an uncanny nose for dissension, rose majestically from his spot near the hearth and went to rest his muzzle on Sue-Ellen's knee. She stroked him absently, and the dog's eyes moved solemnly from her face to Edward's.

The phone, jangling loudly in the hall, effectively censored his drifting mind.

The call was for Sue-Ellen. From some shop in Bournemouth, the largest town in the county. He returned to the sitting room to wait.

"Sue-Ellen Hill," he heard her say. Then, moments later and loudly, "That's not possible. How were they delivered?" More silence. And a little later, "Yes, I'd say there was a mistake. And it won't be repeated. Send the shipment out again—immediately. We'll absorb the extra shipping cost. I'll make sure there's no repeat of what happened today."

"What was all that about?" Edward asked as she came back into the room.

She stood, hands in the pockets of her jeans, just inside the door. Her hair had been pulled back into a rubber band and straight wisps escaped to hang in front of her ears. Sue-Ellen wasn't a woman who spent a lot of time primping. Something else he liked about her. Her skin was beautiful, her features attractive in a wholesome way and her figure... No man would fail to notice that shape.

"Well?" he prompted.

"I think a decision was just made for me."

He didn't like the way that sounded. "About what?"

"Whether or not to tell you the things that have been done to me in the last few days. That was the store where I ordered linens and other supplies. They tried to deliver today but were told to take everything back."

"But . . . do they know who did that?"

She gave a wry smile. "No. The driver got his instructions from the other side of the tradesmen's entrance door. The contractor was also not given a name this morning."

Sue-Ellen continued to talk and he continued to grow more angry. His question "Are you sure you didn't have the wrong time for the contractor?" met with a glare before she told him exactly what had happened with Chalkers. Then he maintained silence and kept his face impassive. Damn. How could he have been such a fool? He should have called a meeting with the old guard and made his position crystal clear. Then, possibly, this mess could have been avoided.

"Nail polish?" That was incredible.

"Nail polish. They ruined my family picture with it, too. How small-minded can you get?"

Finally she finished her litany, including the story of her unpleasant interlude in the cellars. She shrugged and leaned back as if tired. He considered and discarded the idea of telling her that she might come to regret that little trip for more than the grief it caused her at the time.

"Well, I'll give them one thing," he managed a laugh. "They've got imagination." If he could put the whole episode into a lighter vein she might stop taking it so seriously. Then he'd make sure there was no repetition and they could all get on with their lives.

Sue-Ellen didn't appear amused.

Edward blew into a fist, deciding how to drop his little bombshell. Honestly, he supposed, without pretense. "The theft of my aunts' diamonds is a problem," he said finally.

"Hmm? Oh, come on. You know there wasn't a theft."

"Meaning?" This was more than difficult.

"Meaning they've got them stashed away somewhere until it suits them to decide they've been found. Whoever fol-

lowed me around on Saturday night was sent by them.
They're behind everything—''

"Sue-Ellen—"

"No. I'm going to finish. You've just come from a sum-
mit with them, haven't you?''

He nodded, his stomach sinking.

"Are you calling the police immediately?''

"We prefer to sort this out quietly.''

"Naturally you do. Did your aunts, by any chance, suggest that I might have taken their diamonds? And then did
they say I'd been seen out of my room at the damning
time?''

"Yes . . . on both counts.''

"Did they say *who* saw me?''

"No. They said they couldn't give the person away.''

"And you let it go at that?'' She swiveled toward him, a
forefinger raised. "Just a minute. It wasn't you who said
you saw me, was it?''

"No, dammit. You know darn well I wouldn't—'' He
shook his head. Why shouldn't she wonder if it had been
him? "Sorry. I see your point, but I swear I didn't. Every
word I said last night about not wanting to run into them
was absolutely true. We're going to search the house tomorrow.''

The slow raising of her brows let him know he hadn't
slipped the announcement past her. "We're what?''

"Searching the house. All of it. Every nook and
cranny . . . including this place,'' he added, hoping she'd be
impressed by the fairness of it.

"Those old . . . those old bats rig this up and you're going
to search the house? What do you expect to find? Either
they'll put their goodies somewhere to be conveniently
found, then say I hid them, or they'll suddenly remember
leaving them somewhere and produce them, pleading for-
getfulness. At least half the staff members are on their side.
Snobs, the bunch of them. Afraid their cronies will think
less of them if they work in a house that's used for something as 'common' as a hotel. This makes me sick. They're

all working together to try to get rid of me. And you should be concerned, because it'll be your financial loss if I fail.''

Edward stood up, steeling himself. ''I am concerned. But until such time as I have proof my aunts deliberately arranged the disappearance of their own jewelry, I'd appreciate your not suggesting that they have. I do regret that there appears to have been some calculated interference with your work, but I don't think it will continue.''

''Appears to have been?'' She was on her feet.

He genuinely detested having to do this. ''Tomorrow we search. Always in groups of two or more. Bea or I will accompany someone into each room or area. I'll get old Bastible to lend a hand. Everyone trusts him, and he can be counted on not to spread the news around. The rest of the staff won't be told until morning.''

THE REST OF THE STAFF.

When Sue-Ellen left Edward, she set out for the village. Going back to the house immediately was out of the question. In the narrow lanes where one car had to almost balance on a hedgerow to allow another to pass, she hugged the verge. Naked moss-covered trees—yews, chestnuts, oaks—met overhead, formed a tunnel like a gray-green cocoon wrapping woolly mist inside.

The rest of the staff.

The first of the thatched, yellow-stone cottages loomed. They lined the tippy road, crowded in, one upon another like old friends with a secret to share. Gardens, dormant now, scraggly, sprouted in profusion the dripping foliage of hydrangeas, peony stalks, the bare thorny fingers of rose bushes and gentle fronds of used fuchsia bushes. Sue-Ellen trudged on, bound for the cottage tea shop where the owner, a plump and stoic woman, said little but served passable coffee.

Shapes emerged, human shapes.

''If it isn't our Sue-Ellen!''

Colin Bastible's voice boomed from the silence, too full, too cheerful and totally unwelcome. She drew to a halt, shoving back her hair that must be a fright and peering at him . . . and his sister who held his arm.

"I say—" Colin came closer, lowering his voice in the manner of a conspirator "—I hear we've got a bit of a schmoo up at the Hall. We're on our way for a confab with Edward now."

"Schmoo?" Sue-Ellen echoed, looking not at Colin but at Helen who shook her head slightly and raised her eyes heavenward. For the first time Sue-Ellen felt a small kinship with the woman.

"Oh, don't be coy," Colin continued. "You know what I'm talking about. Edward telephoned the old man. Seems we're being drafted for top-secret duty tomorrow. Can't say I mind. Always did like a good poke around the old place."

"Colin!" Helen jabbed a carmine fingernail into her brother's arm. "For God's sake shut up. Daddy told you to keep quiet about this." She inclined her head at Sue-Ellen. "Edward had to tour Dorchester to find me. We weren't due to have lunch until one. He called my father a while ago and said he'd like a bit of help taking a look around for the, er . . ."

"Missing loot," Colin supplied cheerfully. "Hope I find it. I could use an extra sparkler or two to turn into the old ready."

"Colin!" Helen put distance between herself and her brother and glared. "You're absolutely hopeless. Edward asked Daddy for help." She turned to Sue-Ellen. "And Daddy volunteered us to fill out the cast of searchers. I hope we find where the old dears misplaced their treasures quickly, because I need to get back to Dorchester and finish what I started today. I've got a frightful meeting at the Women's Institute—to buy a new silver teapot or repair the old one is the question. Comes with the territory, but I don't have to like it."

Sue-Ellen warmed even more to Helen, who appeared open and not disposed to gossip.

"Right," Colin said. "We'll get on it first thing. Better warn the rest of the staff they're about to be invaded by special investigative forces."

"Colin!"

Sue-Ellen wasn't sure what she muttered as she excused herself, moving blindly around them, and heading down the single street of the village.

The rest of the staff.

She ducked into the corner shop. Crowded into what must originally have been the two downstairs rooms of a cottage, East Puddle's equivalent of a variety store sold everything and anything. The many narrow wooden drawers piled one on another were like a series of genies' lamps. Rub the handles and they produced what the shopper wanted.

The rest of the staff.

When she'd opened the shop door a bell had jangled overhead. Seconds later Betty appeared from behind a faded brown velvet curtain that hung on a sagging wire to hide the kitchen Sue-Ellen had glimpsed. She knew, or assumed that the woman was Betty because that was the name of the shop. And she'd never seen anyone else working there.

Betty, pleasant enough but reserved, as were all the villagers, waited patiently while Sue-Ellen decided on some candy from one of the giant jars set in a row on a counter.

"Bull's eyes," Betty pronounced after Sue-Ellen pointed. "Peppermint. Strong." She extracted a pile of black-and-white striped candies with a metal scoop, weighed them on an old brass scale and poured them into a bag.

"Have you had the shop long?" Sue-Ellen smiled.

"Long enough."

Was she starting to imagine hostility at every turn? "You certainly have a wonderful stock."

"Mmm. Will there be anything else, miss?"

She wasn't imagining anything. "No, thank you. I expect you know most people from Airstone Hall."

Betty took her money and rang a noisy cash register. "I know them all, miss, just as my parents knew them before me. Not much changes around here. We like it that way."

Coins were plunked in her hand, and the paper bag of sweets.

Sue-Ellen returned to the street. Rough paving reverberated the squeaky sound of her shoes. Everyone here liked things the way they'd always been. The less change the better. And she was change.

Rather than go to the cottage tea shop, Sue-Ellen started back for Airstone.

The rest of the staff.

The rush of disappointment, which came each time she thought about the words, was illogical, but until this afternoon Edward had made her feel his equal, accepted. How could she have been so wrong? He'd showed what he really thought of her. She was just another member of his staff and he'd aligned himself with his own kind. Only she wasn't even acceptable as a member of the staff, or anything else around here. That the Bastible twins had also lumped her into the general classification of lesser beings rankled almost more. Sue-Ellen wanted to ignore the reason but couldn't. Being considered less than Helen Bastible in Edward's eyes was ridiculously unbearable.

THINGS WERE GOING BETTER than expected, but the next twenty-four hours would be crucial. If the result planned didn't materialize by this time tomorrow there would have to be some rethinking, perhaps some action. . . .

Finally, at midnight, the light had gone out in Sue-Ellen Hill's room, and after waiting another hour it had seemed safe to come here.

An ear to the wall, listening intently. No sound came from the other side where the Hill woman's bedroom was. Finding the spring was easy. One small stroking caress in a corner of a paneled square, and an opening gradually appeared, a darker oblong into the dark room beyond. Wood slid noiselessly into wood. Deception from another age. A masterpiece, just as everything else about this beloved house was a masterpiece.

Waiting...seconds of waiting with head raised. Then it came, the soft but unmistakable sound of regular breathing.

Carefully, a step, then wait, another step and wait again; enter the room and inch to the foot of the bed. The curtains at the bowed casement were open. One tiny noise would awaken the sleeper and reveal the interloper in the same shaft of blue luminescence that spread over the still form in the bed.

But no sound was made. This ground had been covered before and bore no surprises. And the wardrobe door opened as smoothly as planned. For the last time...or it had better be, for Sue-Ellen Hill's sake.

With the task accomplished, the steps were retraced until there was a moment to look at the slumbering face on its pale pillow. Little fool. She thought she was a match for this house, for those who belonged here. But no matter; it would soon be over...by whatever means proved necessary.

At the opening in the wall, another pause to give a last long look over the shoulder and run a thumb down the knife blade. It was almost a pity there had been no need to use it. Sue-Ellen's neck, in the sapphire light, was so very white.

Chapter Seven

"Let's get this over with," Bea said, leading the way to the staircase that accessed the servants' quarters. "I don't like it one bit and neither does Edward."

Sue-Ellen had to run to keep up. "Neither do I. I can't believe we're going through with it."

"No choice," Bea rejoined, casting a baleful glance over her shoulder. Understanding passed between them. Edward was doing what came naturally—protecting his own.

Helen Bastible trotted behind Sue-Ellen. "This is mad. If Alice and Mabel think there's been a robbery, why not call in Constable Merryfield?"

"You know the answer to that." Bea didn't bother to turn around but her tone was deprecatory. "I'm sure they've dropped the wretched jewelry under a cushion or something, but they won't hear of letting anyone look around their rooms."

"Are you serious?" Helen was panting.

"Absolutely. I stayed behind after Edward left yesterday to try to persuade them. I think they'll be disappointed when we hand them the gems, honestly I do."

"Good grief." Helen was puffing now. "I don't know how Edward keeps his patience with them."

Sue-Ellen's spirits lifted. At last she felt close to these people. There was no hint that they suspected anything more sinister than the old ladies' having misplaced their possessions. And the comments about Edward warmed her. He was a special man—a man loyal to the end.

A final steep and tortuous flight brought them to the servants' rooms.

"Now," Bea said, pausing at the top and waiting for Sue-Ellen and Helen, "Edward said to look in Mrs. Leaming's room and Sylvia's. He and Colin and the reverend will pop up to Grossby's and Mr. Pitts's. So we'll do just as instructed—look—and leave. Everyone's incensed by this and I don't blame them."

Sue-Ellen was ready with a question or two. "What happened to Mr. Leaming?"

"Honorary title," Helen announced as she reached the landing. "Married or not, household cooks have always been 'Mrs.' in this country. Mary's single."

"Oh." That covered that. "What do we do about Connie?" And this was by far the more pressing problem.

"Connie?" Bea frowned.

"She doesn't live here. How can we be sure she didn't make off to the village with the diamonds?"

A smothered noise suggested Bea didn't think this was the moment to laugh. "We'd better hope we don't have to descend on her cottage," she said, winking. "Ernie Butters isn't someone I want to deal with."

Helen groaned. "Me, neither. How a nice woman like Connie got tied up with..." She coughed. "The sooner we deal with this, the better, for all our sakes."

The first room was Sylvia's. Its tidiness surprised Sue-Ellen, and the lack of personal touches. She'd expected clutter, stacks of glossy magazines, makeup containers. The plain white bedspread showed not a wrinkle, and every surface was empty and free of dust. No pictures hung on the pink-flowered wallpaper. No photograph or ornament stood on the simple furniture. As if no one lived here, Sue-Ellen thought; or perhaps as if the person who did live here found no comfort or sense of home in it. The only extras in evidence were a pile of books neatly stacked on a bedside table and, incongruously, a child's metal doll buggy, apparently antique, that stood in a corner.

Bea saw Sue-Ellen looking at the buggy. "Sylvia said that belonged to her mother. All she has left of her family, was the way she explained it." She glanced around. "All right. That's it for Sylvia's. Now Mrs. Leaming's."

At the next door Sue-Ellen hung back, remembering something. "I'll be right with you," she said as the other two women entered. Rapidly she returned to Sylvia's room and went directly to the books. The oversized brown leather volume on the bottom had to be the one Colin had given Sylvia the night Sue-Ellen saw them outside the library. Neither of them should have been in that room, and she was curious about what Sylvia had seemed so pleased to take from it.

She must be quick. Helen and Bea would be through in minutes, and explaining what she had seen that night was out of the question.

Tilting her head she looked for the book's title. There wasn't one, only gold scrollwork down the spine. She ought to leave at once. With a glance at the door, she slid the book from beneath the others and opened the cover.

Voices sounded in the hallway.

Journal. Charles Ormsby-Jones. 1923.

She stuffed the book back in place and met Helen as she poked her head into the room. "I dropped my pen somewhere," Sue-Ellen said, scrambling for the first excuse that came to mind. "Thought it might be in here, but it isn't."

"I'M NOT SURE Edward's thought this through well enough." Bea flopped into a sagging tapestry-covered chair in the oppressive parlor where she and Sue-Ellen had retreated for tea. Helen, late for her meeting at the Women's Institute, had left.

She sipped the strong brew Connie had brought and regarded the massive squares of aged paneling. An ornate frieze topped these, sporting a row of pouting damsels trailing wisps of fabric and flanked at intervals by what Bea had explained were reproductions of the Ormsby-Jones coat of arms. And all of this was presided over by a floor-to-ceiling white stone fireplace, defaced, or so Sue-Ellen had decided, by the sculpted image of some early family member. Dreary. Much as she loved the old and historic, this was one room Sue-Ellen would like to change.

Stirring, she considered Bea's remark about Edward. Could the housekeeper also have drawn the conclusion that the sisters had stolen their own booty? "What did you mean about Edward just now? About him not thinking things through well enough?"

Bea sighed and drank some of her own tea. Her broad hands dwarfed the delicate Limoges cup. "Oh, I'm not really sure what I mean. It's just that I wonder what we shall do if the diamonds don't show up anywhere and we're forced to inform Miss Alice and Miss Mabel to, er . . ."

"Put up or shut up?" Sue-Ellen suggested and laughed.

Several seconds passed before comprehension cleared Bea's eyes, and she laughed, too. "Interesting way of saying it, but yes."

For a while they drank in companionable silence. An idea came to Sue-Ellen, first acutely and quickly closed out, then more insistently.

"Well—" Bea pushed her cup and saucer aside on a minute cloisonné table perched on impossibly skinny legs "—onward. I suppose we'd better report to Edward for instructions. He's got the poor reverend going through the gate house—with Colin's help. Such rubbish."

Sue-Ellen cleared her throat. "I went on an expedition the other night. The night of the crime, in fact . . . to the cellars."

"The cellars?" Bea raised finely drawn eyebrows. "Where I took you?"

"No. Remember I said I'd found a door behind a tapestry in the Great Hall? And you said there were more cellars down there?"

"Ah. Those. They've been locked up for years. I decided they were one more thing to look after and we didn't need them."

This wasn't easy. "I broke the padlock and went down there. Stupid, I suppose, but I wanted to see if there was something we could use."

Bea only stared.

"Anyway, I went late at night, and I do think we could use that area—with a lot of work. But the point is, someone followed me and turned off the light and . . ."

"And?" Bea leaned forward.

"And the aunts don't like what I'm doing and I think they're looking for a way to get rid of me. So I wonder if whoever followed me was also used to put the diamonds somewhere."

"I'm not sure I understand you."

"No. I'm not sure I understand me, either. But I think the aunts plan to make it look as if I'm the one who stole from them. I guess I'm trying to say that it suddenly seems possible that the suggestion could come that the cellars be searched because someone—someone who can't be named, of course—thinks I may have hidden my ill-gotten gains there. So why don't we go and look and say all is in the open . . . about my expedition, I mean. I'd appreciate it, Bea, and I think it might simplify matters if you and I presented a united front."

Bea stood at once. "We are a united front. You're the breath of fresh air this place has needed for a long time. I can't imagine that they'd try to pull off what you suggest. Sounds too farfetched, but we'll do what you want, just in case."

Located next to the breakfast room, the parlor was on the other side of the entrance from the Great Hall. This time Sue-Ellen took the lead, slipping past the foot of the stairs and into the hall with Bea in her wake. They moved as a unit, Sue-Ellen hurrying, hoping to accomplish her objective without having to explain to anyone else.

"You did this alone and at night?"

They stood, side by side, enveloped by the vast and dusty tapestry.

"Crazy, I know." The padlock still hung, unfastened, and Sue-Ellen opened the resistant door, as she had the first time, with her shoulder.

She found the light switch, and once again the yellow light washed around graying walls and over the cold stone floor.

Bea hesitated in the doorway. "We don't have to go on. If there's a move to search this place we'll say we checked it."

The dank smell rose up from the passage, and a chill draft. Sue-Ellen would gladly have turned back, but she couldn't. "I've got a feeling about this place. I can't explain it, but it's as if... It's as if there's someone here." She laughed awkwardly. "Forget I said that. I've always been known for my ability to enter into the spirit of things."

At that Bea grinned. "I hope that comment was an accident. Should we go back?" As quickly as it had come, the grin faded. "Frankly I'd rather. I was only here once before and I don't like it."

The admission surprised Sue-Ellen. Bea didn't seem a woman given to nervousness. "I'd just like to walk through and make sure there isn't a jewelry box conveniently lying around somewhere."

Still Bea didn't move.

"I went into the second room on the left. The one that looks like a little cell with a niche in the wall?"

"I remember it."

Sue-Ellen watched Bea's face, fascinated by the distant unfocused quality of her eyes.

"The first door on the left is locked."

"Yes." A flat statement.

"I didn't get any farther. The Reverend Bastible said there's an old kitchen and more rooms, but the lights went out on me."

Bea shuddered. "Oh, God...it reminds me of the story."

"What story?" Sue-Ellen moved closer to Bea but kept an eye on the passage.

"Oh, nothing. Silliness. Let's go."

Sue-Ellen caught Bea's arm. "Tell me."

"It's nothing really."

Sue-Ellen waited.

"All right. Supposedly that first room—the locked one—was used as a prison for some poor girl who fell out of favor with a former lady of the house."

"When?" She moved another step nearer to Bea.

"I don't know. A long time ago, I suppose. But the story went that the girl became mad in there . . . in the dark, and cold. There was no light, I suppose."

Sue-Ellen closed her eyes and felt the familiar dreaded lightness in her head. She shouldn't pursue this.

"The family, or so I was told, don't like to talk about the tale, and as far as I know there isn't a key to the room."

Faintness slipped in around Sue-Ellen's brain. "She went mad in there."

"If you can believe what I was told. But there are a lot of hints about madness in relation to this house and the family. They talk about it in the village. Always have. If you hear anything, do what I do and ignore it."

The girl in the room. Sue-Ellen barely listened to Bea. "What happened to her?"

She crossed her arms. "Killed herself—"

"Bea! Sue-Ellen!"

The voice was like a blow, and Sue-Ellen flattened her hands on the wall behind.

In the darkness, confined in a locked room, a girl had killed herself down here. Sue-Ellen opened her eyes wide and saw Edward looming behind Bea in the doorway. He ducked his head and peered at Sue-Ellen. "There you are. I thought I was seeing things at first when the tapestry moved. What on earth are you up to?"

Bea raised her brows significantly, and Sue-Ellen's composure settled in again. "It's okay, Bea," she told her. "Edward knows I came here the other night." To Edward she said, "I told Bea about being here and asked her to come and check for the diamonds with me."

His blank expression, the pause, conveyed his total confusion, and Sue-Ellen gritted her teeth. Now there'd be another tale of madness in this house. Her own.

He touched Bea's shoulder. "There's some sort of uprising in the kitchen. Connie's all het up. The staff is threatening mutiny over all this fuss. I sympathize, but I'm not up to dealing with that sort of thing. Would you go and pour a little of your magic oil, please?"

"Of course, but Sue-Ellen—"

"I'll carry on. I'll just take a quick look in the other rooms. Edward can stand guard and make sure I don't cheat or something."

"If you're sure?" Bea was leaving as she spoke, a worried frown deepening the line between her brows.

"She really cares about what happens in this house, doesn't she?" Sue-Ellen said as Bea's footsteps rapidly became distant.

"Yes, she does," Edward agreed and smiled.

For an instant Sue-Ellen didn't think of anything but his face. How had he ever managed to appear...ordinary? Yes, ordinary when she'd first looked at him, apart from his height and breadth. When he smiled there could be no question but that Edward was remarkable. The way his features fitted together, the eyes, sometimes brilliant, sometimes soft, the firm yet sensitive mouth...unforgettable.

"Why did you two come down here?"

His voice jarred her. "I told you I was followed the other time. I told Bea the same thing, and she agreed to come with me in case...in case there was an attempt to, er, frame me."

"Frame..." He shoved his hands deep in his pockets and raised his eyes to the ceiling. "All right, I'll play. Lead the way."

Outside the first door to the left she paused, touched the handle. "Locked," she said, glancing back.

Edward shrugged. "I wouldn't know. If I was ever here I don't remember."

She turned the handle and pushed. "Locked," she repeated and moved on to the little cell.

With a backward glance at Edward she went inside. Just having him there, feeling his solid steadiness, gave her courage.

"See anything?"

She looked behind the door and then went to peer into the niche. Nothing. The only light came from the passage and cast dim shifting shadows that hid corners, but there was no evidence of a box.

The door slammed.

"No!" Sue-Ellen flung out her arms. She couldn't see.

The girl had died in the next room, in the dark and cold. A scream erupted from her, one she'd held back again and again. She flew at the darkness, beat at it with her fists.

"My God. Calm down." Edward's voice seemed to come from far away.

The darkness was hard. It held her. "Help!" It lifted her to her toes, gripped her tightly, held her face on something rough.

She fought. She wouldn't die here like that other girl.

There was a creak and a glow swept in again. "Just hold on, Sue-Ellen. Hold on to me. It's okay."

Sweat streamed between her shoulder blades. Her skin felt pinched and icy.

"My dear, dear girl. You're shaking. Please just hold on to me. The door blew shut behind me, that's all."

Gradually the sickness in her throat, the suffocating ache receded. She could breathe. "I'm . . . I'm sorry."

He enfolded her, gripped her by the waist with one arm, around the shoulders with the other and held her face to his chest. She'd lost control. After years of never letting the demon out, she'd let go . . . and in front of Edward.

"Why would you come down here when you . . ." He rocked her, gathering her to him even tighter. "You've got claustrophobia, haven't you?"

She turned her face away, but he lifted her chin with a finger and thumb. "Why would you push yourself into situations you know you might not handle?"

"It hasn't happened for ages," she said, and he bent to catch her soft words. "I always think I'm over it."

"Tough, huh? Got to prove you don't have any soft spots." He made broad circles over her back, and what he probably thought were relaxing strokes. Sue-Ellen, her pulse no longer jumping, felt a quickening. His body was solid, his chest, the thighs pressed to hers, the heavily muscled arms in their comfortingly warm sleeves. And there was that smell of clean woods again.

She should move away. Instead she relaxed, leaned on him and closed her eyes. "Guess I'm not so tough. I really felt as if I was losing it for a while."

"Do you feel better now?"

Reluctantly she raised her face. "I feel like an absolute fool. Can we forget this ever happened?"

He laughed, tipped up his head to show strong teeth. "Absolutely. But just remember the power I wield over you. I know your dark secret."

Sue-Ellen wasn't sure she was ready to laugh, but she did smile... and he stopped laughing. All the laughter faded, from his lips, his eyes. His glance centered on her mouth.

"We'd better go upstairs," Sue-Ellen said, breathless again.

"Yes, we'd better." But instead of releasing her, he moved his hands to her neck, settled them there loosely. He had big square hands. She'd noticed them earlier. They appeared strong and used, rather than suited to being folded on a desk. "I like having you here," he said. "I'd almost forgotten how it felt to know there would be someone I'd like coming home to."

Sue-Ellen swallowed, at a loss for words. She bowed her head and realized her own hands rested at his waist.

"Now I've embarrassed you. Don't be. I was only trying to say..." He bent suddenly, kissed her temple and, when she looked at him, kissed her cheek... close to her mouth.

Just as quickly he dropped his arms and waved her into the passage. "I was trying to let you know you have a fan. You've got guts, Sue-Ellen."

The tingling in her limbs, the flutter in her stomach might be... silly, but they felt good. She gave him the brightest smile she could muster and walked in front of him.

With matter-of-fact efficiency, she went farther into the corridor and located a horror of a kitchen, festooned with cobwebs and stripped of equipment. No sign of a box. Ten minutes and three rooms later she returned, with Edward holding her elbow, to the blessed openness of the Great Hall.

"There." He lowered his voice to a whisper. "Now you've dealt with two problems at once."

She met his eyes. He was perceptive. "It's almost an obsession," she admitted, not addressing the question of the missing gems, "to confront a weakness and keep testing it. I dread the exercise, but I can't seem to stop."

"I know," he said, and she wondered what he meant. Sylvia approached quickly on tapping heels. Sue-Ellen turned her attention to the woman, resenting having to let go of this time alone with Edward.

"Mr. Edward," Sylvia said, looking from him to Sue-Ellen, "Miss Smallman said to find you."

"Well, you have," Edward said, sounding anything but pleased.

At least the door to the cellars had been closed and the tapestry was safely back in place.

"Miss Smallman said the only places left to go over are her rooms and, er, Miss Hill's. She'd like you to meet her in her sitting room."

Edward frowned, and Sue-Ellen's heart felt too big for her chest.

He kept his hand on her arm all the way upstairs and through the corridors. At the last turn he stopped. "This is unpleasant," he said, not looking at her. "Bear with me, okay?"

What choice did she have? "Okay. But what do you intend to do when we've finished this operation and we still don't have what we're looking for?"

"I've already thought about that. Somehow I think the problem will suddenly be solved."

She didn't tell him she was sure it would be.

Bea let them into her sitting room. "Come in, come in. I'll stand by while you unearth the loot."

They all laughed a little uncomfortably. Bea also had two rooms, her bedroom and the sitting room. Sue-Ellen admired the woman's taste. Here, there was an unexpected Asian influence—black lacquer, inlaid Chinese chests, loose Serapi rugs on polished boards. A couch, love seat and three chairs, covered in heavy satin sprayed with white lilies on a black background stood on straight black legs around a low square table. Between two long windows a lighted curio cabinet, taller than Edward, exhibited a display of perfectly preserved weapons, guns both ancient and modern with photographs of the warriors who might have used them.

"This is beautiful," Sue-Ellen said. "You have wonderful taste."

Bea smiled and blushed. "I'm glad you like it. This used to be Edward's grandmother's suite. These were her things. But we'd better get on. You should open a drawer or two. Look under the bed."

Sue-Ellen shook her head, and Bea slid open a desk drawer, and another. Edward shifted from foot to foot, his hands clasped behind his back. Sue-Ellen caught his eye and he didn't look away. She felt something, was beginning to feel something every time she was anywhere near him.

"The bedroom." Bea crossed the room, clearly oblivious to the current Sue-Ellen could tell Edward was at least aware of. "I insist."

Dutifully Sue-Ellen went with Bea and watched uncomfortably as she opened and closed drawers and cupboards.

Finally it was finished.

"Me next," Sue-Ellen announced, producing a key from her jeans pocket.

Her own suite was smaller than Bea's, and there were fewer places to check.

Now, Sue-Ellen noted, it was Bea's turn to seem disconcerted. Edward simply stood in the middle of the room and gazed into the distance.

"My bedroom, too," Sue-Ellen insisted. This was almost over, and she could hardly wait to see how the two old bats would handle what they must have known was coming. How furious they must be that Edward hadn't sent her packing without questioning her guilt or innocence.

The heavy bedside table had no drawer, only a ledge where she kept a book. She opened the drawers in the Tudor chest and the wardrobe door and stood back, waiting.

"Good enough," Bea said, starting for the sitting room.

She stopped beside the wardrobe and knelt, craning her neck once to see Sue-Ellen. "Looks like someone spilled nail polish."

"What?" She hadn't noticed before.

"Oh." Bea lowered her head again, this time reaching inside the wardrobe. "Oh, Sue-Ellen."

She should have been ready, but she wasn't. Bea held a hand aloft. Diamond jewelry cascaded from her fingers.

Chapter Eight

"Dammit, Sue-Ellen, will you please wait?"

He stopped climbing for a moment, waiting to see if she'd answer his shout, or at least acknowledge she knew he was behind her.

She continued on, trudging steadily up a rise on the westerly side of the estate, her yellow rain slicker and hat bright and wet with rain. The storm intensified by the second. He stuffed his glasses in his pocket, cursed under his breath and struck out again.

His first mistake had been to retreat immediately after the jewelry was found. His second was to let her fester alone in her rooms for two days because he didn't know what to say. Now every line he'd rehearsed to calm her had fled, and all he wanted was to make her believe they'd all get through this.

"Sue-Ellen, will you wait . . . please?" He drew level and reached for her arm.

She shrugged away. "I'd like to walk if you don't mind. Alone." Her face was invisible beneath the floppy brim of her rubberized hat. "Unless the police have finally come to take me away."

"Women." He turned up his palms. The famous Ormsby-Jones control was deserting him. To yell would feel wonderful.

"What does that mean, *women*?" She halted, tilting her head far back to see from beneath the hat. Her eyes were brilliant, whether with anger or from imminent tears was hard to tell. "Tell me. What do you mean, *women*?"

Now she would give him the outraged act. He'd come with an olive branch and she was turning him into an aggressor. "It means what it sounds like. You're all the same. You overreact and you don't wait to work things out. Dammit all." Max shoved between them, soggy and smelling of molding leaves, and making Edward aware that he was standing very close to Sue-Ellen.

Carefully he stepped back, bent to pat Max's soggy muzzle and gently pushed the dog away. The look on Sue-Ellen's face, the hurt, sapped his own energy.

She wiped the back of a reddened hand over her brow. "We won't get into a discussion of the negative traits of women in general. And there's no need to say what you came to say. I've already made my decision and I'm sure you'll be relieved."

He'd been afraid of this. "You don't know what I came to say, not exactly. If you did you wouldn't find it necessary to run away when I ask to see you."

"I'm not running away. I just don't see the point in discussion. Your aunts got exactly what they wanted. I'll be gone as soon as I can make arrangements. If you'd prefer, I can move out today."

"Dammit! Will you be quiet for long enough to hear me out?" Immediately he felt contrite. "I'm sorry, that was unforgivable. You've got every right to be upset. But these past few days haven't been a picnic for me, either. We have to get things sorted out and get on with it. There's no time for stupid delays."

She folded her arms. Again he was presented with the top of the ugly hat. He recalled the blue woolen creation she often favored and decided she had the worst taste in hats he'd ever encountered.

"Sue-Ellen," he said, lowering his head to try to get a glimpse of her face. "Did you hear what I said?"

"I heard. I don't get it, though. By now the entire household must know the diamonds were found in my wardrobe, and no doubt they're rubbing their hands and waiting for me either to be arrested or to slink off in disgrace.'' She let out a disgusted breath. ''Like something out of a Victorian melodrama.''

The rain grew heavier. He wore nothing on his head, and rivulets ran inside the upturned collar of his oilskins. ''You're not going anywhere.'' How could it be that even when he set out to make things smooth he managed to sound like a dictator?

Sue-Ellen's face turned up to his. ''Meaning?''

''Oh, come on. You know what I mean. Do you honestly think I believe you took the jewelry and put it in your own wardrobe where it could be conveniently found on cue?''

''It was found in my wardrobe.''

Edward knew her pride was severely wounded, and her ability to trust. ''Look, can we forget this whole thing? It really would be the quickest, most sensible way to cope.''

''I don't think so. Someone put those diamonds in my room and it was done for only one reason—to get rid of me.''

He was skating on eggs and he wasn't used to the feeling. ''I don't give a... This house is my responsibility. I decide who stays and who goes. And I've decided you stay.''

Her shoulders raised, and she glared at him. The effect would be amusing if he didn't know the trauma she'd been through. ''Does that mean you've decided to judge me innocent? I suppose you'd feel quite comfortable in that role—fits right in with your line of business.''

The sky had darkened, was darkening steadily, and not only because the afternoon was waning. A stillness fell and the rain slackened. Edward looked at the lowering sky and prayed for inspiration.

''That was a mean thing to say,'' she said in a softer voice. ''I do comprehend all you've been going through. And I assume you know I didn't touch that ridiculous jewelry. But the fact remains that it looks as if I did, and if I tried to carry on here it would be with a household who already wish I'd go to the moon. They think I'm the cause of changing their so-called elevated status with the people who live around here, and in some cases, they see me as the bringer of un-welcome loads of extra work."

"But—"

"Please. I have to finish this. Add a lot of talk about me being a pardoned thief, and what hope do I have of work-ing amicably and successfully with them?"

"That's what I'm trying—" Lightning, splitting the sky in two, drowned out his words. "Good Lord, this is awful. Come on, come back to the gate house."

Before she could respond, thunder roared in a deafening roll and in seconds the sky was torn by another angry white stroke.

"Sue-Ellen?" he shouted. The heavens grumbled, and what felt like a crashing wave of water descended on them.

Edward put his arm around her shoulders, pulling her closer. The slicker she wore wasn't meant for this sort of cloudburst. He remembered the pavilion, and there was no time to think about not wanting to go there. Sheltering her as best he could, he led her not downward, but farther up the slope and into a straggly stand of pines.

She didn't resist and they slipped and slithered. Mud turned to slime squelching over their feet.

"Where—" she strained to see him, water running down her face "—where are we going?"

"Old pavilion." He pointed, blinking. Without glasses the distance was a blur anyway, and the rain made a gray wall of everything.

Beneath his arm she was stiff and shaking. Struggling, he unsnapped his oilskins and wrapped her inside. The fit was snug, but possible. Walking was almost impossible.

Into the trees and up an old flight of rough stone steps, and they arrived at what had once been a pretty vine-covered structure of white stone. Now, after years of neglect, the stone still stood strong, but the vines were a morass of brambles.

The front was open, pillars supporting the roof at inter-vals. He urged Sue-Ellen inside, and they turned as one to stare out at the sheet of water that fell from the eaves. In here the noise was a steady drone. Max had raced ahead to flop down, panting, in a corner.

"What is this place?"

He felt her steady shivering and kept her close. If he had to guess he'd say the shaking was as much nerves as cold, but whatever the cause, holding her was far from an unpleasant task.

"Edward?"

"Left over from another age. My great-grandfather had it built back in the days when they used to ride to hounds. It was a kind of halfway spot for those who'd rather drop out of the hunt and have a glass of sherry or whatever." He laughed, feeling anything but cheerful, and avoided looking at the stone seats that ran around three sides. "I believe some people rode straight here and never ever considered doing more."

She leaned against him and he liked the sensation. He'd like it a lot more if they were anywhere else but here.

"How long ago did you stop keeping horses?"

"We haven't had any since I was a small boy. Too expensive and no time."

"But . . ." She frowned up at him and as quickly looked away.

"But?" He took off her hat and touched her cheek. "But what?"

"Oh, nothing. Just something Bea said. I'd assumed there must have been horses here quite . . . well, not so long ago."

He pressed his lips together. Staff talked. It was natural. But somehow he hadn't expected Bea to confide some things. "Bea told you about Lenore?"

"Yes. I'm sorry."

Everyone had been sorry. But what else was there to say? "Thank you."

"Do you mind if we sit down?" Sue-Ellen said. "I haven't done a whole lot of eating or sleeping in the past few days and I think it's catching up with me."

Not here, he wanted to say. "All right." He let her go and
she went to the seat at the back, farthest from the rain.

He faced the downpour. What he felt about it all now
wasn't guilt. He hadn't made Lenore go riding that day, and
anyway, she'd been a wonderful horsewoman and the conditions had been good.

"Sit with me, Edward."

The request startled him, and the small voice. Sue-Ellen
was asking for comfort and that had cost her something.

Wordlessly he joined her and sat with his arm against her
shoulder. One thing he mustn't forget was that not one, but
two women had died after getting involved with him. Su-
perstition was foolish, he'd always pushed it away, but the
niggling sensation that he was a jinx kept returning.

"Bea said Lenore died in a riding accident."

"Yes." Right out there. Right where the rise dropped off.
And they'd brought her in here. He'd come rushing to help
only to find her already dead.

"What happened? Or maybe I shouldn't ask."

"It's all right." Or parts of it were. "She was riding
alone—borrowed horse from the Sidleys who have an estate a few miles from here. Evidently something spooked the
horse and it threw her."

Sue-Ellen was silent and he put an arm around her, for his
own comfort, he realized. "I'd never felt so helpless. It was
a puzzle. She must have hit her head in just the right . . . no,
the wrong way, because she was hardly bruised apart from
that."

"How horrible." Sue-Ellen's voice was hushed. "Could
the horse have kicked her after she fell?"

"They didn't think so. He bolted, and the blow didn't
seem consistent. There was a lot of talk about something
hitting the horse's neck and causing him to rear. He had a
puncture as if a sharp object struck him, but that was so
much conjecture and Lenore was dead, so what good was
hashing it all over?"

"None." She turned to him. "Except sometimes it's good for us to remember the things that have affected us most in our lives."

He remembered the phrase about being able to see someone's soul through the eyes. She was sensitive and comforting, and having her slip her hand around his neck and press her cheek to his felt the most natural thing in the world.

"How did we get onto this?" He laughed, and she smiled and moved away a little. "All history now. Just this place, I suppose. This is the first time I've been here since."

"I'm not surprised."

They fell silent, but the storm raged all around.

"Sue-Ellen, I haven't managed things very well in these last few days. Please, bear with me. I know everything's going to work out well."

The subtle change of light in her eyes suggested she was far from sure. "The point is that the less said, the better," Edward said.

She sat straighter, lifting heavy damp hair from inside her collar. So appealing, particularly now when he felt, for the first time in years, that he needed someone—someone close.

"Nothing hurtful's been done," he told her, and before she could bow her head, he took her face in his hands. "No real harm, huh? And I don't think there will be now. It would be one thing if there'd been some hint of a dangerous incident, but there hasn't and there won't be. You don't have to worry about gossip. Bea's the only one who knows where the old ladies' treasures were found, and she's not about to discuss it with anyone else."

"Your aunts know."

"Not in theory...the theory of what's supposed to be actuality." He smiled down at her and saw the corners of her mouth turn up. "We took the gems back and said they had been in the safe all the time—hidden at the back. Must have slipped there, was what we told them."

Sue-Ellen started to grin, then she giggled. "And did they have apoplexy?"

He brought his face closer. "I don't know what you're suggesting."

"Don't you? Well, never mind. But remember that it's unlikely either Miss Alice or Miss Mabel put the things in my wardrobe themselves. They had help."

Close up, there were darker specks in her eyes. "All I'm going to say is that common sense tells me we forget all this and carry on."

She appeared to consider this. "All right. Yes, all right. I do want to stay—very much. And, Edward, if I can get the staff solidly behind me, things will go so much faster. We're going to have a huge success on our hands, I just know we are. This is a marvelous house, a marvelous estate."

Her enthusiasm was infectious. "I agree with you. So, do we get on with it? After all, no one got hurt, did they? It was all pretty innocuous nonsense."

"Yes, it was. Edward?"

"Yes?" He could smell, faintly, that light scent of flowers that always surrounded her.

She wasn't smiling now. "I won't mention this again. But thank you for your confidence. It'll keep me warm at night...." Her lips were parted as the words trailed away. A rosy blush shot over her cheekbones.

"I'm very pleased about that," he said and heard his own husky tone. And, without planning to, he kissed her. Lightly at first, perhaps intending to seal their agreement, nothing more, but the touch of their mouths took on its own life.

For an instant she didn't move. Then they came into each other's arms and the movement of their lips became a seeking sexual thing. He closed his eyes and felt his heart beating heavily.

They drew back. Her eyes showed the shock he felt, but the color had left her face and he felt no embarrassment of his own. "I'm glad," he said, and meant he didn't regret the kiss.

Sue-Ellen stood and offered him a hand. "Why did we do that?" she asked as he held the hand and stood beside her.

"Because we're both under stress. The moment was right. And because we're attracted to each other. Think that sums it up?"

"I think so." She came to her toes, kissed him hard and full on the mouth and returned to her original spot, all so abruptly he could only smile and hook an elbow around her neck.

"Well," he told her, studying her face, "I suppose we'll have to be very careful about that. Although I'm not sure I want to be."

"Me, either. But we'd better get back."

The rain had abated slightly, not that it seemed to matter anymore. At the gate house he tried to get her to come in for tea, but she smiled and said, "I think we'd better say goodbye for now. But it gives me a good feeling that we like each other. It'll make working together nicer." He watched her go, uncomfortably suspicious that she might decide to make sure there were few opportunities for a repeat of what had just passed between them.

OH, SHE'D STAY. Of course, she would. Nothing would persuade her to leave now, and the main reason seemed to have changed just slightly. She smiled with self-derision. Sue-Ellen Hill, career-woman-of-the-untouchable-heart, might just be getting "a case," as they said. She tromped soggily to the back of the house and through the gate that bisected the stables and tack rooms.

He'd told her about Lenore and sounded so open. There were people who, when they loved, loved with all that they were. Sue-Ellen would stake her life on Edward's being one of those people. An odd twisting sensation wound about her heart. She'd better not blow a chance encounter out of proportion. He was a busy, directed man, and she had ambitions of her own to fulfill. Now was not the time to give into...into what? Simple attraction didn't cover what she'd felt in his arms. Something strongly sexual came closer, but even that didn't express it all.

A hot bath and then bed would feel wonderful. Then it must be work as usual. Whatever came, she'd confront it. Glancing up, she stopped in the middle of the stable yard to peer intently at the second-floor windows. There had been a movement, a curtain slipping shut . . . hadn't there?

She took a few more steps and paused again. The only rooms in use that overlooked the stable yard right there were hers.

A slow hammering started in her chest and sounded in her ears. She set off at a run. The first thing she'd do in the morning was arrange for the lock on her door to be changed. It had already become obvious that the two keys in her possession couldn't be the only ones in existence.

Inside the door from the yard she slipped off sodden shoes, took off the slicker and hat and hung them with a jumble of outdoor clothes belonging to the staff. Hurrying, but anxious not to attract attention, she slipped through the spartan passages between kitchens and pantries, mudrooms, and by the door leading to the wine cellar. And stopped again. Muffled voices came from the other side of the wine-cellar door. She recognized one clearly: Helen Bastible's.

"You'll do it, then?" Helen said.

A man's voice, low, said something Sue-Ellen couldn't hear, and the handle rattled.

There was nowhere to go, except the way she'd come. Shuffling quickly backward, turning, moving as fast as she dared, she made it to the hanging coats and wriggled between them, praying neither Helen nor her companion would discover her.

She felt, more than heard, them come. There would probably be no one in the kitchen by now, so Helen and friend were in little danger of being seen; if they didn't want to be seen, as seemed the case.

"There's a lot riding on this," Helen said, so close Sue-Ellen flinched. "For both of us."

"Don't worry. You know you can trust me."

The blood in Sue-Ellen's veins stopped running. Miles Grossby, the butler. Talking to Helen Bastible as if they were old and comfortable friends.

"I try not to worry, Miles, but this isn't the first scare, and I don't know how many more I can live through. He means so much to me."

"I'll let you know," Grossby said softly. "And in the meantime, relax."

A click. Receding footsteps, then quiet once more.

Sue-Ellen let minutes go by before venturing from her hiding place. This house seethed with intrigue.

Skimming the ground, she slipped through the passages once more and shot upstairs.

Colin and Sylvia. Helen and Grossby. The aunts and their meanness. Even Michael Bastible and his stories. They all added to a sense that there were multiple levels of activity all around her.

At the door to her room she hesitated. How did she cope with this? She'd swear someone had looked at her from her own bedroom window. That whoever it was would be gone was a foregone conclusion. That they'd come here with a mission was also a given.

She unlocked the door and threw it back against the wall . . . and smiled a grim smile at her own dramatics.

After what felt like ages, she'd searched every inch of the bedroom, bathroom and sitting room. That movement she'd spotted must have been imagined. There was no sign of anything out of place.

Now she would close the door she'd left open like a child afraid of being alone.

The handle was in her hand when she had another thought. Her two rooms were the only ones occupied on the second floor of this wing and facing the stable yard. *Occupied*.

Slowly, instinct begging her to turn back, she walked in damp socks along the corridor. The only window she could have mistaken for her own was that in the empty room beside her bedroom. She'd looked inside once and seen nothing but the draped shape of a single chair against one wall.

She half expected to find another lock had been closed against her. It hadn't and she went in.

Night had fallen. Heavy damask drapes were pulled back to reveal lace curtains beneath. Disuse scented the air.

The chair was there, but not against the wall, and not draped. Instead it had been moved close to the window.

Sue-Ellen walked around it, her stomach rising, afraid that as she passed the wing chair she'd confront some evil staring face.

No one sat there.

Relief flooded her, so strong she gripped the chair back for support.

Fool. She was loosing the iron-hard composure she'd always been so proud of.

With her breathing returning to normal, she went to the window and moved the curtains aside. The wet cobbles glittered. Above the stables hung a luminous band of navy blue caught between blackness above and the faint light spread upward from lamps on the old brick walls.

Time for a bath and bed. Someone could have come in here, but it was doubtful. She took a step and tripped...over an ebony cane with a silver handle.

Chapter Nine

"I don't know how you talked me into this. You probably put something into my tea this morning."

"Yep. You guessed it," Sue-Ellen agreed. She walked beside Edward toward the conservatory where they were to meet with Michael Bastible and Massing, the head gardener. Max strutted ahead, glancing back from time to time.

Edward was in the mood to make the most of his good-guy act. "I wouldn't do this for anyone else, you know. And I can already hear the kind of reception we'll get."

Sue-Ellen punched his arm lightly. "Who's the boss around here, you or the reverend—and your gardener? Whose conservatory is it? Who has the right to make some money out of it?"

"Mmm," was all she got in response. But being with him was a delight, even when they didn't speak.

In the ten days since the debacle over diamonds, she and Edward had spent several evenings together discussing business. Things were going well. Renovations were solidly under way, and contacts within the travel industry had produced promising results. Even the staff had calmed down and begun to accept both Sue-Ellen and her project.

There had been no repeat of the physical closeness that occurred in the old pavilion.

Sue-Ellen thought of this now and couldn't resist a side-long look at Edward. He strode beside her, or rather she trotted beside him. A big confident man with the ability to

turn her heart just by his presence. There was a sense of
waiting between them, a tension. Occasionally Sue-Ellen
caught him watching her and the effect was always the
same . . . a sharp longing. At night, in the bed that had been
his, she visualized the way he looked at her, that mixture of
pensive sizing up and desire.

She'd decided against mentioning the cane in the empty
room next to hers. Her first instinct had been to demand an
explanation for its being there. This idea had been discarded. She had no right to ask the question. If she did so,
an airtight excuse would undoubtedly have been trumped up
to cover its presence.

All that night she'd sat propped on the couch in her sitting room, straining for a sound of someone coming to re-
trieve the cane she was certain belonged to Mabel. At six
she'd awakened, stiff and groggy and expecting that when
she checked, the cane would still be there. It wasn't. But so
much for that. At least she was becoming even more certain who her enemies were, and they were harmless, except
as nuisances. Still, the possibility of a presence on the other
side of her bedroom wall did little to lull her to sleep at
night.

"Now," Edward said, marching along a path of crushed
red rock that bisected geometrically precise beds of dormant rosebushes. He drew to an abrupt halt.

A step ahead, she turned back. "Now, Edward?"

He lowered his chin to his chest and stared at her, hands
thrust into jeans pockets beneath his tweed sport coat.
"What was it I was supposed to say to Bastible and Massing?"

She let out an exasperated breath. "You agreed, Edward, agreed, to back me up in what *I'm* going to say. This
is no big deal. Just assume a masterful air and mutter
agreement from time to time."

He laughed. "Quite the manipulator, aren't you? I love
it. But we'd better not take too long. Helen called earlier and
said she had to see me. Something dire, or so it sounded. I

promised her lunch at the Arms. A man's Saturdays aren't his own anymore.''

Without commenting, Sue-Ellen started for the conservatory, a separate building in a walled courtyard off an unused wing on the far right of the house. This wing was undergoing extensive repair and conversion, and the results were exciting.

Something dire. Sue-Ellen had had a lot of time to think over the various tidbits that had been fed her recently. Helen had needed Grossby's help because someone very dear to her was causing her problems. What kind of problems, Sue-Ellen wondered, and who was the ''he'' who mattered so much? She wished Edward's name wasn't always the one to come to her. And she also wished that she didn't have the insistent conviction that she might be part of whatever troubled the fair Helen, who, Sue-Ellen was at least a little suspicious, considered her a potential rival. How far would a woman in love go to eliminate competition? Would she enter into a conspiracy with two bitter old women…and the butler? If it didn't have sinister overtones she might find the picture funny.

''Oh, hell,'' Edward muttered as they entered the conservatory courtyard, ''reception committee. Massing looks murderous.''

''Leave this to me,'' Sue-Ellen said through her teeth. ''Good morning, gentlemen,'' she hailed. ''Nice of you both to come.''

A chorused grunt didn't bode well, but she breezed into the circular domed building with its elaborately etched glass panels and stopped, arms outstretched, lips parted. ''Oh, I had no idea how beautiful it would be.'' She turned, overwhelmed by what she saw. Orchids, rows and rows of orchids of every size and color, and begonias; a profusion of so many exotic flowers she scarcely knew where to look, what to sniff. ''This is absolutely magnificent. And the air, the smell in here…heavenly.''

Massing—sinewy, weathered, gray-haired, dressed in brown corduroy and leather gaiters—remained impassive.

He was, Sue-Ellen didn't fail to note, an impressively fit-looking man.

"We're proud of the place," Michael Bastible said, a glow in his eyes. The expected sheepskin was in place over his collar and blacks, and he'd kept his wide-brimmed hat on and rakishly dipped over his eyes.

Some time later, Sue-Ellen wasn't sure how long, Massing, muttering slightly, had departed, and she was left with a vaguely disgruntled Michael and Edward, who appeared remotely dazed. But all had been agreed upon. When the house tours started up again in the spring, and before that, when the first bed-and-breakfast guests arrived, the conservatory could be viewed for a small fee. And, in fair weather, small tables and chairs would be set in the courtyard and light refreshments served.

There would be packaged seeds suitable for mailing and strips of slides showing the gardens as they were in full bloom, and potted plants for those who lived close enough to transport them. A carefully selected group of books on British horticulture and tasteful bookmarks would be offered. These would be sold in a small shop to be prepared in the stable area and presided over by someone not yet known, but easily, Sue-Ellen was sure, found among the young of the village, many of whom were looking for work.

With Michael and Edward, Sue-Ellen stepped out into the crisp morning, for once blessedly free of rain or fog. Her spirits were higher than they had been in days.

A stone bench stood nearby. "Will you gentlemen sit with me for a while?" Sue-Ellen asked expansively, and sat down without waiting for an answer. They joined her, one on each side. Edward whistled and Max came to thump down, panting, at his feet.

"Now, Michael, you are comfortable about all this?" Sue-Ellen smiled at him, and after a second's pause he smiled in return and nodded.

"Good. I'm delighted with the way everything's going."

They sank into a not-very-comfortable silence. She had something else on her mind and now seemed as good a time as any to jump in. She shifted and crossed her legs.

"I've been thinking about those cellars."

Edward made an indistinguishable noise, and when she looked at him he shook his head.

Undeterred, she turned to Michael. "Remember how we talked about them?"

"I remember."

"Did Edward tell you I went down there...twice actually." As soon as she said the words, the slow bump, bump of her heart began, as it did every time she thought of the episodes.

"He didn't mention it," Michael said without inflection. Edward made no comment.

"What I really wanted to ask you two about was a story I was told about one of the rooms down there."

"What story would that be?" Michael took off his hat and ran the brim through his fingers.

"It's all right if I ask what you know about it?"

He raised his brows. "Why shouldn't it be? I doubt if I know anything."

"Well, as far as I can tell there are a few tales going around that no one wants to talk about—or at least that's the way the thing was presented to me. But I was thinking we might like to capitalize on what seems like a juicy piece of myth." She could hardly admit that since hearing the story she'd been haunted by the possibility of a girl dying in that dark closed place, and that she felt an almost obsessive need to find out more.

Edward, silent until this point, leaned forward. "I'm not aware of any stories. Who told you?"

"Oh—" she made an airy gesture "—someone did. I was sworn to secrecy," and she made herself smile wickedly. Pretending the whole thing was a joke seemed the best approach. "Anyway, I thought Michael might know, since his family's been around East Puddle and Airstone for a long time."

"Not as long as mine," Edward said, sounding cryptic. "And apparently this story is something to do with my home."

There was something there, a reticence, as if he'd prefer the topic dropped. But Bea had said the family avoided the tale.

"I was told that a girl committed suicide in the first room you come to—the locked room."

Absolute silence followed. Then Edward made what sounded like a disbelieving snort. "That's ridiculous. I'm amazed you'd listen to such old wives' tales." He laughed. "Suicide in our cellars. Good Lord. When was this supposed to be? In the year dot?"

"A long time ago," Sue-Ellen said, embarrassed but stubborn enough to be determined to get more than a brush-off. "Evidently she offended a former lady of the house who shut her up until she went mad and killed herself."

"My...oh, really." Michael turned sideways to face her. "You know, you really should take a lesson from this. There's no place more given to silly stories than a little village like East Puddle where almost nothing happens. What else did you hear?"

Sue-Ellen crossed her arms. "That there's been more than one case of madness in this house." She immediately regretted the comment. Avoiding looking at Edward, she concentrated on Michael Bastible and prayed no one would think she was referring to Sir Arthur Ormsby-Jones, whom she'd forgotten until this moment.

"That," Michael said, his face turning an unusual mottled hue, "is the most outrageous tattle I've ever heard."

"But it doesn't surprise me," Edward said quietly behind her. "I suppose my father's name came up?"

Sue-Ellen would willingly have disappeared. She slipped back on the seat until she could meet his eyes. "No, of course it didn't. And I shouldn't have said something so thoughtless. It's just that I've become fascinated by it all. I thought one of you might have heard something." In Edward's set features she saw distress, the deep and quiet distress of a long-shouldered burden. Damn her childish curiosity.

"I think that's about enough said." Michael got to his feet. "I'm speaking for Arthur now, Edward, so let me have my say. This family has put up with quite enough nonsense from the ungrateful inhabitants of East Puddle. Gossip mongers left and right, I'm afraid . . . much as I try to guide them. This is one story that won't be repeated again, do you understand?"

Startled, Sue-Ellen could only stare into his angry face.

"I say, Michael—"

"No, Edward. You're too gentle, to everyone. I'm not blaming Sue-Ellen for bringing this up. How was she to know it might be hurtful? But I can tell—suggest most firmly, for the family's sake, that no further mention be made of the subject, and—" a big forefinger punctuated the sentence "—stay out of things that don't concern you. That means stay out of the cellars if that's what's going to start you on this sort of thing. Stay out."

NO MORE WAITING. The time was approaching for Sue-Ellen Hill to get the final message. She'd get it and understand it. If not, there would be no more warnings.

Two weeks since the expedition to the pavilion. That should never have happened, but who could have guessed that a chance walk would take them there? What had Edward told her? He was bound to have mentioned Lenore. No one was ever to go there again. No one was to remember. In remembering there was danger, danger of some missed nuance that could drag up the truth and lead to the ultimate revelation. That revelation must not be allowed.

At least there was no question of stumbling on the spot where that other girl— No, no question, because that had been beautifully done, no traces left behind. An evening at the Arms. A few too many drinks and an unscheduled swim in water too cold for the poor thing's heart. Perfect.

Expecting this Hill woman to be easy to get rid of had been a mistake. But who could know that the first open warning had been ill-timed, that it would make the diamond theft appear ridiculous?

But thanks to a little luck and some conveniently dropped remarks by an innocent or two, the trap had been baited and the bait taken—so far. Now it was time to close the trap.

THERE WAS A STORY HERE.

Sue-Ellen shut herself into her rooms with its shiny new lock and tossed her notebook onto the couch.

Stay out, the Reverend Bastible had ordered with fire in his eyes. And later, when they were alone, Edward had only smiled indulgently and alluded to her overactive imagination.

She wasn't convinced. Upon returning to the house she'd spoken to each staff member. A risk, but one worth taking. Mary Leaming didn't know much, only what the previous cook, a lady now dead, had told her—that there had been some rumors about a sinister death in the house.

Sylvia knew nothing, neither did Connie, who'd looked horrified at the suggestion, so scared that Sue-Ellen had been grateful that she hadn't disclosed the location of the supposed suicide. Grossby had listened somberly, shaking his head all the while. He'd never heard the story, and Pitts couldn't stay awake long enough to respond.

She went to look down into the stable yard. Workmen were packing up their tools for the day. Already the stables and tack rooms had been cleared and a kitchen roughed in. She puffed out her cheeks, overcome by a sensation of being at loose ends. Edward had issued no invitation to join him this evening, and there was no pretending she wasn't disappointed. In his quiet way and despite the evident amusement over her revelation, he'd made her feel that he was withdrawing from her again. Damn, she didn't want that. Maybe she should drop this preoccupation with the cellars and concentrate on the job she'd been given to do. Then there could be a chance... Why did she have to come halfway around the world to a place where there was no time for personal diversion, only to become hopelessly diverted?

Picking up the notebook, she stretched out on what had become her favorite thinking spot on the couch . . . and saw a folded sheet of paper slide beneath the door.

She took a second to react, a second too long. By the time she reached the door and threw it open, the corridor was empty.

With a feeling akin to a million crawling insects climbing across her skin, she trod slowly to the room next door.

Seconds later, with a stomach that felt wrung out, she was back on her own couch, the paper in hand. No one had been secreted in the hateful room.

Not wanting to, but knowing there was no alternative, she unfolded the sheet and read:

HER NAME WAS LETTIE. SHE WAS NINETEEN. WHY IS THE DOOR LOCKED?

Blood pumped in Sue-Ellen's ears. The note was printed in block letters and unsigned.

Lettie. Having a name made the girl real.

Trembling, Sue-Ellen got up and pushed the paper into her pocket. Why *was* the door locked when none of the others were? She felt for and found her Swiss army knife. A regular lock would be more difficult than a padlock, but she had to try.

It was late afternoon. The staff would be closeted in the kitchen putting final touches to dinner for the aunts, Bea and Sue-Ellen. Bea always spent this part of the day going over household accounts, and the aunts would be taking their naps.

Sue-Ellen encountered no one on her way to the Great Hall. This time the door to the cellars opened more easily, and she was quickly inside with the dismal light bulb on.

She'd also brought a small bottle of baby oil that she kept with her toiletries. A little lubrication might help the old lock mechanism give up its hold. She went directly to the first door on the left.

The feeling came, swelling inside her head, grayness at the edges of her vision. She would not turn back. Fingers on the handle, she flipped out a narrow blade on the knife and bent . . . and the handle turned, turned easily, and the door opened inward. It had been unlocked.

She slid to her knees, gripping the jamb. A dim glowing wedge spread inside and she pushed the door wider, all the way back.

A small windowless room. Bare stone floors, graying whitewashed walls and a single narrow cot covered with a drab blanket. Beside the bed, a wooden chair and, on its seat, a new candle, matches and a jam jar filled with fresh daisies.

Sue-Ellen stumbled to her feet and took a few steps inside. She struck a match, lighted the candle, and jumped when shadows shot, dancing, over walls and ceiling.

The air smelled of incense, and she saw a small glowing spill upright in a holder that stood in a niche like the one in the next room.

Then she saw the marks on the wall, scratched numbers in rows—rows and rows. Dates? Here and there she made out recorded days from 1922 and 1923. The numbers had been made, not with pencil or pen, but with something sharp that scratched through the whitewash to the dusty stone beneath. And beside the numbers something . . . red. No, rust, something once red turned to rust, like old old bloodstains . . .

She couldn't breathe. Someone had prepared this place for her visit, had known she would come once she saw the note. Someone understood how affected she'd been by the story of Lettie. *Lettie.* Now the girl had a name, almost a face, if Sue-Ellen closed her eyes.

The thumping pulse in her ears also vibrated her throat. The bed, the flowers, the candle . . . preparations for a new occupant, readiness for another victim?

She saw the square of pale fabric as she backed away. Light blue. Something soft on the pillow.

Fascinated, terrified, she inched up beside the bed, one arm stretched back, ready to grab the door if it should start to close.

The thin stuff fell open as she lifted it and she leaped away, clutching it to her. A place had been prepared ... for her.

What she held, and quickly dropped, was one of her own nightgowns!

Chapter Ten

Why wouldn't she leave well enough alone? "I think you should sit down," Edward said, feeling helpless and angry at the same time. She seemed determined to invent a skeleton for the Ormsby-Jones's closet, and he didn't like that one bit. In fact he was going to have to stop her. Airstone didn't need some sordid little story to make it attractive to tourists.

Sue-Ellen stormed back and forth across his sitting room, dodging Max who tried to stop her at each turn. "You aren't listening to me, Edward. Today someone tried to scare me half to death. They tried to scare me so badly that I'd go away. Which is exactly what's been going on most of the time since I arrived. The past couple of weeks—while everything seemed so quiet—have obviously been used to plan the next offensive, which has now started."

He looked at her closely. Her face was pale and her gesturing hands shook. If she wasn't frightened she was a very good actress. Damn, the feeling was there again, the pull of fascination with her. What was it that drew him? That they were opposites in so many ways?

Time to get the hormones under wraps. "Sit down." He planted his hands on her shoulders and plunked her into a chair. "Tell me the whole thing again, slowly."

Sue-Ellen did as he asked, then said, "I hated it. It was awful." Her eyes filled with tears.

Again he was getting a glimpse of the side she usually kept hidden. He hadn't forgotten kissing her in the pavilion. He hadn't forgotten or stopped fantasizing about kissing her again . . . and much more.

She wasn't all tough, perhaps not even a little bit tough. Scared would sum up the way she looked right now, and the effect that had on him was predictable. "Hey, it's okay. Relax." He couldn't take her in his arms. He mustn't, or they might start something that shouldn't be started. But that was exactly what he wanted to do.

"I'm not going to be frightened away. They can do what they like but I won't give up."

Brave words, but a tear slid from the corner of one eye. He pulled an ottoman close to her knees and sat down. "Of course you won't give up. Please . . ." Uncertainly he rested an elbow on the arm of her chair and wiped the tear from her face. She turned her cheek into his hand, pressed it there, and his stomach contracted.

"I'm sorry," she said very quietly. "I guess I pulled my usual stunt and did what you said we women always do— overreacted. But there is something going on. And I've got this nasty feeling that whoever's behind it isn't about to stop."

His fingers found their way into her hair, briefly, and to her neck. He'd like to kiss her again, and to hell with what he ought to do.

She leaned back and he withdrew his hand, but there was a subtle change happening between them, had been happening since the day they met. He was going to have to tread carefully, unless he was prepared to get into a situation that might turn sticky.

"Why don't you give me the details again, slowly this time?" He didn't know exactly how it had become so, but having her trust him was important.

Fingers tented, she launched into her story once more.

"I can't believe any of my people would do this," he said when she'd finished.

"You think I'm a liar?"

"No," he said in haste and got up, "no, absolutely not. But you'll admit it sounds farfetched and unreasonable even if some of them don't like the idea of the hotel. Work is already well advanced and we're obviously going ahead, so why would anyone bother with this?"

She rested her head against the chair and looked up at him. "I thought of that. So what's the answer? Why is someone trying to get rid of me? And they are."

"I don't know." He shrugged and went to pour whiskey into two glasses. He should insist she stay out of the cellars and stop wasting time on imaginary grudges. The decanter cracked against the silver tray. His practice needed all his attention right now. "Can you try to forget about this nonsense, Sue-Ellen? I think it would be better for all of us."

"What makes you so sure I'll be allowed to forget it? I think I represent a danger to someone, a big danger neither of us has guessed at. And I'm pretty sure it has something to do with Lettie."

This exasperated him. "You don't know there is, or was, a Lettie. It's probably a practical joke, and you're buying it."

"I want to find someone who might know. Who's been at Airstone the longest?"

He was tired. "I don't know. My aunts, I suppose. Or Pitts. And none of them is capable of doing what you say was done today."

"They could have had help. But I'm more interested in someone who might have heard the story in greater detail. Someone who might give a clue as to why I'm a threat around here. Perhaps your father?"

"No," he said, closing that avenue. "If anyone would know it might be Michael, and he obviously doesn't." Although Michael's almost violent reaction to the subject did puzzle Edward. "Bea's been visiting East Puddle for almost as long as I can remember. She was related to our old cook, I believe. But she only moved here from Yorkshire to live about nine years ago, after my mother died. So she's not likely to be any great help." Damn, he was starting to sound as if he gave credence to this nonsense.

"You don't believe me, do you?"

He offered her a glass, which she ignored.

"Do you know about the room next to my bedroom?"

What now? "There is a room, yes. I think my grandfather used it as a study. Bea told me she's in what was my grandmother's suite. Where you are now, where I was, used to be my grandfather's."

There was a small pause. "Your grandparents had separate rooms?"

He barely stopped himself from saying, so what? "That wasn't uncommon. Still isn't for some people." Not that it was an arrangement he'd ever understood.

"Your parents...?"

"My parents used the wing that opens onto the conservatory courtyard, and no, they didn't have separate rooms." Her blush gave him more pleasure than it should, mostly because he was intrigued by the flashes of naïveté she showed from time to time.

"Well," she said, "that's not the point. That room doesn't have a thing in it but a chair."

The fascination she held for him was becoming stronger and clearer. Sue-Ellen wasn't worldly. But she was sexy. Sexy and innocent, and the combination hit him like an erotic pain. He wanted her.

"Did you hear what I said? About the room?"

"It isn't in use." He needed the whiskey and he drank some now.

"That's what you think. From time to time someone sits in there and peers out the window—watching me. The other night that someone left an ebony cane with a silver handle there."

An ebony cane with a silver handle. She had to be joking.

"Surprised? So was I, and of course the thing's gone now. But it *was* there and we both know who owns it."

Now he'd have to be firm. "My aunt Mabel probably isn't the only person in the world to own a cane like that—"

"I—"

"Please. Quite apart from that, she can't walk without it. She can hardly walk with it. So, if she did leave it behind, how would she make it back to her suite?"

Sue-Ellen shook her head. "It all points back to what's been shaping up in my head. I'm supposed to think the aunts are actively trying to dispose of me. There's something going on here, Edward, something horrible, only you won't admit it."

"You must watch too much television."

"That's it." She stood up. "I'm being victimized and you make jokes. I want you to come with me now. You'll see I didn't make any of this up."

He grinned and instantly realized his mistake, but she was cute when she was mad. "Okay, okay," he said and set down his glass, "I'll go, but only to humor you."

Her glare was impossible to miss. Angry or otherwise, she was irresistible, and that was something he'd better get over. Even if he hadn't decided after Lenore's death that the female population might be safer if he avoided serious attachments, Sue-Ellen wasn't the type to settle in one place permanently. She'd fulfill her task here for as long as it interested her and move on. And he'd been left alone and more than a little bloodied from loving and loosing a couple of times too often. Not that love was the question here—he wouldn't let it be.

The first person they saw on the way to the house was Michael Bastible. He ambled into view from the direction of the conservatory and waved.

Edward felt Sue-Ellen check her stride. When he looked at her he saw her eyes narrowed on Michael and guessed what she was about to do. "Sue-Ellen," he said in a stage whisper.

Too late.

"Good evening, Reverend."

Michael drew closer. "Hello, you two. How goes it with the Airstone Plaza?"

"Very funny," Edward said and placed a hand at Sue-Ellen's waist. He had to divert her from annoying poor Michael again. "We're going to check a few things out now. Sue-Ellen thinks we'll open ahead of schedule."

"Not if some people have their way." She resisted the pressure from his hand, and he let out a low whistle.

Michael stopped in front of them. "Problems?" he asked Sue-Ellen.

"It's—"

"Come with us, Michael," Edward interrupted. "We might need you. How long is it since you did a bit of exorcism?"

Michael's brows shot up.

Edward felt, as much as saw, Sue-Ellen's frown. "Seems we've got a ghost to dispose of," he said.

"I never said anything about a ghost. I told you—"

"That some ghoul is trying to frighten you. Michael, Sue-Ellen's convinced that old tale she was told about the cellars is true. Now I think she believes she's slated to be the next Airstone mad suicide."

"In that case," Michael said, a twitch moving his mustache, "lead on. I think I've got my forked stick in my pocket."

Edward grinned. "Wrong prop, old chap. We're not looking for water." He glanced at Sue-Ellen, at her flaming cheeks and the glittering blue eyes set straight ahead, and he felt despicable. Dammit all, what had he got into with this money-making scheme of his? A small quiet place formed behind the question before he wondered if he would have done otherwise had it meant he was never to meet this woman.

She didn't slow her pace until they'd passed beyond the tapestry and into the cold passages beyond. Then they reached the first door, and she stood absolutely still.

As he watched her, his body tightened. He felt her tension and remembered that every time she approached a closed space she skated on the edge of panic. Whether she was imagining these passive attacks on her or not, she had courage.

She threw open the door and stood aside. "There. See for yourselves and tell me if I'm imagining things."

With his own inward shrinking, he entered slowly, Michael close behind. He should have had the foresight to bring a flashlight.

"What are we looking for?" Michael asked sotto voce.

Edward glanced around a bare cell, the twin of the one next door. No bed, no chair with a candle and no nightgown. He rested an elbow on the other forearm and rubbed his face, meeting Michael's confused eyes. The place smelled unpleasantly sweet.

"Oh!" Sue-Ellen came to stand beside him. She gripped his arm. "This is impossible. It was here, I tell you, all of it." And to Michael, "A bed and a chair. There was a candle on the chair and matches, and I lit the candle." She looked upward. "Shadows were all over the ceiling and then I found my nightgown on the bed, as if I was going to sleep here."

Michael was silent.

Edward transferred her two hands into his own and smiled. There seemed nothing to say. He wouldn't have done this to her for anything.

"This is vicious," she muttered. "You can believe me or not, but I know what I saw. Look around you. Don't you notice anything?"

He did as she asked. Michael said, "I don't see anything."

"Right," Sue-Ellen said. "Nothing. No dust or dirt. Everything's clean as a pin. If this place has been locked up forever—and, by the way, notice the door isn't locked now—where's all the dust and cobwebs? Someone cleaned this room, right down to sweeping the floor."

Muscles in Edward's jaw tightened. She had a point.

"And look at this. Here on the wall." In a flurry, she went to jab a forefinger against the stones. She peered closer.

"They tried to rub it away but it's still here. See. Scratched numbers. Dates, I'm sure . . . and this rusty-looking stuff. It looks like old blood."

"Oh, I say," Michael said, "hold on. My dear girl, you've got to calm down or you'll make yourself ill."

Edward transferred his attention to Michael. In the dim light from the passage the man's face appeared rigid. His hands, held at his sides, were tight fists. What was Michael exhibiting? Anxiety? Or just distress over Sue-Ellen's wild suggestions?

"It was all here, I tell you," she said, but her voice broke and she leaned against the wall. "It was." From her pocket she withdrew the note about Lettie and handed it to Michael. "It was as real as this."

Michael read and reread the note, then patted her shoulder. "What you thought you saw seemed very real. But I'm pretty sure I know exactly what happened. The marks are there all right. We can all see them. You came down here to look around. You saw the marks and suddenly the story you'd been told came back."

"No!"

"Were you nervous when you got here?"

"Well . . ."

"Of course you were. And when we're anxious the subconscious can play tricks. That's what happened. I've seen the same sort of thing before."

Edward watched the play between the two of them. Sue-Ellen, her palms held up, appeared desperate, and he wanted to go to her, but there was something about Michael, something different. He spoke rapidly, waved his arms, and his eyes moved repeatedly to the door.

"I didn't imagine it," Sue-Ellen said, but the fire was gone from her voice.

Michael peered at his watch. "Heavens, I'm late. Will you excuse me? Got to go."

"Yes," Edward said, feeling drained and muddled, and Michael hurried away.

Without looking at her, Edward held an arm toward Sue-Ellen. Seconds passed before she came to lean against him, and he stroked her hair.

"You believe me now," she said. "I can feel it."

"Yes." The bond was forming, the ability to understand each other without knowing why or how.

Still holding Sue-Ellen, he reached into the niche and held before him a partly burned stick of incense. "They forgot something."

GLITTERING RIME clung to the grass beneath her feet.

Fools. Always fools. They came, pleading their cases, swearing allegiance, promising that, by them, she'd be better served. And always they failed her. There was no one to trust, no one to help. She was alone. But that was best.

But this new fool had been unexpected, a potential problem that would have to be removed . . . after Sue-Ellen had her accident.

She walked on, savoring the frozen night. For a while it had seemed possible that the American could be eliminated quickly, without energy, but now that had become unlikely, even undesirable. Yes, the demise of Sue-Ellen would be delightful. Tonight the stage had been set. Everything was in place for the execution.

Still, one thing rankled. The new fool. Blackmail. That had been the not-subtle message.

First Sue-Ellen. Then the blackmailer. Both would be eliminated.

The swelling in her veins, the pumping, thrilled her. Twice before she'd felt this pounding joy. For her own sake she'd thought it would be better never to feel it again, but now...now she knew what she was doing was right. Too bad she dared not risk watching this time.

There would be the other matter to take care of, and soon, but until she'd accomplished her mission of tomorrow night, she must wait for the other—wait with anticipation.

At the death of the fool blackmailer, she would be the lone spectator.

Chapter Eleven

Sue-Ellen depressed the telephone cradle on her desk, waited an instant, and dialed Edward's office number.

"Mr. Ormsby-Jones, please."

She squeezed the bridge of her nose. He believed her, but she still wasn't sure he felt the ominous threat of danger she'd been carrying with her since yesterday.

"Hello. Edward Ormsby-Jones here."

"This is Sue-Ellen. Would you meet me at St. Peter's in East Puddle?" *Brilliant.* When would she learn to put things in their correct order? "The Reverend Bastible just called and said he'd like to talk to me at the church this evening. At seven, after his service."

She heard a clicking, as if Edward tapped the mouthpiece, before he said, "Did he say why?"

"No. But I think I know. He's going to tell me about Lettie."

A long sigh. "If there ever was a Lettie."

Ridiculously she felt like crying. "You said you believed me."

"I believe someone is playing not-very-funny-tricks on you and I don't know why. But I do intend to find out. The Lettie thing is still a gray area in my mind. Why do you want me to come with you?"

It was her turn to sigh. *Because I want you with me. I want to see you and be close to you. You make me feel safe, and I think I'm falling in love.*

"Sue-Ellen?"

"I'd like you there, that's all," she said. "I need you." Now he'd feel threatened. Quickly she added, "It seems important for you to hear anything that has to do with what's been going on."

"I'll go straight there on my way home. Seven. I've made a note of that. Sue-Ellen?"

"Yes?"

"Would you like . . ."

She held her breath.

"Um, if you like I'll bring you into Dorchester one day. You can have a look around. The break would do you good."

Expectancy fled as swiftly as it had come. "That would be wonderful." Maybe she was tilting at windmills, but she'd swear he'd almost asked her something quite different.

MIST CURLED in a shifting swath above the ground. She'd forgotten how dark it would be by the time she left for East Puddle.

Huddled in the orange down parka she'd brought from Augusta as a last-minute precaution, she scrunched along the gravel drive toward the gates. Thank God for the ski parka. Incredibly the damp cold here was more bone chilling than any weather conditions she'd experienced on her infrequent trips to the slopes.

She put up her hood, stuffed her hair inside and tied the string securely beneath her chin. The effect, the way it added to the sense of being closed into an echo chamber with the sounds of her swishing coat, her footsteps and breathing, made her swing around to walk backward, searching the shadows. Then she smiled, hunching her shoulders. Silly. Like a kid afraid of the dark.

The gate house loomed. She didn't like the place when there were no lights in the windows, because it meant Edward wasn't there. Damn, she was getting a bad case on the man.

Once in the lane she walked quickly, more and more aware of the darkness and her solitude. Here the mist became a shifting sea, milky, tinged blue by a cloud-skulking moon.

A tap-tap, tap-tap, came from her right. She stopped, ducked to peer. The hedgerow was higher than her head, as high as the lower branches of the naked trees beyond. Tap-tap, tap-tap. An animal. Hoofs. Sue-Ellen scurried up the left verge and flattened herself against stickery foliage. Were there wild horses here?

The moon emerged, fleetingly sent a wash over the scene, and she covered her mouth. The light touched great antlers, glimmered on soft eyes. Then, so close she felt the power of muscle and sinew, a giant stag darted past.

The thumping in her ears kept pace with the pulse in her throat. Why hadn't she arranged to have Grossby drive her, or asked Edward to pick her up?

Shrugging her shoulders to loosen cramped muscle, she started off again. She was twenty-seven, competent, a world traveler, and she could cope with anything that came her way.

The next sound was like that of a far-off siren. Sue-Ellen kept walking, planting each foot hard and loud. Why did she get the feeling that if she looked down she'd appear to float in the mist, legless from the knee down? Not a siren. This was ridiculous.

The thing sailed out of the pale rim of a cloud, swooped through branches upheld like bony arms...and barely missed her head. An owl. No, a bat. The sound was the whistle of air currents in the filmy membranes of its wings.

She ran, beating the air before her face. She wouldn't stop running until she reached the church.

I NEED YOU. Edward parked the Jeep at the side gate to the churchyard, told Max to stay, and leaped to the ground. She'd said she needed him. Of course, that could be no more than a statement of needing his support in this, whatever *this* was. On the other hand... He liked the possibility of the other hand, not that he was sure what to do about it.

The gate squeaked. Any last stragglers from evensong would have left by now. He walked up the path at a leisurely pace. Tombstones appeared luminous, detached from the earth by mist. He liked the peace here, the feeling that, as his father had always said, among the dead one was safe. Threat hung with the living. Fifteen minutes to go before seven. He needn't hurry.

A shape to his left, a spade over one shoulder, lumbered along between gravestones. "Hey up, Ernie. How goes it?" He didn't like Ernie Butters, grave digger, but out of deference to Connie, his wife, he made a point of being polite to the man.

"Ah." Came the expected grunt. Edward had never decided just what *ah* meant in the context of a salutation.

"Taking a shortcut," Ernie said, shocking Edward into immobility. Ernie never said anything but *ah*. "Been to the shop for Connie. Could have gone around to get to our place, but might as well save a body a few steps, I always say."

"Yes, indeed," Edward said, astonished as Ernie touched the greasy cap that always decorated his head and walked away.

Almost at once the man was swallowed by vapor and trees, and Edward carried on.

He entered the church by the heavy brass-studded door that led into a crossing aisle halfway down the tiny nave. On Christmas morning, St. Peter's fifty or so seats often had to be augmented by a few folding chairs brought in by parishioners. For the rest of the year, except perhaps at Easter, Michael tended to preach to a congregation of twenty or so, most of whom snored gently through the proceedings to qualify for the tea and buns Helen served in the church hall afterward.

Why did Michael do it? Edward mused. Habit, tradition, because his father had done so before him? As on so many previous occasions, the thought came strongly that

Michael Bastible could have been so much more. He'd read theology at Cambridge and, from what Edward had been told, had done brilliantly and been offered a job as gofer for some bishop or other. That might have led to great things in the Church of England. But Michael had chosen instead to return to East Puddle in time to take over for his father, Frederick.

Edward's shoes hit stone flags with the impact of pistol shots. He supposed Michael wasn't such a puzzle. In a way they were similar. They liked where they were and what they were. But Michael hadn't had much luck, apart from being where he wanted to be. Marriage to a woman much younger than himself had ended in divorce, leaving Michael to bring up Colin and Helen, at the time two years old. And from then on that had been his life: raising his children, tolerating their foibles, looking after his tiny flock and, obviously his greatest joy, presiding over Airstone's conservatory.

"Michael!" His voice echoed back. There was no reply.

He should put some lights on. Michael didn't need to see where he was going in here, and neither did Edward, but Sue-Ellen was likely to be intimidated by the oppressive blackness.

"Michael, where are you?" He stood still, frowning. Michael had an appointment with Sue-Ellen in a few minutes. Where was he? He shouldn't have turned off the lights and expected her to fumble her way in here. Instantly Edward considered going to meet her. Why hadn't he suggested picking her up? Too much time had passed since he'd been accustomed to thinking of the niceties of a woman as part of his life.

He patted the bulging pockets of his camel-hair overcoat. The purchases had been impulsive, and now they seemed ridiculous. He probably wouldn't give them to her.

A clatter came from the right, toward the front of the church where he'd entered. "Michael, is that you? Where are you?" The belfry, unused for at least twenty years, was there, and two small rooms used to store vases and hymnals.

The clattering grew, something metal, or perhaps wooden, on stone. Damn Michael and his peculiarities. The noise came from the belfry. Money might be short here, but surely not so short that it was necessary to work in a cramped belfry with no lights on.

Where were the light switches? All the way back by the main door, if he remembered correctly. The ancient latch to the belfry door raised easily and he entered, squinting. "Michael—"

The noise, the reverberating noise, shattered him. Something fell, so near that his hair moved with the current of the passing mass. Then came the deafening clang that sent him to his knees. He covered his ears, bent over and swallowed against nausea.

My God. What was that? Sue-Ellen found a light switch inside the church door and turned it on. Tiny sconces slicked pointed patches of brownish glow on the walls. Where had the awful crash come from?

To her left were a few rows of pews. The same number of pews on her right reached a minute sanctuary with a simple altar.

She heard a muffled voice from the left and went that way, to a glass-paneled door that stood ajar.

"Reverend?" she asked tentatively, going into a cramped gray space. "Oh!" For an instant she couldn't think. Edward, kneeling, his hands over his ears, didn't move. His head was bent low, and inches from him was a big brass bell, about two feet in diameter, corroded green and snaked about by filthy rope and the thick red-and-white sallie section that must once have been held by bell ringers. At the top of the bell, a broken curved piece of metal hung from a welded bracket.

She looked from the bell to Edward and, with horror, knew what had happened.

"Edward. My God, Edward." She knelt beside him and pulled his head to her shoulder, gripped him so tightly her fingers hurt.

He peered up at her, dazed. "I don't believe it. The thing just came down like a boulder off a cliff. It was dark and I didn't see it. If it had hit me the curtain would have come down without my knowing I was part of the last act."

She began shaking, and with the shaking came tears. Things were getting crazier here. Pulling him closer, she touched his face, his hair. "You would have been killed."

He laughed without mirth. "Understatement, darling. I'd have been a pile of jam."

Sue-Ellen shuddered and he shook her gently. "Sorry you walked in on this. You aren't exactly being treated to a lot of cozy British interludes, are you? Oh, my—" he brought his face close "—don't cry, please. I— Please don't cry."

"You might have been killed."

"Yes. Painful, but not such a loss to the world, hmm?"

She stopped crying, sniffed and laughed. "If I didn't know you were very British and therefore incapable of fishing for compliments, I'd think you wanted me to argue that. But we both know you don't want it." Not kissing him, over and over, was going to become impossible if she stayed where she was.

When they both stood he was smiling, but weakly, and he kept an arm around her as if he needed to convince himself he was still alive and feeling.

"What do we do?" she asked him.

"Michael said to meet him in the church at seven? You're sure of that?"

"Certain. It was Helen who called, and she said her father would wait for me after services."

Edward looked past her and frowned. "Well, he didn't wait, did he? I don't understand that. He's not the forgetful kind."

"Should we just go home?" At this moment she wanted to put distance between herself and this place. If possible she'd like to forget they'd ever been here.

"We're going to the vicarage. This—" he pointed at the bell "—must be taken care of so there are no more accidents. And I want an explanation from Michael as to why he let you come here alone in the dark and didn't even bother to stick around. I won't have you treated like that."

The tough tone swelled her confidence while it warmed her. Edward cared what happened to her. He might not understand or agree with some of what she wanted to do, but what she felt emanating from him was more than casual concern.

Rather than being attached to the church, the vicarage had been built in its own walled garden, which could be entered from the main street in the village or from the graveyard. Sue-Ellen held the hand Edward offered and let him guide her among gravestones to a metal gate and a path leading to the door of a rambling stone house built to complement the Norman church.

Helen answered their knock. Her wide smile and the warmth in her eyes blanked when she saw Edward wasn't alone. But she said, "Come in, come in," waving them inside and kissing Edward's cheek before hanging on his arm.

Sue-Ellen didn't like what happened inside her at the sight of the two of them so close, but there was nothing to be done about her reaction in that area anymore.

The way Edward felt about Helen's attention, or the way he didn't feel about it, quickly became evident. He gently removed Helen's hand from his arm and gave her a vague smile. "We came to see Michael," he said, and Helen's lips coming together, the shift of her eyes to Sue-Ellen and then to the ground, filled Sue-Ellen with an uncomfortable combination of relief and pity. Helen was in love with Edward and her feelings weren't reciprocated. If she could be totally glad about that it would be easier on her, but she had never learned how not to feel for other people's unhappiness.

Michael sat in a lumpy but comfortable-looking chintz chair in a shabby room that faced the front of the house. As they came in he pushed aside a pile of newspapers and got up. "Edward, Sue-Ellen. What a lovely surprise. Sit down, sit down. Helen, did I polish off that bottle of Scotch the Sidleys brought at Christmas?"

"I don't think so," Helen said faintly.

"We won't have anything, thanks," Edward said, darting a questioning glance at Sue-Ellen. "Did you forget an appointment this evening, Michael?"

Before Michael could respond, Colin ambled in dressed in navy blazer, gray flannels and a startling yellow-spotted pink cravat. "Hello, kiddies. Come to break the monotony? God thanks you. *I* thank you," he added, grinning at his father as if he dared him to comment on his choice of terms. "Shall we drink here or at the Arms? I'm easy. Of course, if we stay here pater will have to break out his private stash, wherever he's got it salted away. Haven't found it yet."

Sue-Ellen was more interested in Edward's reaction than Michael's. "Sometimes, Colin, you are a royal pain in the ass," said the usually mild-spoken Edward. "Stay and shut up, or go and shut up. The choice is yours. Sorry," he added, taking in Michael, Helen and Sue-Ellen.

"Oooh. Touchy, aren't we?" Colin, his brows raised almost to his artfully tousled hairline, subsided into a chair that matched his father's.

"I was asking about your appointment this evening, Michael," Edward continued after a short and painful silence. "Why did you ask to see Sue-Ellen at the church, then turn out all the lights and leave?"

Michael stared.

"Don't be silly, Edward," Helen said, going to her father's side. "Daddy wouldn't do any such thing."

Sue-Ellen's turn to stare.

"Didn't you say it was Helen who called?" Edward asked her.

"Yes. Helen, you called this afternoon and said your father would like to see me after evensong at seven."

Helen frowned. "I didn't call you. Why should I? Daddy didn't ask me to."

"Yes, you did," Sue-Ellen insisted, feeling foolish. "You called and said your father had some things to discuss that would interest me and I agreed to be at the church at seven."

"Just a minute." Michael spoke in an explosive rush. "What's all this about? Why should I make an appointment to meet you? Which I didn't, by the way."

"Must have been a ghostly summons," Colin said, examining his fingernails. "Probably wanted to give you a message from beyond...something about a locked room and a dead girl."

"Shut up," Edward said and made no attempt to apologize. "Michael, this is serious. Sue-Ellen asked me to join you both there because she thought you might know something about what's been going on at Airstone Hall."

"What's been happening at the Hall? Apart from diamond thefts and things that go bang in the night and—"

"Shut up, Colin." Michael spoke this time. "Sue-Ellen, what did you think I might be going to say?"

"Well..." Sue-Ellen glanced at Edward, who nodded. "I'm... Edward and I, actually, are beginning to think that this plot to frighten me away from my job may have little to do with what I'm doing—with opening the hotel, I mean. We think I must be some sort of threat to someone, only we don't know what it is. And we, well, I've been wondering if you might know more about it. I thought you intended to let me in on the reason tonight."

"No." Michael shook his head slowly. "No, I don't know a thing. In fact, as I told you yesterday, I think you're imagining things. There's no plot to get rid of you. Why should there be?"

Sue-Ellen gritted her teeth. "I'd like that note back."

"What?"

"The note about Lettie. You took it with you yesterday. I'd like it back."

Michael colored. "Oh dear. I was really hoping you'd forget all about that. I decided it would be better if I got rid of the thing. I burned it."

"That's unbelievable!" Sue-Ellen raised her hands and let them drop. "What right did you have to do that? Ever since I got here unpleasant things have been happening to me, then the evidence gets disposed of. And I'm supposed to believe you only got rid of that note for my good?"

"Yes." Michael looked directly at her. "Anyone could have written it, including you. Don't you use a notebook with the same sort of paper? Isn't that what I see you carrying around?"

"Well . . . yes."

"All right. We'll drop this for now," Edward said. Muscles in his jaw jerked. "I got to the church first this evening, Michael. I thought I heard something in the belfry, and when I went in there that old bell, which has been out of commission forever, fell. If it hadn't missed me by about a hair I wouldn't be talking to you now."

"Good Lord." Michael sat down. "No one's supposed to go in there. It's dangerous. The bell was shored up as best as possible. We hope to have it repaired one day."

Edward looked as if he didn't give a damn what happened to the bell, as long as he never had to go near it again. "Let's go," he said to Sue-Ellen.

"Someone called me," she said, stubbornly holding her ground. "And that someone said she was you, Helen. Why would that happen?"

"How should I know?" Helen's pale face was even paler, and Sue-Ellen didn't have to guess that she was considering the possibility of Edward's being killed. "But I didn't call you. Perhaps you simply aren't liked here. Have you considered that? Perhaps you don't fit in."

Sue-Ellen laughed, she couldn't help it. "I don't have to consider the possibility. It's a fact. But I don't intend to walk out on a job I've been hired to do and one that I know I'll do very well. So, whoever's decided to launch this very unpleasant offensive can go . . . can go fly a kite, as they say where I come from. Edward, would you give me a lift back to the Hall?"

ONE DAY there would be a Sue-Ellen Hill award for valor. She didn't know exactly the circumstances under which it would be awarded, but she hoped she'd be around to help judge the applicants. But if her heart didn't stop trying to leap out of her chest she'd be lucky to make it through this night without cardiac arrest.

She slipped down the main pathway to the church. Rather than diminishing, the mist had thickened. Almost blessedly. On the way back here she'd at least been able to pretend there was nothing beyond her narrowed field of vision, nothing lurking or lying in wait.

Now her heart pumped uncomfortably in her throat. She turned the big ring handle, made of a length of twisted metal, and almost groaned when the door opened, whined and creaked inward on complaining hinges.

This had to be done. It had to be. All the way to Airstone, perched beside a silent Edward in his Jeep, she'd argued with herself. He obviously hadn't figured out exactly what had happened in the belfry. Should she tell him and enlist his help, or try to find some evidence first? Finally, at the door to the Hall, she'd turned to him, looked at his sharp troubled profile and decided he didn't need anything more to worry about.

But she should have asked him to come back with her.

Murder, she should have told him. *Someone was supposed to die in that belfry, and since we know who was called there on a wild-goose chase at a specified hour, we know who that someone was. You, Edward, made the mistake of arriving first and unexpectedly.*

It had to be ten-thirty. She'd left just before ten. At least there hadn't been any bats on this trip. Bats in the belfry, she thought, and felt the start of hysterical laughter. This wasn't the time to go to pieces.

She shut the noisy door behind her and walked rapidly, close to the outer wall, until she reached the belfry and crept inside. The breaths she took hurt. Why was she creeping? She was the only one here.

From her parka pocket she took a flashlight and turned it on. There was the bell. Her stomach rose. It was huge, huge enough to crush the life out of a man, or woman, in one second. The space between it and the door was narrow. That Edward hadn't been smashed to pulp was a miracle. She sent up a prayer of thanks. After all, this was the right place to do that. She couldn't manage a smile.

The flashlight beam showed walls built of large rectangular blocks of stone. Above, far above, was a wooden apex. Twenty or so feet below this, iron stays crisscrossed the space. The bell must originally have hung from the rusted hinges and brackets attached to the stays. She didn't understand how church bells worked. A length of rope, evidently the other end of what lay haphazardly about the fallen bell, was draped from the brackets to a ladder that scaled the wall and traversed the roof of the tower to give access to the...

She'd found it. Up there was her proof. Casting about, she found a graying wooden stool and dragged it to the ladder, the bottom rung of which was too high from the ground to reach without help.

Climbing with the flashlight in her hand wouldn't work. She shoved it in her pocket and felt her way up, clinging, trying not to think of the dark, of how long ago the old ladder had been driven into the wall, of how precarious those fastenings in crumbling mortar must be by now.

A swish across her face. *Oh, God.* She closed her eyes. The rope. She'd reached the rope. *Please don't let me scream.* Whoever had done this—if they'd done what she was sure they had—was quite capable of coming back.

With her left arm wrapped around the ladder, she worked the flashlight out again, and then she knew. Yes, the rope was old, frayed, but the final break had had help. From a few straggling strands trailed a thin piece of twine... No, fishing line. Now she must see where the other end of the line led. While she and Edward had huddled together on the floor, someone had stood nearby, decided whether to await a chance to escape or to attack. That person had possessed the strength to yank the fishing line hard enough to unravel the last strands of rope holding the bell. The thinking was obvious. No actual cut, no evidence. But why hadn't they removed the line?

Managing to hold the flashlight she made slow downward progress.

A creak.

Instinctively she clicked off the light.

Soft footsteps—tennis shoes?—coming this way through the church. She was going to be sick.

How far was she from the ground?

She'd been slated to die tonight. Had she been followed? Was she still on the death docket?

Leaning away from the wall as far as she dared, the flashlight in her free hand, she waited. Accustomed to the gloom, she could see the paler rectangles that were the glass panes in the door. A long shadow moved over them, and they narrowed as the door was opened against the wall.

No time.

Not so far to fall, and she had no choice.

She did scream, screamed as she jumped, arms flailing, onto the big solid body beneath.

Chapter Twelve

Edward's head hit the bell with a dull boom. Someone was all over him, thrashing with a hard object. With a satisfying thud, Edward's fist met soft flesh. From the indrawn breath and groan, he'd have said it was the solar plexus.

Rolling swiftly, using what he could tell was his height and weight advantage, he straddled the creep, pinned his biceps beneath his own knees and pried the weapon free.

It was all surprisingly easy. For several moments he bowed over the figure, clamping the wrists to the ground while he caught his breath. A steady pounding had started inside his skull.

"Please!"

He went cold, then unbearably hot. The voice was feminine and unmistakable. "Holy . . . Sue-Ellen? What the hell are you doing here?"

"I . . . can't . . . get my breath."

She couldn't get her breath because he'd punched it out of her. Good God, what a night. "I could have killed you! I would have in about another minute."

"You wouldn't. You . . . wouldn't kill anyone. I hurt."

"Oh, hell." Her arms were still crushed beneath his knees. He swung to sit beside her, pulled her to a sitting position. She gasped and doubled over.

What he'd taken from her was a flashlight, and he switched it on. "Oh, no."

She looked at him through matted hair, shoved it back to reveal a purplish welt across her forehead. Gingerly she touched the spot. "You pack quite a punch, and my middle feels worse. I haven't been winded since I played touch football."

He didn't care what that was. He'd attacked her like he would a man and his advantage showed. "You have to be one of the most infuriating females I've ever met. You really don't think you need anyone. You're a one-woman army."

She smiled and the effect was ghastly.

"You think this is funny?" he said. "If you could see your face you'd cry."

Her grin broadened. "It is funny. I hung up there like, like—" she laughed and immediately hugged her belly "—like a bat in the belfry." She laughed louder, then moaned and hiccuped.

"You, Sue-Ellen, are a nut. And I'm not amused."

She peered up at him. "We are not amused?"

"How can you make a joke of this? Someone tried to kill you here tonight. Don't you realize that?"

Her smile vanished. "Of course I do. That's why I came. To look for some evidence. I almost said something to you, but I figured you had enough to worry about."

"That's what I mean...old Superwoman herself. You can take it but no one else can, right?" But her pallor, her scrunched-up form, the way her blue eyes appeared huge and shadowed, dissipated his anger. Gently he put a hand on each side of her face and tilted her chin. The welt was darkening. "We've got to get a cold compress on that."

She sniggered again.

"Okay, let me in on the latest joke."

"A cold compress. You sound like an old medical manual. Ice will do the job, if you've got any. Only we're not going anywhere until we finish what I started." She moved so rapidly he almost lost his balance. Her arms shot around his neck and she kissed his brow.

He couldn't help wincing. Lovely as her mouth felt, her ardor didn't help his headache.

She pulled away and frowned. "Sorry. I just felt like doing that. I didn't mean to offend you."

"Sue-Ellen—" he slipped his hands around her, beneath the arms of the awful orange parka "—right now I can't think of anything I'd enjoy more than being kissed by you— except about five aspirin. I hit my head on the bell and I feel as if I've had my own clangor implanted in my brain."

"Oh," was all she said, but she smiled, a soft smile that crinkled the corners of her eyes. She kissed him again, very lightly, on the lips.

They were moving in only one direction, and he couldn't think of a way to stop it. The reason to go no further came easily, but not the means.

"Come on." She got to her feet, moving slowly, grimacing as she straightened. "As far as I can make out, the bell was shored up with the rope, because the bracket that held it was broken. Up there—" she held his wrist to direct the flashlight beam on the wall "—there's the place where the rope wore through, only the last couple of good strands were helped to give out by a piece of fishing line. The line was tied to the rope and yanked to make the break at the crucial moment."

"When I walked through the door."

"That's it. The line's still there and we have to see where the other end of it is, because that's where our friend stood while we were in here. If we'd thought to look around we'd have caught him. I'm only surprised he didn't take the line with him."

She had it all worked out.

"Maybe he got too scared to take the time. Hell, my head." He got to his feet, and Sue-Ellen slid a hand around his waist as if to take his weight. "Maybe we'd better lean on each other," he said, and wished he didn't like the feel of her quite so much.

Walking side by side was impossible. Sue-Ellen moved in front of him to skirt the bell. She took the flashlight and followed the almost invisible trail of transparent line that looped from the ladder.

"Look at this," she said.

He followed her to a corner where a narrow bookcase, crammed with dusty volumes, stood a few feet from the back wall. The line had been strung over this, and its end dropped by an open doorway not visible from the other side of the bookcase.

"Maybe there's some way to get out in here." Edward went through the door and up a spiral staircase, so narrow his shoulders touched the sides with each step.

A trapdoor stood open at the top. He levered himself out onto a parapet, which ran around the wooden apex of the belfry, and hauled Sue-Ellen up beside him.

They stood close together in the still dampness.

"This is creepy," Sue-Ellen whispered.

He wanted to agree, but instead he said, "Stay here. We don't know how safe this is," and took several careful steps to the edge.

A sharp object cracked against his shins and he stumbled.

"What's the matter?" Sue-Ellen, wading in as usual, was beside him and holding his arm.

"This." He shone the flashlight downward on a rotting stool that stood against the parapet wall.

"The same as the one down in the belfry," she said. "Now we know what happened."

"We do?" As the lawyer, the one supposed to be adept at putting details together, he wasn't doing so well.

She let out an exasperated sigh. "There's a stool that matches this down there. The... He couldn't be sure how long we'd wait around for the Reverend Bastible. He hid, probably behind the bookcase. Then, as soon as we were out of the belfry, he took the stool and came up here."

"And?"

"And he used it to get himself high enough to get a firm hold on that tree so he could climb down and get away."

The limbs of an ancient chestnut stretched nearby, but not quite near enough. Edward stood on the stool and found he could then grab a sturdy branch with ease. "Clever you."

Sue-Ellen changed places with him and leaned far out.

"Don't!" He grabbed her, but she pushed him away and managed to snare first twigs and then a substantial limb.

"There. A little swing and even I could do it."

"Wonderful. Now come down and let's get out of here. I'm taking you back to my place where we can talk. But first we take that fishing line. There'll only be our word for it that it was used as we say it was. But without it we have nothing."

Sue-Ellen dropped down to the steps and he followed, stopping to close the trapdoor. By the time he reached the bottom she was already in the belfry. "Hold up," he told her, "I should be able to pull the line free."

"Too late," she said indistinctly.

Rather than being caught on the ladder, the frayed length of rope now swung free.

The line was gone.

DENSE BUSHES at the side of the gate house provided a perfect hiding place. The Jeep approached, its tires crunching the gravel. It was the Jeep that had prevented disaster. If Edward hadn't taken it to the church where the sound of its engine gave warning that Sue-Ellen Hill wouldn't be alone for long on her return expedition, this night might not have ended even as well as it had. And it hadn't ended well.

Lights went on beyond the mullioned panes in the sitting room. Seeing inside was simple. Edward had brought Sue-Ellen home.

Now he was taking off her jacket and his own, brushing back her hair, looking at her face. And she was looking at his. It was happening exactly as could have been expected; she was letting him know with her eyes, her hands on his chest, his neck, that she lusted after him. And Edward, damn him, was ready to give her what she wanted.

There was no more to be done tonight. Let Edward be the kind of man his male ancestors had destined him to be—carnal, inside his civilized shell. Without the right woman's influence he couldn't resist his instincts. But Sue-Ellen would get only his body, just as all the Ormsby-Jones men had always given no more than their bodies—and empty promises—to similar women. One of their women had been different, a victim, and the debt against her was still to be repaid. There should be room to feel pity for Sue-Ellen Hill with her parted lips and wanting eyes, but there would be none. This woman deserved what she would ultimately receive—nothing. Edward's destiny was already set.

Tonight there had been a close call—twice. Now there must be a time of waiting, a lull, before the next strike. Without evidence, these two could do no more than lodge a complaint with Merryfield, who would scratch his idiot head and help the cause by agreeing that they should do nothing.

Edward was pulling her down beside him on the couch, kissing her. Their mouths opened. He stroked her shoulders, her back, and she put her hand on his thigh. The rise and fall of their pressed bodies could be seen from the window. Two survivors of a deadly battle who needed to prove they were still alive.

Let them cling, for now. Let them start to relax. There had been Lenore, and poor little Jennifer. They were gone. And eventually Sue-Ellen would be gone.

"EDWARD, LISTEN." She didn't want to stop him, didn't want to stop at all, but the timing was wrong. "We should talk. We need to decide what to do next."

"I'd rather hold you," he murmured against her hair.

Whoever had said Englishmen were cold had never met Edward. He aroused her with the simplest touch of his mouth, his fingers, the pressure of his palms, aroused her as she had never been before.

"Edward."

He kissed her neck, and his hands rested where his thumbs met the sides of her breasts. Her breasts strained, began an exquisite ache.

"Edward, please, talk to me." While she could still talk.

He raised his head. He'd taken off his glasses, and the amber eyes were lambent now, soft and faintly out of focus. "Talk? You're beautiful. Sexy. I've been thinking that from the first moment I looked at you."

"Thank you, but that's not what I meant." But she did like what he said—was absolutely crazy about it.

"And I've also been wondering how I was going to cope with the way you make me feel, because we are definitely not a matched pair."

She had to smile. "No, we're definitely not a matched pair. I think that by tomorrow morning, when you've got over the shock of what happened to us tonight, you'll go right back to thinking I'm a crass flake."

His eyes cleared. "I never said I thought you were a crass flake."

"You thought it, Edward. You still do. And we're going to fight to the bitter end over every decision I try to make around here."

He frowned, looking like a man faced with a novel idea. "I've agreed to most of your ideas. But I do have to draw the line when the cost exceeds current resources."

"I'm not worried about our business venture. Not at this moment." She put a few inches between them, but he continued to hold her. "Tonight my opposition passed into a new phase. They went from petty malice to murderous intent."

"We should have gone straight to Merryfield."

"And said what? That the old bell rope finally gave out and we decided someone deliberately made it do that because they wanted to kill me, only we don't know why?"

Edward rolled back on the couch and pressed his temples. "Why didn't we take the damned fishing line before we went up to the turret?"

"It's probably just as well we didn't." She avoided looking at him.

"You think," he said, reaching for her hand, "that he might have killed us both to get it? Sue-Ellen, I can't have you exposed to this kind of danger."

Her scalp prickled. "Are you saying... What do you mean?" That he was terminating her employment, that she had to leave? Leaving now, leaving him, was out of the question.

"I'm not sure, except that I won't let anyone hurt you. If I had any sense I'd call the project off and make sure you were somewhere safe, but I've got this feeling you're right. It isn't the hotel that's the problem anymore."

He didn't want her to go. She said, "One thing we know for sure is that whoever was in that belfry tonight was strong. And agile. In other words, your aunts are out. Although not, of course, as instigators."

"They're out," Edward said shortly. "Please don't suggest they could be part of this. I know otherwise."

The sharpness in his tone made her legs tingle.

"Did anyone know you were going to meet Michael?"

"Apart from Helen, you mean?"

"Helen says she didn't make that call."

She breathed in slowly, fighting down irritation. "And you believe her word over mine?"

"I believe Helen doesn't lie. We've known each other a long time. It's more likely that someone else made the call, which is why I asked who knew you were going to St. Peter's."

They'd known each other a long time. "Mary Leaming knew, because I told her I didn't want dinner. Connie was in the kitchen at the time and so were Grossby and Sylvia and Bea."

"Damn. Why didn't you stand on the roof with a loud hailer?"

His attitude rankled. "I didn't know I was supposed to be murdered tonight. Stupid of me not to guess. Next time I'll be more careful."

"I'm sorry." He still held her hand and he raised it to his mouth, kissed her palm and curled her fingers over his. "This is getting to me, that's all."

He was saying the right words, but that special tension had gone out of the moment. Edward was drawing away again. She felt it, felt him realigning himself with his own kind. The passion of a few minutes ago had died.

"I'd better get you back to the Hall," he said and stood up.

Sue-Ellen followed suit. "I'm not going to be intimidated out of doing what I came to do," she told him, even though she was beginning to wonder if her presence here was causing more trouble than Edward's new business was worth. "I'm not a quitter." That she no longer doubted she could become very much in love with him was as much his fault as hers, and she wouldn't give up in that area, either—not until she was sure there was no point in trying to find out what they could have together.

He was holding her parka and she let him slip it on. Rather than use the opportunity to hold her, he immediately stepped away and put on his own jacket. Running for cover, Sue-Ellen thought with some satisfaction, afraid of his own feelings.

"Oh—" he picked up his camel-hair overcoat that had been tossed on a rosewood chest "—I almost forgot to give you these." He tugged a package from each pocket and thrust them at her. Deep color rose over his face.

From the first bag she took a pair of sheepskin-lined gloves.

"It's cold here. Your hands always look cold."

She tried not to give in to the rush of emotion that came. "Thank you. I guess they do look as if they need help." She'd always taken refuge in a joke.

"You've got nice hands. Capable. I like them." He was deep scarlet now. "Open the other one."

The second bag produced a ball of soft black mohair. She straightened it out and found it was a hat, a sumptuous hat, casual yet stylish in a 1920s' way, with a flower also of mohair on one side.

"It goes on like this," His big hands fumbled, pulled the hat onto her head, tucked her hair inside. Then he stood back. "Not right. It needs to be farther down, like this, all the way to your brows. And the flower goes over one ear. A saleslady showed me how it's supposed to be. It really shows off your eyes, like it did hers." He blew upward, concentrating deeply, and his mussed hair moved. "That's great. Now you can get rid of those other monstrosities you wear..." Horror left him with his eyes and mouth wide open.

Sue-Ellen laughed. "Edward Ormsby-Jones, you truly are a charmer."

HE TRULY WAS a charmer. And he was truly mixed up. On the one hand he could hardly stand that he'd taken her home and was faced with lying in bed alone, thinking about her, all night. On the other hand, he suddenly knew he must think.

He stood in the shower, grateful for the soothing beat of hot water on his skin. Surely the idea that had come to him was off the wall. But was it? What had been uppermost in her mind when she'd insisted they talk? The supposed would-be murderer? No. It had been Sue-Ellen who insisted they shouldn't go to the police because there was no evidence, and then all she'd wanted to talk about was his reaction to her plans.

Could the little drama of the bell have been intended to cement his support? It seemed fantastic, but she was ambitious, though how ambitious he had no real means of knowing. But she'd been the one to tell him of the meeting with Michael, and after the accident she'd been the one to suggest they simply go home without going to the vicarage. And Helen denied making that call, and he believed her.

Then there was the fact that Sue-Ellen had appeared almost the instant after the bell fell. Could she have been sure he wouldn't be hit? She didn't want him dead—why should she? Timing the drop just right would have been possible, and so would escaping up the turret, down the tree and running around to reenter the church. Demonstrating she could reach the tree might have been a neat smoke screen. Had she returned later specifically to remove the line and managed it in the seconds before he joined her in the belfry after leaving the turret?

The hat was wonderful on her, and the surprise of receiving it had made her look so sweet and young. He still wasn't sure why he'd decided to give her the gifts after all, or why he'd chosen that moment. But he was glad he had. Spontaneity was all too rare with him and it felt good.

This doubt of his had to be madness. She was blameless. He must be on watch to make sure nothing happened to her. Even if he did keep his own guard up at the same time.

The doubt was madness, wasn't it?

Chapter Thirteen

Edward must be scared. He'd probably felt himself letting go with her, and it had frightened him...so badly that he'd gone into hiding.

Making her way to the kitchen, Sue-Ellen repeated this to herself. She'd repeated it many times in the four days since Edward had brought her home from the gate house and then, apparently, dropped from sight. At his office he was always in conference. And if he ever came home she saw no evidence of him.

Well, let him hide. Sooner or later he'd have to surface, if not to face what had gone beyond simple attraction between them, then to deal with the final phases before the hotel opened, which would be soon.

Meanwhile, she didn't intend to wait a day longer to get back to what had become her obsession—Lettie. Lettie, Michael Bastible and, she was certain, a number of others, were tied into the scares she'd had. She didn't buy Michael's explanation that he'd disposed of the note to save her embarrassment any more than she believed Helen hadn't made that call. Her real troubles here had stemmed from her interest in the cellars—the place that held Lettie's secret. Now Sue-Ellen intended to dig out that secret and put a stop to all this very dangerous cloak-and-dagger stuff. And she'd do it with or without Edward's help.

Edward's cooperation would be so nice, though, she thought as she breezed past Sylvia in the scullery and entered the kitchen. She missed him, spent every unoccupied moment thinking about him.

This interview would be kept as short as possible. "There you are, Mrs. Leaming. Could we have a word?"

The cook, up to her elbows in flour, stopped kneading a ball of dough in a huge bowl and rubbed the back of a wrist across her chin. A white smear made her look even more flustered than usual.

Grossby was in his customary spot, hovering over the silver he seemed to be forever cleaning.

"I take it you know the story of the young woman who committed suicide in the cellars of this house?" Sue-Ellen believed in the value of shock.

Stoic Mary's mouth fell open.

"Oh, you must have heard all about it," Sue-Ellen said. "I understand it's common knowledge in the village."

Mary found her voice. "I'm sure I don't know what you mean, miss. And if I heard any such nonsense in the village I should put a stop to it, I can tell you. Such nonsense." She went back to her pastry with renewed vigor. "Gossip and nonsense."

Grossby had turned to lean on the counter. He crossed his feet in their glistening shoes. "Would that have happened recently, Sue-Ellen?"

Why did she hate his use of her first name? "No, it would have been a long time ago. Probably in the 1920s."

"They wouldn't listen. They'd never listen."

Startled, Sue-Ellen jerked around and noticed Pitts, almost buried in his old chair. She went over to drop to her knees beside him. "What wouldn't they listen to, Mr. Pitts? What happened to the girl in the cellars? Who was she?"

His rheumy eyes moved aimlessly. "Just a story, the said. We was all to remember it was just a story." His hands, twisted by arthritis, rose and fell against the chair arms.

"Mr. Pitts—"

"Don't bother him," Grossby interrupted. "Mr. Pitt picks up words here and there and gets a bit muddled. But we all understand."

The obsequious incline of his head, the lowering of his lids, caused an acid taste in her mouth. But he was probably right.

"I've never heard the story, either," Grossby continued.

"Can't imagine why you'd want to know," Mary Leaming put in. "Meddling, I call it. Next thing we know you'll be letting out haunted rooms to some of those Americans of yours."

Sue-Ellen quelled the impulse to say that was a good idea. "I'm not meddling, Mrs. Leaming, just trying to find out if something I was told is true." And if she was in danger because of it.

"It's undoubtedly no more than some idle chitchat, and there's plenty of that in East Puddle," Grossby said. "But if I do hear anything I'll let you know." His intense smile suggested he'd be glad of any excuse to ingratiate himself with her. Because he had an overactive libido? she wondered, or because he thought she might be useful to him in some other way?

With a nod she returned to the spotless scullery. Sylvia sat manicuring her nails. This should irritate but it didn't. After seeing the maid's room and every other area she touched, it was obvious that, despite her protests against extra work, she was thorough in what she did do.

Sue-Ellen was about to leave when she remembered she hadn't put her question to Sylvia.

With a pleasant smile, she said, "I wondered what you could tell me about a girl who killed herself in the cellars."

Sylvia swiveled on her stool, almost knocking over her nail polish. "Why are you asking me? Er, I mean, what girl?"

Sue-Ellen almost grinned with satisfaction. Here, at last, was what she'd hoped for, a glimmer of reaction. "In the early 1920s, as I was told, this girl was locked up down there and then she took her life."

Sylvia shook back her hair. "I don't know a thing about it. Not a thing. If I was you I'd forget about it. Someone's having you on." And she went back to a minute inspection of her hands.

"You're probably right," Sue-Ellen said, retreating.

At the foot of the stairs she did a jig. One tiny slip added up to a point for her side. Sylvia had heard of Lettie all right. Now the aunts. The thought took any spring out of her walk.

The smell of lavender floor polish assailed her in the corridor to their suite. Lavender was definitely on her list of hated odors.

Connie opened the door the instant Sue-Ellen knocked. "Hi, Connie. I'd like to see the aunts— You've been crying. Is something wrong?"

"Nothing you can do anything about, miss. Come in and I'll ask if they'll see you. They're in a bad mood."

"Is that why you're upset?"

Connie shook her head and began to weep softly. "Ernie, my husband— You don't want to know about my problems."

Sue-Ellen felt uncomfortable but sorry for Connie. "If I can help in any way, let me know."

"You can't, but thank you. He's taken off again. Been gone for days this time."

Sue-Ellen made a sympathetic noise. From what she'd heard, Ernie Butters was no prize, but that didn't mean Connie didn't love him.

"He's a quiet man, my Ernie, not much for conversation. But he's, well, he's my Ernie and I worry about him. He's never been gone this long."

"He didn't leave a note or anything?" Sue-Ellen asked. Clearly Connie wanted to talk.

"No. He'd been doing a bit of overtime. Grave digger he is. The reverend knows we're often a bit short of the ready and he finds ways to pay Ernie extra when he can. Had him filling in old Mrs. Hawker's grave after hours. I knew it was so it could be called overtime, but Ernie just accepted it. Anyway, he hasn't been home since and I don't know where to turn."

"How about the police?" She felt phony even suggesting it.

"Merryfield?" Connie dried her eyes. "I did mention it, and the reverend said to give it some more time, since Ernie's done this before. Reckons Ernie probably took what he was paid and went into Dorchester to get drunk where no one knows him, then didn't like to come home. Reckons he'll turn up."

"And does that make sense to you?"

Connie shrugged. "Sort of. But I wish he hadn't done it when the rent on the cottage was due." She sniffed again, squaring her shoulders. "There, and I promised myself I wouldn't say a thing to anyone. You forget I did. I'll be fine. Just having a bad day with them." She nodded to the curtained door leading to the inner sanctum and excused herself to ask if Sue-Ellen might be received.

Minutes later, she was seated in the witness chair, waiting for the best moment to broach the subject of Lettie and figuring out how best to do so.

"We're surprised you have the audacity to come here, Miss Hill," Mabel said after a lengthy silence. "Perhaps you've decided to let us know you agree that what you're doing to our home is unacceptable?"

She ignored this. "I've come to you because I believe you may be in the best position to throw light on a puzzle I've encountered."

Alice's yellow eyes shone up at her. "A puzzle?"

"A puzzle. Something rather sinister that happened when you and Miss Mabel would have been very young women."

Alice set her needlepoint on the table. "You would know nothing of anything that happened to my sister and me, now, or at any time." She was at her imperious best.

Undeterred, Sue-Ellen plowed on. "Do you know of a feud between a member of your family and a girl named Lettie? Do you know what happened to her?"

The two women became a frozen tableau before they spoke as one: "No."

"No," Mabel repeated, "there was nothing. We are above reproach in this house. Only someone like you, someone who doesn't understand what is and is not said, would make such a suggestion. How dare you."

"How dare you," Alice echoed. "Leave us at once, please. And be sure that if we hear any more of this viciousness, we'll insist that Edward get rid of you. And he will, you know." The old triumphant lift of the chin returned. "Edward understands family responsibility."

Again Sue-Ellen had what she wanted. The moment of silence before the denial, followed by the venomous threats, said it all. They knew. She escaped to the anteroom where she was surprised to find Bea comforting Connie. Both stood when they saw Sue-Ellen.

"How did it go?" Bea asked. "I heard you'd been asking questions and that you were coming here. I tried to head you off but I was too late."

"Why did you try to head me off?" Sue-Ellen was very satisfied with the outcome of her interview.

"Let's go to my suite," Bea said, glancing significantly at Connie who seemed more composed. "I think we could both do with a cup of tea before lunch . . . and a chat."

They left Connie to answer the jangle of the aunts' bell.

In Bea's elegant sitting room, Sue-Ellen declined the offer of tea. "How did you know I'd gone to see the aunts?" She found the couch less comfortable than it was eye catching.

"I followed your trail," Bea said, smiling. She stood before the delicate white plaster fireplace. "Mary contacted me in high dudgeon and said you'd been asking questions about that story I told you. Miles Grossby thought you'd gone upstairs, and when I didn't find you in your rooms I decided you were fascinated enough by the fantasy to ask Miss Mabel and Miss Alice about it."

Should she confide in Bea? She needed someone else in her corner. "Who told you the story, Bea?"

"Well—" she coughed, colored slightly "—now I really feel silly for mentioning it at all. I knew the former cook here—"

"The woman you were related to? Edward told me about that."

"No relation." Bea sounded...snappy? "I used to spend vacations in Dorset when I was a young woman, and I often came to East Puddle. I met the cook by chance—at the tea shop—and she invited me to visit here. I couldn't hurt her feelings so I came. Then I was invited back to stay—by the family naturally. It turned out that we had acquaintances in common in Yorkshire, where I come from. Then when dear Lady Louise died and Sir Arthur asked if I'd consider running the house for him, well, I was torn, of course. But my own parents had passed on and there was nothing to keep me in Podsbury. So, I came, and I like to think I did the right thing, for everyone."

"I'm sure you did," Sue-Ellen said and meant every word. "You deserve a medal for diplomacy alone. I couldn't cope with..."

They laughed.

"The story's true," Sue-Ellen said when they'd fallen silent. "The story about Lettie."

Bea moved slowly to sit on the edge of a chair. "Lettie?"

Sue-Ellen explained the note she'd received and what had happened afterward.

"Oh, my dear," Bea said when she'd finished. "I don't know what to say. You should have told me at once."

"I did tell Edward—and the Reverend Bastible."

"And I hope they told you this is all silliness. What I don't understand is the reason for it. Oh, I know some of the staff are reluctant about the hotel, but they're getting over it, don't you think?"

Sue-Ellen nodded. "The Reverend Bastible thinks I'm starting to imagine things."

"Well—" Bea spread her hands "—I'm sure he didn't mean to be unkind. He simply meant that in this type of setting and with the right stimulus it might not be too dif-

ficult to think you see things you really don't. But I blame
myself for this. I should never have repeated this story. But
you see how it works? Make the setting right and that type
of thing just pops into your head. Tell me, did you check to
see if your nightgown was missing?''

Sue-Ellen grimaced. Bea, as usual, had both feet firmly
on the ground. ''It isn't. It wasn't by the time I got back to
my room. But I know I didn't imagine what I saw.''

''I'm sure you thought you didn't. Wasn't the lock on
your door changed?''

Sue-Ellen's heart sank lower. ''Yes.''

''And you have all keys?''

''Yes. And yes, I know—it doesn't sound as if it was
possible for anyone to get at my things. But I could have
forgotten to lock my door or something. I don't remem
ber.''

''Of course it's possible, dear.'' Bea moved to her side.
''Everything's going to be quite all right for you here. Please
don't allow yourself to get overwrought.''

Mentioning the church bell was out of the question.
Something near suffocating pressure built in Sue-Ellen's
head. There was no one she could turn to. Bea thought she
was cracking up. Edward seemed on her side, but had cho
sen the time when she needed him most to become unavail
able. And who knew what she should think of any of the
Bastibles?

She got up and walked around the room, pretending in
terest in the many objets d'art, which no doubt had also
belonged to Edward's grandmother. Strange, to give such a
suite to a housekeeper. But Sir Arthur must have felt enor
mous gratitude to Bea for taking over in difficult times.

''These seem unusual in this room.'' Sue-Ellen scanned
the shelves of weapons behind their locked glass doors.

Bea joined her. ''Those were my father's. They're the only
thing I kept of his. He loved them so. Some are very valu
able.''

''How about the photos? Did he know these people?''

Bea put a hand over her mouth, but not before Sue-Ellen saw her smile. "My father wasn't a strong man, which probably had something to do with his fascination with guns. He couldn't even go into the forces during the war. No, he merely collected photos to match the weapons, their era, the war, or whatever. I wish I knew more, but he never spoke about them much. My father was a quiet man." Her hand went to her throat, and the small pause suggested suppressed emotion. "My father was special, a gentleman in every sense of the word. I'll always know what he was even if... the world can be very unfair."

Sue-Ellen slipped her hands into her jeans pockets and shifted her weight from foot to foot. "Was that the last one he got?" she asked, pointing at a gun newer than the others.

"Ah, yes." Bea straightened her shoulders, smoothed her cardigan over her hips.

"The photograph's missing."

"There never was one," Bea said, all business now. "He died before he could find just the picture he wanted. One day I must see if I can do it for him."

"They must be wonderful to have," Sue-Ellen said, oddly sorry for this aging woman who seemed to have no close friends, no family.

Bea's sudden smile transformed her somber expression. "They are. Lenore said..." She paused, narrowed her eyes. "How extraordinary. I was going to say that Lenore liked them, which she did. I'd forgotten all about that."

"Did you like Lenore?" Sue-Ellen asked. Lenore was none of her business, except that she had loved Edward, which meant that, at least potentially, they had something in common.

"I liked her very much." Bea said, serious once more. "At first, when she and Edward got together after Jennifer drowned, I didn't think it such a good idea. Particularly since she and Colin had been close. But I soon changed my mind."

Seconds passed before Sue-Ellen sorted through what she'd just been told. Lenore had been Colin's friend first? And how, she wondered, had the apparently egotistical Colin felt about the defection?

Then the other comment took over. "Who was Jennifer?"

"Oh, dear. I'm doing it again. I don't talk to many people and I tend to think everyone here knows everything I know. Please, I think we shouldn't talk about it anymore. Oh, dear."

Sue-Ellen should leave it at that. But she was who she was. "Did Jennifer drown in the fountain pond?" What was she saying? Michael Bastible, that was who—he'd told the tale of the lovelorn girl drowning beneath the fountains.

"The fountain pond? Good heavens, no," Bea said. "Whatever made you suggest that?"

Embarrassed, Sue-Ellen opted for the truth. "Just something the Reverend Bastible told me about a woman having an argument with her lover and running into the pool. He said the weeds caught her and held her and she wasn't found for a long time."

"Oh." Bea reached for the back of a chair and held it. Her naturally healthy glow disappeared.

"Bea, what is it?" Sue-Ellen guided her to sit.

"Michael had a hard time with that," Bea said, her voice faint. "I didn't realize how hard. He must think about it and get it muddled sometimes. He found her, you see. But not in the pool. She was in the rushes by the river that runs near the village."

Sue-Ellen felt ill, but she still wanted to know it all.

"Jennifer and Edward were quite serious," Bea continued. "Poor Edward, he hasn't had any luck with love."

Perhaps Sue-Ellen didn't want to know more.

"They'd been out together at the Arms. Colin and Lenore, Edward and Jennifer. And Helen was with them, of course."

"Of course." Poor tagalong Helen. She deserved more sympathy than Sue-Ellen had ever imagined.

"Jennifer was young in some ways. Anyway, evidently she drank too much. She said she was going to the bathroom and then she never came back. Poor Michael was out walking when he found her. That was weeks later." Bea shuddered. "Not that he knew it was her until the postmortem, although we guessed. Heart attack, the coroner said. They thought she probably decided to swim in the river, who knows why. It was December. Need I say more? Too much alcohol and all that cold, and the dense weeds in the river."

"How awful."

"Ghastly. Colin and Helen and Lenore were all absolute rocks for Edward, and somehow or other, who knows how these things work, Edward and Lenore became very close—and you already know what happened to her."

Sue-Ellen went to the window and stared out. Bea's view was different from her own, to the north across the most densely forested portions of the estate. "That's about the worst thing I've ever heard. Edward must have been devastated . . . devastated twice."

"Yes," Bea said. "It's sad to think of a fine old family like the Ormsby-Joneses dying out. He's the last of the line, you know."

Sue-Ellen turned. "He's only thirty-five. There's no reason he shouldn't still have children."

"Normally I'd agree with you. But Edward doesn't see it that way, I'm afraid. I think that between the business about mental illness in the family and the fact that he seems to be a curse on anyone who gets close to him, he's decided that any future involvements had better be purely casual."

Chapter Fourteen

An entire week without a word from him, and now she was not only to be ready to meet Edward, but ready to meet him immediately. But he had sounded subdued on the phone, and he'd also accepted with grace her response that she couldn't be at the gate house for an hour.

She'd changed quickly from her uniform of jeans and sweater into a soft gray skirt, gray turtleneck and matching heels. She carried the Burberry raincoat that had been her treat to herself upon arriving in London.

The mission she intended to accomplish before meeting Edward would have been made easier by tennis shoes. As swiftly as her high heels allowed, Sue-Ellen followed the ground-floor passageways behind the family's rooms to the stairs that led to the servants' quarters.

Not until early this morning, as she awoke from another restive night, had she remembered what should have come to her days ago.

Without pausing, she crossed the landing at the top of the stairs and went into Sylvia's room. She and the rest of the staff were at lunch. Before coming here Sue-Ellen had made a point of stopping by the kitchen to say she was going out immediately.

She must do this very quickly, before she lost her nerve. First, because she couldn't risk being caught and, second, because she hated intruding on someone else's privacy.

Her fingers shook as she moved the pile of books on the bedside table, reaching for the bottom volume.

Gone. The leather-bound journal was gone. She looked around the room, her heart thundering. Sylvia had hidden the book, she was sure of it. After the questions about Lettie, Sylvia had probably been spooked and disposed of the journal, which showed a date that matched the ones in the cellar room—1923.

Tears of frustration sprang to film her vision. All she could do was leave. Sylvia wouldn't put the thing anywhere obvious. She might even have returned it to the library. Still, Sue-Ellen looked under the bed, ran a hand along the top of the wardrobe. Nothing. Feeling ridiculous, like an amateur detective, she lifted the mattress . . . and found the journal. Unbelievably Sylvia had hidden the thing in the first place anyone would think of. Perhaps that wasn't so dumb.

Sue-Ellen checked her watch. A few more minutes were all she dared stay. She opened the cover, read the inscription again and started leafing through. Fortunately only a dozen or so pages were used. She scanned each one. Notations of expenses. Odd entries about meetings with the "Master of the Hounds." Mention of Sir Charles's concern for his daughters. That would be Mabel and Alice, and Sue-Ellen thought, he might well have been concerned. Not that it had done any good.

Then, with a sense of disappointment, she reached the last page. Here the ink was smudged, the words illegible in places, as if something had been spilled on them. She put the open journal on the bed and knelt to peer closely. *Esther will have her revenge.* Sue-Ellen's spine prickled. Then there was more splotched ink before the comment: *The boy is to be named George . . . the couple are good people. He'll do well up north—the best arrangement, just as Esther said.* The next two lines were obliterated, then: *She's dead,* stood out clearly, and *Thank God for Frederick.* The last sentence read: *Can't find the lock . . .* but *lock* had been only part of the word; the rest was a graying streak smeared down the page.

Slowly Sue-Ellen closed the journal and replaced it beneath the mattress. The death of someone female and the word *revenge* were all that matched. These and the dates. Perhaps she'd found something related to Lettie, perhaps not. But now she must go and find out what Edward wanted.

The door to the gate house stood open. She knocked lightly, called, "Edward?" and went in. A misty rain fell outside, and her hair and raincoat were dusted with moisture.

Edward appeared immediately, jogging down the narrow stairs on the opposite side of the hall from the sitting room. She'd dressed up. He'd dressed down. And, she decided, he look eminently touchable in his washed jeans, baggy navy sweater and sneakers.

"There you are," he said, sounding tetchy now. "I thought you'd never get here. I came back from Dorchester especially to get you."

"Thank you," Sue-Ellen said, oblivious to what she was thanking him for. He looked different, and it wasn't just the clothes. Drawn, haggard? And beneath his eyes, dark lines that suggested lack of sleep.

"You look lovely," he said, shocking her. "Classic clothing suits you. You should wear that kind of thing more often."

Instead of her usual grubbies? "Thank you. I like the way you look, too."

His amazed expression gave her pleasure. The women he was used to probably never made that kind of comment.

"Let me grab an anorak," he said, still eyeing her curiously. He riffled through the heaped coats on a row of hooks in the hall and pulled out a green waterproof parka with a hood.

"Where are we going?" He shouldn't object to her wanting to know.

"I've been thinking about what's happened," he said, his big hands spread on narrow hips. "In fact I haven't thought of anything else for days."

So why had he left her alone to jump every time she saw a shadow?

"I've tried to piece things together and I can't. And that's because we only have little bits of the whole puzzle," he continued.

"The puzzle about why someone wants me away from Airstone badly enough to kill me if necessary?" Sue-Ellen added.

He wrinkled his nose and shoved his glasses up. Max wandered from the sitting room and sat between them. "If someone tried to kill you, yes. We could have been wrong about that. It could have been intended as just one more scare tactic."

"Oh, sure." She crossed her arms. He was doing his best to explain everything away in a palatable fashion. That would make him more comfortable. "You didn't tell me where you're taking me." The weary set of his features disarmed her. She'd like to hold him and tell him she knew all he'd been through and that she wasn't afraid to risk getting close to him.

"To see my father," he said and waved her back outside.

Sue-Ellen opened her mouth to ask more questions but changed her mind. Let him be the one to initiate communication. Max swept past her and leaped into the Jeep where he took the passenger seat.

"No, boy," Edward said, his amused smile having its usual warming effect on Sue-Ellen. He half pushed the resisting dog into the back seat and turned to her before they got into the Jeep.

"Have you been afraid?"

He asked it so abruptly she paused, her hand in his. "Yes. I wondered where you were, Edward. You could be right, I suppose, and there's nothing more sinister going on than an effort to make me run away, but I doubt it. Thinking there could be someone waiting to kill you isn't my idea of a good time."

"I know." He rested a forearm on her shoulder, his golden eyes very serious. "But I have kept track of you. I needed time and distance to think, that's all."

"To think about what?" She looked directly at him. "That you—" No, she wouldn't mention what Bea had said. "To think about the best way to gracefully make sure there's no repeat of what happened between us last week? After all, I'm not your type. I'd probably be an embarrassment to you if one of your friends saw us together. You wouldn't want that, so it's best not to get involved, right?"

"No, dammit." His broad chest expanded. "You don't know what you're talking about." And with that he did what she'd known he wanted to do.

The force with which his lips met hers lasted only an instant before it softened, became a gentle caress of her mouth. Their tongues touched. She clasped him beneath the parka, around his waist, and he pressed so very close. They were standing, in broad daylight, in the rain, outside the gate house where anyone could walk by.

"Edward," she whispered into his ear. His arms, crossed about her, held her on tiptoe. "Someone could see us."

He arched his neck to see her face. "And they could eat their hearts out. I've needed to do this for days. But we'd better resume at a more convenient time."

Sue-Ellen stepped away and he handed her up the steep step into the Jeep. When he sat beside her she said, "Resume at a more convenient time? Isn't that legal stuff? The judge calling a recess or something?"

His sidelong glance held tension. "I'm not a judge. I meant what I said. We've got some problems to overcome, and some might say that since I employ you, any personal involvement would be unwise. But there will be a more convenient time and I intend to take advantage of it."

She didn't respond. Bea had said he'd decided to avoid any but casual relationships. Did Bea know for sure, or was she surmising?

The drive to The Lawns was longer than she'd expected. The Jeep took with ease the winding lanes that rose and fell between reddish bracken hedges. Clouds brought a heavy sky low over the land, and as the Jeep crested each hill, a blanket of gray obscured the bottom of the next dip. Through the streets of the quaint village of Cerne they went, past houses of mellow gold stone overhung with the brittle vines of sleeping wisteria and clematis.

Another hill and a long, long downward sweep, and Edward pointed to the right. "This isn't the best time of year to see him, thank God, but the Cerne Giant's on a hill down there. We're headed south." And he turned left.

"Who's the Cerne Giant and why don't we want to see him?"

Edward laughed, tipping back his head in the way she liked so much, showing a dimple beside his mouth. "He's just a big carved outline on the side of a hill. Hill drawing, they called it. Supposed to be an ancient fertility symbol. There are those who'd like to put clothes on him, but the local historical society prevails."

She thought she got the picture and smiled. England, the history that steeped every inch of it, was fascinating, and she hoped she'd get to experience much more before she moved on. She settled lower in her seat. Moving on wasn't something she cared to think about—not now, maybe never.

The Lawns was aptly named. Studded with majestic deciduous trees, acres of winter-pale grass sloped up to a Gothic manor.

Edward hadn't spoken since they'd driven through the massive stone gateway. The closer they drew to the house, the more Sue-Ellen felt him withdraw.

In a towering entry hall crowned by jewel-colored windows, he held her arm and stood still. "This isn't easy for me. I never know how he'll be."

Sue-Ellen ached for him. "We don't have too much control over the way we grow old," she said. "Perhaps today will be a good day."

"I decided to bring you here because... Oh, hell, I'm not sure, except that I wanted you to meet him. I also wondered if he might know something about this dead-girl thing."

He didn't say any more, only walked ahead, his stride deliberate. Several men sat in the room he entered, a breathtaking library walled with endless lusciously bound books. Edward had spared no expense in choosing a domicile for his father. Sue-Ellen glanced at him: tall, straight-backed, handsome and intensely disturbed by all this. He must love his father very much. But from what Bea had said, he must also see in his father what could happen to him, or to his offspring, if there was an inherited tendency to mental illness.

She would have known Sir Arthur Ormsby-Jones even if she'd come alone. He sat in a leather wing-backed chair with a book open on his lap. His hair was white, his skin cross-hatched with wrinkles, but his back was as straight as his son's and his eyes the same amber color.

"How are you, Father?"

"Hmm?" The old man raised his chin, and gradually the light of recognition lit those fine eyes. "Edward. How nice of you to come."

Edward brought a chair for Sue-Ellen and made much of settling her in it. His nervousness made her jumpy. He remained standing.

Sir Arthur smiled at Sue-Ellen. "You shouldn't have wasted a lovely spring afternoon on an old man, Lenore."

Sue-Ellen turned icy. At her shoulder she felt Edward stiffen.

"Not Lenore, Father. This is Sue-Ellen Hill. She's an American from Augusta, Georgia, and she's managing the necessary renovations to Airstone."

Sue-Ellen offered her hand and Sir Arthur grasped it firmly. "I'm very pleased to meet you," she said.

"Why?"

She looked at Edward who shook his head slightly. This was not going to be one of the good days. She'd do anything to ease this for Edward.

"Are they treating you well?" Edward asked.

"I'm quite well."

Edward shifted. "I don't think there's any point in staying."

She reached for his hand and squeezed. "Relax. Sir Arthur, Edward's told me so much about you and the family. It's all so fascinating."

"Why?"

Edward was pulling her to her feet, but she resisted. There might never be another chance to at least try to see if this man knew any key facts.

"Sir Arthur, I've been researching some of the old stories about Airstone and I'm hoping you can help me."

"It's pointless," Edward said.

"Is it possible that..." How could she put it without causing offense? "Was there ever a young woman who tried to usurp the place of the true lady of the house?"

Sir Arthur turned a page of the book on his lap.

"Perhaps even a rival of your mother's. The girl I have in mind would have been at Airstone when you were a small boy."

Sir Arthur turned another page.

"Let it be." Edward sounded urgent now. "I've got to get out of here."

"Give me a few more seconds. Could there have been a secret death in the house, a suicide?"

"Just talk," Sir Arthur said, startling Sue-Ellen. "All that talk about Lettie. Nothing to it, of course. Mother wouldn't have had it."

"Oh, my God," Edward said under his breath.

Sue-Ellen held his hand tighter, willing him to take strength from her. "Lettie. You knew Lettie?"

The book fell to the floor and the man leaned forward. "Lettie Tinker," he said. "Difficult, so difficult. Old Reverend Bastible knew all about it. Frederick was a good friend of our family." He closed his eyes and slumped back, as if exhausted by his effort.

A woman in a simple blue dress bustled in. "He's tired, Mr. Ormsby-Jones," she said to Edward. "Best let him rest now."

"Yes." Edward leaned over his father and kissed his cheek. "Be well, Father. I'll come back soon."

It was Sue-Ellen, her throat painfully constricted, who led the way out, still holding Edward's hand. *Thank God for Frederick,* the journal had said. And Frederick must have been Michael Bastible's father, the former vicar of St. Peter's. She wouldn't mention the journal to Edward yet. He'd gone through enough for one day.

"Next stop, East Puddle," Edward said after they'd started for home. "I think we should have a word with Michael. His father must have said something about this Lettie."

A quiet half hour later brought them to the door of the vicarage where Helen, with a frosty stare at Sue-Ellen, announced, "My father isn't here." She turned her attention on Edward, and longing shone from her face. Sue-Ellen felt again a deep sympathy for Helen. To love someone who thought of you as part of his comfortable scenery had to slowly destroy the heart and soul.

"When will he be back?" Edward asked.

Helen, wearing a coat and with gloves in hand, glanced past them. "I don't know."

"Where's Colin?"

"Out," Helen said, her lips tightening. "He sleeps here but we hardly see him. Probably means... Colin has a way of keeping busy."

"Quite," Edward said as the sound of an approaching engine drowned out any further conversation.

"Got to go," Helen said, a pink flush washing her cheeks. She closed the door behind her and walked rapidly past them. "I suggest you call later if you want to see Daddy."

With that, she half ran through the gates and climbed into a late-model red Austin.

Edward frowned at Sue-Ellen. "Why the cold shoulder, I wonder."

She didn't intend to explain. And she was more interested in the red Austin. "That's Grossby's car. I didn't know he and Helen were friends." Although she hadn't forgotten the overheard conversation at Airstone.

"Hmm?" Edward squinted at the departing vehicle. "Neither did I, but I don't suppose there's any reason they shouldn't be. Well, where do we go from here?"

"The graveyard," Sue-Ellen said. "Isn't that where they usually put dead people?"

Edward grimaced. "I still can't accept this story about Lettie. If it's true, I'd have heard about it by now." But he walked beside her to the soggy turf dotted with old and new stones, some leaning perilously.

"We'll take a quick look," Sue-Ellen said, not wanting to remind him that, whether or not Lettie had died at Airstone under unusual circumstances, Sir Arthur had known of her.

An hour yielded nothing but damp shoes and, for Sue-Ellen, aching calves, as she tried to avoid sinking her heels into muddy earth.

Close to the church was a new grave covered with wilting wreaths. "I expect that's Mrs. Hawker's," Sue-Ellen remarked.

Edward laughed. "How would you know Mrs. Hawker, or that she died?"

"Because that's the grave Ernie Butters was filling in the night he disappeared."

"Ernie disappeared? When?"

"Oh, a few days ago. Evidently he does it from time to time. Connie said he probably went to Dorchester to get drunk in private and hasn't had the guts to come home yet."

"Fits," Edward said, turning the corner of his mouth down. "That man is no good.... Oh, hell, look at this, will you?" He took several paces, passed a child's grave and dropped to his haunches.

Sue-Ellen joined him, ignoring her shoes to hunch down at his side.

Moss etched the inscription on a small gray marble headstone. Edward rubbed at it with a thumb.

Letitia Tinker. Born June 9, 1903. Died February 17, 1923.

Chapter Fifteen

"So, Edward and Sue-Ellen, you found her."

Sue-Ellen almost overbalanced. Edward caught her elbow and they stood to face Michael Bastible.

"And you knew about her all the time," Edward said. There was more to this, much more than he and Sue-Ellen had discovered yet. "Why didn't you tell us and save us all this cloak-and-dagger stuff?"

Michael pulled his battered hat lower over his eyes. "There isn't much to tell, and I know your father would have preferred the subject avoided."

"Someone other than you knows the whole thing," Edward told him. "And that same someone is using the trappings of what must have been a tragedy to try to get back at me."

He felt Sue-Ellen look at him but didn't meet her eyes. "That has to be what it's all about. Someone doesn't want Airstone turned into a hotel, and I'm not talking about a simple dislike of the idea. If I had to guess, I'd say I have an enemy who wants me to fall into financial ruin, and they know that after what I've invested, if it doesn't go through I could even lose the Hall."

"Edward—"

"Let me finish," he said to Sue-Ellen. "This sad death has been used as a convenient black flag to wave at Sue-Ellen and scare her off. I only hope it's stopped now, because there won't be any turning back from my plans. There can't be.''

Sue-Ellen touched his arm. ''I never thought of that—of someone simply wanting you to fail. But, Michael, what did happen to Lettie Tinker?''

''It's not a new story,'' Michael said, his eyes screwed almost shut against the rain that was blowing now. ''I heard my parents talking about it when I was a small boy. The girl was a maid at Airstone and became pregnant out of wedlock. Sir Charles and Lady Esther Ormsby-Jones took pity on her and cared for her. She was in that awful cellar room at the end because they had to make sure no one saw her and spread gossip, you see. Even her family didn't know. That kind of thing ruins a girl in a village like this, or it did then.''

Edward glanced at Sue-Ellen, who watched Michael intently.

''As you see—'' he nodded at the grave ''—Lettie died. It happened a few days after her baby was born.''

When he didn't continue, Sue-Ellen stepped closer to him. ''How did she die? Did she kill herself? What happened to the baby?''

''I don't know,'' Michael said, backing away. ''She didn't kill herself, of course. Probably just complications after childbirth. The baby was probably adopted or something.''

''Michael—''

''Got to get on,'' Michael said, cutting Edward off. ''I'd drop the whole thing if I were you and concentrate on your new business. I don't suppose you'll have any more trouble now it's just about fait accompli.''

Edward breathed deeply through his nose. It no longer seemed even a remote chance Sue-Ellen had caused that bell to fall. His overriding fear was for her safety. Should he send her away? He wasn't sure he could, not until he'd made up his mind about what he wanted, or didn't want, to happen between them. Thinking about it made him feel calculating and vulnerable at the same time. The sensation was new.

More to himself than to Sue-Ellen, he said, "I hope Michael's right."

BEA HAD WARNED HER that Edward could be difficult. He was being difficult now.

"No," he said.

"Oh, come on, Edward. Use your head."

"Drop it. We're going out for dinner, and for the first time in two weeks we aren't going to talk hotel."

Sue-Ellen crossed her arms. "Just agree and then we will drop the subject."

"So help me, don't push this. I've said no and I mean no. I've given in on one thing after another, but this is too much." He glared at the list in his hands. "A Henry VIII Room? Special features: plaster heads of dead wives, a block, an ax. I don't believe it."

Sue-Ellen dropped to sit on his leather couch and counted to ten in her head. "It'll work. These are the type of things people go for. You should visit Universal Studios in California and see how the tourists lap up the corny stage effects."

"This isn't Universal Studios. I'm not in the motion-picture business." His face was red. "A Little Prince's Room. Sickening. Flagstone outside door to mark supposed burial place of murdered boy king, Edward V, and his younger brother. Lord, this is appalling. And a Powder Room? Guy Fawkes in effigy atop dummy kegs of gunpowder?"

She might have guessed he'd been hiding his stuffy side. Either he did this her way or she wasn't doing it at all. "Are we or are we not planning to open a hotel in ten days?"

"Yes, but—"

"Is the idea for us to make money? As much money as possible?"

"This kind of stuff is rank tasteless commercialism." He tossed the sheet at her.

"Commercial is the only term that interests me and it should be the only one that interests you." She felt like say-

ing he was becoming the biggest problem in her life around
here. Even Bea had found the idea of naming the rooms and
suites clever. And Bea, who warned her that Edward might
not agree, had urged her to push for her own way.

"I don't want to fight." He picked up his keys and jin-
gled them. "Tonight we're celebrating, remember? You've
finally started taking reservations. So we're going into
Dorchester for dinner and we're not going to talk about
corny names for rooms."

She fashioned a sweet smile. "Go out for dinner—that's
what we're going to do. But only if you agree to let me use
those names. What difference does it make to you really?
You don't have to give the subject another thought after you
agree."

He shook his head slowly. "Let's go. If I'm going to catch
the last train out of Dorchester for London tonight I don't
want to waste a minute of the time I plan to spend with you.
By the way, do you know what cream silk does for your
body?"

He was doing it to her again. Her body tingled as if he'd
stroked every inch of her naked skin.

"This case will only keep me in town for the day tomorrow. When you pick me up at the station can we get together for the evening?"

An erotic remark tossed away and then the matter-of-fact
invitation. "We haven't gotten through this evening yet.
And we may not if we keep hassling."

"We're not going to keep hassling. Call the blasted rooms
anything you like. I just want to spend whatever spare time
we've both got together."

Just like that. She could have her way. In the two weeks
since they'd agreed to drop the subject of Lettie, there had
been no more unpleasant incidents, and Edward, in his
subtly sophisticated manner, had found ways to let her know
he wanted her. Sometimes she'd wondered why he held
back, why, when he'd taken her in his arms in a quiet moment, he hadn't attempted to finish what he obviously ached
to do.

She got up and slid her arms into the coat he held for her. He pulled her against him, moved his hands over the silk he'd admired until his fingers rested beneath her breasts. He kissed the side of her neck and she closed her eyes, felt the weakness in her legs.

"We'd better go," he said, but his palms made a fleeting journey over her nipples before he spun her around, buttoned and belted her coat and told Max to stay.

Shaky, Sue-Ellen made no attempt to move. Edward knew what he was doing with his slow seduction.

The memory of Bea's words were there, almost buried in her mind, *Poor Edward, he hasn't had any luck with love.... He seems to be a curse on anyone who gets close to him. He's decided that any future involvements had better be purely casual.*

While he met her gaze now was he thinking of her as a casual encounter? If he was, and later he walked away for good, would she be more broken up then she'd ever dreamed she could be over a man?

"I'm mixed up, Sue-Ellen. Do you know that? I've never felt less sure of what I should do than I am now."

At first she didn't register what he'd said. All she could do was stand and wait for whatever he would say next. When he didn't continue she said, "I don't think I could eat. Could we stay here?" She looked into his face. "Edward, what is it? What's really troubling you?"

He shook his head. "Will you have a drink?"

"Gin would be fine. Gin and anything." The moment was fragile. So easily they could pull apart, retreat to safely stilted ground.

She followed him to the liquor trolley and watched him pour gin into Waterford glasses.

"Tonic all right?"

"Mmm."

"Are you sure you don't want dinner?"

"Absolutely certain." She took a glass and instead of going to the couch, went to sit at the table by the window. She still wore her coat and Edward his. There was a sense of transiency, that this was an encounter that could be taking place in a bar, by chance, and that they would in a while say, "Good night. Nice to see you," and go their separate ways. The coats were armor against familiarity.

Edward sat beside her. Wind rattled the windows gently, and the ever present rain tapped the panes like the skittering claws of many cats.

For a while they sipped in silence before Edward said, "You must think me very odd, Sue-Ellen. A man who gives a beautiful woman mixed messages and expects her to be patient with him." He drank more deeply. "Or perhaps you don't think anything about it at all. I've got a nerve to assume you're waiting for me to..."

She leaned against him, stroked the soft fabric of his sleeve. "Whatever we say now is so important it scares me. We both know what it is we feel, and there aren't always the right words."

"There are things you don't know about me. Oh, you've been told I lost a fiancée. That hurt. I loved her very much, but I'm at a point when I can remember her and be glad she was mine for a while. But that isn't all, and I'm not ready to spill everything."

And he did have to be the one to tell it all voluntarily. He must trust enough to share all of himself without prodding. "You're a special man. I'm glad I came, glad I met you. My life would be less if I hadn't."

He moved away slightly, took off his glasses and set them down. "But we're on the edge of something, aren't we? And neither of us knows whether or not to jump off. I can't say I want a commitment. Even if I could, I believe you wouldn't be able to accept it. You're a doer, my girl. And in time, when you're done here, you'll leave."

She nodded, liking him so deeply it hurt. "So you're saying that we shouldn't jump—at all—because one of us could end up shattered?"

"I'm saying I don't know what to do. It's that simple."

Sue-Ellen pushed aside her glass and Edward's, and stood up. She offered him her hand and he took it. When he was in front of her she pushed the coat from his shoulders until he stopped her and finished removing it himself. She put her own on the seat of the chair.

He bent slowly over her and she raised her face to his. He touched her loose hair, ran his fingers over it and watched as he did so. Then they kissed, but not with the tenderness of his caress on her hair. Their mouths came together forcefully, and Sue-Ellen drew in a sharp breath. She thrust her tongue into his mouth and they began to slide, downward, clasped together, to kneel, thigh to thigh. Her hands were beneath his jacket on his shirt where she felt hard and shifting muscle, warmth. Edward moaned, pulling her close, roughly, pressing her back, her buttocks through the slick fabric, urging her nearer when there could be nothing nearer as they were.

"No!" he said loudly, clutching her shoulders with shaking hands. "Not like this."

He stumbled to his feet and caught both her hands, pulling her up, leading her, into the hallway, up narrow stairs to a short landing. They passed the first door and he opened a second.

He made no attempt to turn the light on, only stood on the threshold while she walked into the blue-gray shaft of paleness that spread from a single window across wooden floors and the green quilt on his bed.

"I feel . . ."

As he spoke, she turned. His face was invisible.

"This is a place I've never been before. There hasn't been a woman in my life for a long time. No woman. Do you understand?"

"Yes."

He came closer, shedding his jacket, loosening his tie until he could pull it from beneath his collar. His shirt shone in the darkness. Next came his buttons. He fumbled, but she didn't try to help him.

Naked to the waist he moved into the luminescence from the window, and the spatters of rain on the glass made patterns of shadow over his face and the solidly contoured muscle of his chest and arms.

"Undress me," Sue-Ellen said.

"No. I want to watch you do it."

Blood rushed into her neck and face. "Please, Edward."

"If you want this, show me."

She reached behind her neck, struggling with the zip. Tears sprang to her eyes and she felt a fool. "Edward?"

He came to her, pressed his body to hers. She wore no bra and through the thin dress she felt the arousing roughness of his chest hair against her nipples. Her hands were still behind her neck, her elbows trapped above her head by his grip. He stroked her slowly, gently, bent his head to kiss her breasts, making of the silk a wet erotic thing.

"Sue-Ellen."

She felt his control break like the bursting of a dam. He spun her around, yanked the zip open and tore at the dress until it fell at her feet. The rest of her clothes followed until she was naked before him, and he covered her with his hands, followed his hands with his lips, his tongue. He lifted the weight of her breasts to his face, teased, kissed, until she arched her back, trembling, longing for more and more of the almost pain he made, the beautiful pain.

She pressed a palm to his tensed abdomen, pushing down beneath his belt over more enticingly coarse hair.

He stopped her, muttering words she couldn't hear, and dealt with his pants and shorts. She heard his shoes clatter somewhere and then he was against her, walking her backward until he could throw off the quilt and blankets from his bed and tip her onto cool linen sheets.

"I can't wait," he groaned. "I'm sorry."

She wasn't sorry. With something close to ecstasy, with a strength and knowledge born of wanting, she guided him into her. She heard his moan, felt the pumping within her and heard her own words of desire.

Beneath him she let go of her inhibitions. He fell on her, exhausted, and buried his face in her neck. Sue-Ellen pushed her fingers into his palely gleaming hair, wet at the temples, plastered to his neck.

"I'm too heavy." He tried to shift, but she stopped him.

"I love the way you feel. I love your weight." His body, the way it covered all of hers was an aphrodisiac she couldn't resist.

In time, she didn't know how long, they made love again, still not languorously, but to a climax that came more slowly.

When he lay with her cradled in his arms, the quilt pulled loosely over them, she kissed his neck, the space beneath his collarbone, his jaw, and felt the steady rise and fall of his chest.

Perhaps now the trust would come, she thought, but tears welled once more. *I can't say I want a commitment,* he'd said. *Even if I could, I believe you wouldn't be able accept it. You're a doer, my girl. And in time, when you're done here, you'll leave.*

She didn't want to leave, but she couldn't change rules she hadn't refused to play by.

Against his sleeping throat she silently mouthed, "I love you."

Chapter Sixteen

Too many chances. Too many mistakes. No more.

Edward had been treated kindly. He'd been allowed to flourish and to pretend. Oh, he didn't know he was pretending, but that was part of the game, letting him think all was as it appeared.

What happened in the past wasn't his fault. But what happened from now on he could claim as his own creation. If he'd done as planned and taken the woman to Dorchester last night, all would have been accomplished and over, and they could have returned to their appointed places.

From the room next to Sue-Ellen Hill's bedroom, the view was perfect. With binoculars the gate house could be plainly seen. All there was to do was wait.

Last night, Edward should have driven the Jeep to Dorchester, leaving Sue-Ellen Hill to bring it back. Only she would never have arrived. An unfortunate accident on Yellowham Hill would have sent her over the precipice. And if she hadn't died immediately... well, Lenore hadn't died immediately, either.

But their lust had ruined the perfect plan. Oh, it didn't take imagination to picture the two of them locked together. And they'd stayed all night until daylight made the plan impossible.

There came Sue-Ellen now, driving the Jeep, not to the Hall as expected, but to the gate house. A glance at the time showed she must have taken Edward in to catch the first

London train of the day. The binoculars showed her hair windblown about the collar of her raincoat. Smiling, she climbed down with Max at her heels and unlocked the front door as if she belonged there.

Rage threatened to suffocate. She didn't belong. Obstacle after obstacle had been thrown in the way of eradicating the woman, but her luck was running out.

Soon she would belong nowhere.

Soon she would have smiled her last smile.

SUE-ELLEN HAD BEEN the one to insist that Edward not change his plans to go to London. They each had work to do, she'd reminded him, longing for his argument, silently begging him to refuse to leave her.

For an instant before he jumped aboard the train, as he'd held her tightly, she'd thought he would stay no matter what she said, but then he'd sighed and said he'd already lost too much valuable work time. This case was an important one. He'd see her when she picked him up.

Sue-Ellen walked rapidly into the sitting room, anxious to grab the list she'd left behind and get to work. Being here without Edward, seeing him wherever she looked, remembering, was more than she wanted to cope with. Max was to return with her to the Hall where he'd stay, sulking, Edward had laughingly said, in the kitchen. She chuckled, thinking of how they'd awakened this morning to a heavy weight on their feet and looked into what appeared to be a huge doggy grin. Max was, Edward informed her, expecting her to protect him since he wasn't allowed on the bed.

Before she could get back outside, the doorbell rang. She froze, glancing down at herself. No one would need a particularly sharp eye to notice that she was disheveled and hardly dressed for a day's work.

The bell rang again and reluctantly she opened the door.

Colin and Helen Bastible.

Helen's eyes widened before her mouth clipped into a tight little line. Colin grinned, and dislike tightened Sue-

Ellen's forehead. She could see into his mind, and he disgusted her. Women were nothing to him but things to use.

"Where's Edward?" Helen pushed past, and Colin, dark brows raised, followed with Sue-Ellen bringing up the rear. In the empty sitting room, Helen looked around as if she expected Edward to leap out of a cupboard or slither from beneath a rug.

"Edward's left for London," Sue-Ellen said. "I drove him to Dorchester and came back to get this." She held up the folded list.

"I told you we shouldn't have come rushing over here at this hour of the morning," Colin said, a petulant droop to his lips. "Not that I understand why you give a damn about Ernie Butters anyway."

Helen ignored him. "What time is Edward getting back?"

"About six. What's the matter with Ernie this time?"

Colin waved an expansive hand. "Seems the old sot cut out some time ago and Connie's feeling the pinch. Not that grave diggers are exactly big providers, I shouldn't have thought."

He couldn't mean that Ernie had been gone for several weeks. Sue-Ellen hadn't seen more than glimpses of Connie since Ernie's disappearance, and they'd had no reason to talk. "You mean he's still gone?"

"This isn't anything that concerns you," Helen cut in. "Connie came to the vicarage for Daddy's help, and I said I'd come over."

"Poor Connie," Sue-Ellen said. "Bea's more the one to help than Edward. She deals with all those things."

Sue-Ellen caught Colin's warning grimace before Helen turned a reddening face to her. "Why Bea? Because she managed to push herself into a job I could have done better? She wheedled her way in with Sir Arthur, came rushing down from wherever she lived when Lady Louise died and virtually threw herself into the position she'd always wanted—"

"I say, steady on, sis. Bit strong, don't you think?"

"No, I don't. If I were Edward I wouldn't put up with her taking charge the way she does. She's no more than an employee who came begging for a job, and she should be reminded of that from time to time."

Sue-Ellen observed, fascinated. The story was quite different from that given by Bea, but then, jealousy could color the vision, and Helen was a jealous woman if ever there was one. She'd wanted to move in as mistress of Airstone, had been thwarted, and she wasn't about to forget...or perhaps to give up?

"We'd better get on," Colin said to Helen, winking at Sue-Ellen. "By the way, how's our tycoon doing? I must admit I'm a bit surprised things have gone so far with Edward's little venture."

Sue-Ellen breathed slowly, ordering her thoughts. Did Colin hope the hotel would never get off the ground? And if so, why? Maybe he carried an old grudge, as in a smarting ego, because he'd lost a woman to Edward....

"I've got to leave, too," she said. "But we're doing beautifully. We could see our first guests in ten days or less, depending on their final itinerary."

Gratefully she left the Bastibles in the driveway and started the Jeep. At the door to the Hall she braked, switched off the engine and glanced at her list of rooms.

Her jaws chattered together. It hadn't been there last night. It couldn't have been or Edward would have mentioned it. *Letitia's Folly. Special features: a victim-girl's deathbed. The weapon that killed her.*

The added listing had been typed at the bottom of the sheet. Sue-Ellen scrambled to the ground and dashed up the steps leading to the house. Without pausing, she marched across the Great Hall and lifted the tapestry. The hidden door stood ajar.

The naked light bulb shone, and she hurried through the anteroom to the corridor and down to the first room.

She splayed trembling fingers on the door and it creaked open, groaning on its ancient hinges.

Again, her nightgown on the bed, the chair with its single candle, flickering and gummed to a metal saucer. Again, the incense stick in the niche.

Drawn by the sick fascination of it all, she went farther inside until she stood beside the bed. Oh, but this was more artistic, a much better effort. Open on the floor lay her overnight case. She knelt to check its contents: underwear, another nightgown, toiletries, a comb. Nestled beneath was a sweater and her small Bible. Everything a woman might need for a peaceful retreat . . . in a dank cellar that terrified her.

From the corner of her eye she saw something else. A metal tray had been set on the flagstones behind the door. She went to it. A spoon, a tin cup full of water . . . and the jagged shards of a broken bowl amid a glob of congealed oatmeal. This was crazy.

The door slammed.

For seconds Sue-Ellen stood very still, holding her breath, willing herself to be calm. She tried the handle. Locked. "Let me out," she called. No response. "Don't do this." and now she screamed.

She screamed and screamed, and the sweat broke out, burst from every pore. She couldn't breathe. The walls were moving in.

"Help!"

Footsteps, becoming distant, were the only reply.

"No. Don't do this to me." Flailing her arms she spun around and the flickering candle shadows died down. *Shh, shh. Quiet. Don't breathe or shout or the candle will go out. The only candle.* Standing very still, her eyes closed, she remained so for a long time.

When giddiness caused her to wobble, she slid to sit beside the tray and picked up a piece of broken pottery. Thick but pointed and sharp, like a knife. The list was still clutched in her hand. *Special features . . . the weapon that killed her.* Sue-Ellen stared, fascinated by the razor edge of glaze turned to dagger strength by the thickness of the fired clay within.

Her vision blurred, then cleared. Spears of light flared and withered over the walls and ceiling, like flexing fingers.

No one knew she was here. No, someone did know she was here, but they wanted her to stay. Wild flutterings started behind her eyes, minute beating pulses, and the fog pressing around her brain. She hugged her knees, buried her face. Sliding, sliding.

She must have passed out. Now she didn't want to move, only make herself smaller. Beneath her, where she lay on her side, the ground was icy, and she shivered. She stayed there, slipping in and out of a comalike oblivion until she remembered the candle couldn't last forever. Carefully, slowly, she stood and went to try the handle again. The door was still locked. As a child she'd been good at picking locks, but the only implement in sight, the spoon, would be useless. She sat on the edge of the bed, crossing her arms tightly, willing herself to hang on, not to give into the pressure that swelled and ebbed in her head.

The faint scratched numbers were beside her. They started in October, 1922. Sue-Ellen ran a finger over them, coming to rest on the last one: February 17, 1923. My God! She hadn't noticed that the first time. The day Lettie died.

Sue-Ellen leaned on the wall. October to February, five months in this place. Had the girl gone mad? Had she killed herself. Sue-Ellen knew *she* could never kill herself. About the other, she was less sure.

Sir Charles and Lady Esther Ormsby-Jones, Edward's grandparents. Had they been so kind? In the journal it said: *Esther will have her revenge.* Those *kind* people had kept that girl here against her will, Sue-Ellen was convinced of it. Now she was being kept here against her will.

Time passed. Who knew how much time. The candle must be the kind that burned for hours. Eventually it would go out.

"Help!" The word echoed back at her and she slumped over. There was no help.

The brown stains on the wall—were they Lettie's blood? Sue-Ellen looked up again. The marks were smeared as if deliberately wiped. She shuddered and forced herself to get up and walk, her hands thrust deeply in her pockets. She walked and walked.

Her fingers closed around a familiar object she always carried and she found comfort in caressing it. Her Swiss army knife!

Trembling so badly she dropped it once, Sue-Ellen selected the metal spike and went to work on the lock. Her breathing came in loud irregular bursts and she sweated more profusely. It wasn't working. Rust must be packed in around the mechanism.

She had to relax. Sitting on her heels she willed a quiet place in her mind and then tried again.

There was a click—so soft she barely heard it. With icy fingers she tried the handle. It turned.

For minutes she stayed where she was, the edge of the ajar door clutched in her hands. She cried. And the candle died.

When she moved it was in a great rush. She threw open the door, ran into the corridor with its dim light and up to the anteroom. It was locked. She picked the lock but couldn't budge the door, and when she peered along the jamb she saw the shank of a newly installed bolt. There was no way out!

She ran again, back to the corridor, but away from the room. If she was to die, it would not be in that room.

Other cells opened on the right, but none had windows. Then she was at the end, in the cobweb-strewn kitchen with its rodent droppings and the smell of decay. No escape.

She leaned, panting, against the black iron sink and prayed. *Please let Edward come to look for me here.* Surely he would come.

In here the light was almost nonexistent and the air stung her eyes. Once people had worked here, probably to serve at functions held in the Great Hall. Above her must lay the kitchens in use now. They were old but much newer than these and built when the Great Hall ceased to be the center of the house.

Up there. Sue-Ellen looked at the ceiling, helplessness overwhelming her. For a while, when grand parties were held, both kitchens were probably used, or at least the old ovens to augment the new ones. She closed her eyes and drifted again, her mind tired. Time seemed to seep away in empty chunks. When she looked around again her gaze settled on a square gap in the wall. Inside was a single shelf, and she could see vertical ropes. A dumbwaiter. Of course they would have used one to move food to the main kitchen, or the buttery. She edged close.

The ropes felt chalky and dry. Sue-Ellen leaned on the bottom. It was stout. Could she do it? Could she voluntarily close herself into a box smaller than her own coffin would be?

She crawled in headfirst, dragged her hips and legs in until she was curled into a tight ball. Her pulse thundered and she lay still awhile, fighting nausea.

The first pull almost defeated her. Her whole weight resisted her arms and shoulders as she tugged. But then the box within the walls moved, crept, inch by inch at first, gathering speed as the pulley action took over, and steadily, steadily, she was borne upward in blackness. Freedom, she promised herself. Hell first, but then freedom. Unless there was no way out at the top.

When the motion stopped it was with a bone-jarring thud. A crack of light showed at the bottom level of the waiter. Sue-Ellen worked her numbed fingertips under a lip of wood and put all the strength she had behind tearing the sliding door upward.

Gradually the gap widened and there she was, peering up into the wide eyes of Mary Leaming, who instantly covered her mouth but didn't quite smother a scream.

"It's all right," Sue-Ellen said, scrambling out to confront not only Mary but a staring Grossby. Bea stood near Sylvia, who promptly dropped a tray of glasses. "Just experimenting," Sue-Ellen said, not knowing where her wit came from.

She sped past them all, past a squinting Pitts and several members of the cleaning crew who were donning outdoor clothes to go home. How long had she been in the cellars? All day? On the front steps she sidestepped Michael Bastible who said, "My dear," and looked puzzled, and muttered something about a heater being out in the conservatory. She cannonaded into the driveway.

Dark. It was dark and the Jeep was gone.

She didn't stop running until she reached the gate house where she did find the Jeep—and Edward. His hair stood on end, and behind his glasses his eyes were wild.

"Where the hell have you been?"

She recoiled, speechless.

"I've been out of my mind. What are you trying to do to me?"

Sue-Ellen found her voice. "Edward, we've got trouble. So much trouble—and it isn't going to stop."

"Answer my questions." He didn't appear to hear what she'd said. "How did you get back from the station?"

"In the Jeep," she said slowly. "I came back as soon as I dropped you off."

"Not this morning," he almost yelled, "when you went back later and left it there. I thought you'd either been kidnapped or decided you'd had it with things around here—and with me—and left."

She shook her head. "I don't understand. I never drove to the station after I came back this morning to the gate house—and found a name added to that list I showed you." She fumbled in her pockets and didn't find it. "I must have left it in the cellars. You've got to come with me, Edward. We can talk as we go."

"Helen and Colin said you seemed distracted when they saw you, so naturally we concluded you'd taken off."

"Helen and Colin," Sue-Ellen repeated, half dragging Edward toward the house. "Oh, this morning. I wasn't distracted, just busy. While I took you to catch the train, someone added another room name, *Letitia's Folly*, to that list, and when I went to investigate the cellars, I was locked in. And I was supposed to stay locked in. I almost went—"

"Mad?" Edward finished for her. "We're not taking any more of this. It's time for the police. How did you get out?"

"I picked the lock, then used the dumbwaiter in the old kitchen. Edward, I thought I'd die down there." She paused and glanced at him. "I believe I was supposed to die."

"I don't want to think you're right. But someone drove the Jeep back to the station. Can you imagine how I felt when I found it there with no sign of you? The keys were in the ignition. Then when I got back here no one had seen you all day, except Helen and Colin, and that had been early this morning. Your room's locked and I couldn't bring myself to break in until I was certain you had left. Maybe I was afraid I'd go in there and find everything of yours gone."

He pulled her to a halt, and she saw what stress had done to him, the lines of strain. She felt the start of tears and kissed him quickly before they ran on.

"I can't go in there," she told him when they stood before the tapestry. "Go and see what I mean. It's sickening."

He hugged her and went, and Sue-Ellen closed her eyes as the hanging swung down over the wall. There would have been no reason to suspect she was down in the cellars. The stage had been carefully set. *Sue-Ellen Hill simply couldn't take it anymore and she ran off.* And when she didn't show up anywhere, she'd have become a missing person, but by then who knows what would really have happened to her. She shuddered, fairly certain of the answer to that question.

In moments Edward was back. "How long did it take you to get from the house to me?"

She frowned. "Fifteen, twenty minutes."

"Then we talked for maybe five. And took another fifteen to get back here. Almost an hour."

"Why is it important?"

"Because it was long enough. There's no point in going to the police because we don't have a thing to show them. Our friends have done it again. The place is stripped."

Chapter Seventeen

"We've gone over and over it," Sue-Ellen told Edward as they walked along the village main street. "I know I've been put in danger more than once. And yes, I'm scared—but there's no turning back now."

"I don't know about that." Edward opened the door to the East Puddle Arms, and they were met by a rush of heat from a coal fire. He seated her at a round oak table that reflected flames in its burnished surface. "What'll you have?"

Sue-Ellen fiddled with her jacket buttons. A drink wasn't what she wanted. Assurance that Edward wasn't about to scuttle all she'd worked so hard to accomplish would be much more welcome.

"All right," he said when she didn't answer, "I'll think for you." He returned moments later with two glasses of gin and tonic.

He wore the oilskins that made him appear massive, and these he unsnapped and unzipped and threw over an empty chair before sitting beside her. In the much-darned, navy-blue sweater she liked so well, and the worn jeans and knee-high green rubber boots, he looked big and substantial and very masculine.

The bar was old, seventeenth century. Walls of rough stones supported an oak-beamed ceiling that sagged in places. Brass glittered everywhere, and polished harnesses. Small wall lights made dull glimmerings on unidentifiable farm implements, which had been placed, no doubt someone thought, artfully, but which managed rather to create a delightful hodgepodge of rural antique.

Sue-Ellen sipped for a while, listening to the distinctive flat brogue of the Dorset locals who could probably be found holding up the bar any lunchtime of the week.

"I think we should call the whole thing off," Edward announced abruptly and took another sip of his drink.

Sue-Ellen set down her own with a smack. "You can't mean that." Eight tense days had gone by since the episode in the cellar, three sets of guests had arrived yesterday, and although she still felt shaken and nervous, giving up had never entered her mind.

"I do mean it. I should have acted on my instincts before people were in residence."

"But they are in residence and everything's working beautifully. I couldn't be more delighted with the woman we hired to run the tearoom and the one new maid dealing with the extra workload. We've only just started. We can't stop now."

"We can. I want to. If necessary we'll cope while this lot is here, then it's all over."

It was her, it had to be. He felt them drawing closer and closer, and he couldn't cope with that. And he'd decided to use the excuse that he wasn't prepared to risk more episodes like the ones they'd been through. Well, perhaps he didn't know her as well as he thought he did.

"I don't want this," she told him, pushing the gin away. "And you can give me hell for overstepping the mark, or getting above my station, or whatever else you call it here, but I've gone through a great deal to get to this point at Airstone. I've put a whole lot of my talent and energy—and my heart—into accomplishing what I'm just seeing come to life. Look at me, Edward. Look closely." She held out her arms and he did look, and she grew very warm before she pressed on. "Do you see any scars on me? I'm all right and so are you. And you don't have to worry that I'll try to push myself any further into your personal life because I won't. You can also forget any notions about my airing possible ghosts in the Ormsby-Jones closets. We'll probably never know just what happened with Lettie and your grandmother, and frankly I'm beginning to lose interest. I figure that as long as I don't go near that damned cellar or into any dark churches I'll probably be just fine. All I ask is that you let me do my job. And I'll stay away from you, if that's what you want."

He appeared to swallow several mouthfuls of air before he clasped her wrist so tightly she bit her lip. "How can you say that? To hell with it. You don't understand me, but why should you? We're oil and water and we always will be. You're driven, more so than any man or woman I've ever met. Fine. Go head. It's time I stopped concerning myself with someone who works for me."

Every tiny hair on her spine prickled and her legs turned to water. If she weren't too proud she'd cry. Instead she took a leisurely swallow of her drink, stood up, and walked out.

"WHERE ARE THEY?" Sue-Ellen asked Connie, who led the way along the corridor outside Sue-Ellen's suite. After an exhausting day she'd finally decided she could collapse with a good book in her sitting room. No such luck. Evidently there were irate guests to deal with.

Everything had been going so well for the past three days. Edward had made an apology of sorts for upsetting her, then simply done one of his disappearing acts. She was desperately miserable, certain that what she'd feared most had happened: they'd moved apart. But at least he hadn't repeated his threat to close the hotel, and she was gaining confidence with every day. Why did something stupid have to ruin it now?

Connie, who should have gone home hours ago, was visibly drawn, but this was no time to talk about her problems. "They're waiting in their room," she said of Mr. and Mrs. Reginald Harvey of West Virginia—one of four parties now at Airstone who had appeared delighted with everything . . . until tonight.

"What are you doing here so late?" Sue-Ellen asked, descending one short flight of stairs and turning toward the east side of the house and the conservatory wing.

"Miss Mabel hasn't been feeling too well, or so she says, so I've spent the last few nights here. With Ernie gone and my boy being so difficult, I was glad to get away."

"I'm sorry. But why were you sent to deal with this instead of Sylvia?"

"Oh, miss. You've been too busy to notice, I suppose. Sylvia's taken off. Just packed her bags and left without saying a word to anyone. Mrs. Leaming's in a right lather, but Miss Smallman's finding someone else as quick as she can. It was Miss Smallman who called up to the aunts' rooms and asked for me to get you."

Sue-Ellen wished Bea hadn't done that. Alice and Mabel were better kept without ammunition against the hotel.

Mr. and Mrs. Harvey waited outside the door of their room. Mrs. Harvey was small and blond, rounded and fluffy and, at a guess, twenty years her husband's junior. At the moment she clung to his beefy arm and wept.

"There you are, girlie," he said to Sue-Ellen, who managed to keep her smile in place. "You've gone too far with this thing. The idea was cute, I'll give you that, but when you frighten a little woman this way you ruin everything. Baby," he said to his wife, "don't you worry now. Old Reggie'll fix everything. Doesn't he always?"

Baby—Sue-Ellen had no idea of the woman's first name—nodded adoringly up at her balding husband.

Sue-Ellen cleared her throat. "If you'll tell me the problem, Mr. Harvey, I'm sure we can have this sorted out in no time."

"Oh, come now, Miss Hill. We chose the Henry VIII room because we thought it was cute. You know what we found in there tonight, and now you know it isn't cute anymore. We want our money refunded. All of it. Then we'll be on our way. It's late, but we'll find somewhere to stay."

Goose bumps crept over Sue-Ellen's arms and legs. She'd changed from the suit she'd worn during the day into sweats, but they didn't keep her warm.

"I don't know what you're talking about. Why don't you show me?"

He shrugged. "If you want to keep on playing games it's okay with me. Stay here, baby."

The room was terrific. Sue-Ellen considered it her masterpiece, with a lofty four-poster bed and acres of crimson-and-gold brocade hangings, Jacobean pieces to hold the heavily expensive ambience...and the shelf where the plaster replicas of the heads of Henry's wives....

"Where are they?" She turned on Harvey, furious. If this was *his* idea of funny, *she* didn't appreciate the effort. Those heads had cost plenty, and he wasn't making off with them on some flimsy excuse, such as being shortchanged by their absence.

Harvey walked around her and went to the bed. He threw back the covers. "That's sick," he said in a flat voice.

The heads lay in a row. Trailing from beneath the necks were what appeared to be the bloody entrails of some animal. Sue-Ellen covered her mouth and turned her head.

The pressure of a heavy arm around her shoulder surprised her, and she looked up into the concerned eyes of Reginald Harvey. "I'll be damned. You didn't know, did you?"

She shook her head.

"That's bad," he said. "Real bad. I'd say you've got someone to sort out, and if I was on my own I'd stick around to help, but—" he inclined his head toward the door "—baby can't handle this kind of thing, so you'll understand if we move on."

Sue-Ellen could do nothing but apologize and agree to the Harveys' wishes. She trudged back toward her rooms only to be intercepted by Miles Grossby.

He looked slightly mussed, and she assumed he, too, had been dragged from what he'd thought was his own time. "You'd better come down," he said.

Was the serious set of his lips what she should take as the sign of his true feelings, or the hint of amusement that lurked in his dark eyes?

She didn't bother to question him, only waved him ahead of her and followed him to the front entrance of the house.

Connie and Mary-Beth King, ex-librarians from Wyoming, stood with . . . Mabel Ormsby-Jones.

"I felt compelled to come down and help these two poor ladies," Mabel announced, and Sue-Ellen had no difficulty recognizing triumph in her glittering eyes. "Really, we did warn you about this sort of thing."

Connie and Mary-Beth King, both sixtyish and papery, colorless as if they'd dehydrated among all those books, made unintelligible twittery sounds.

"Alice and I already know what happened to those other poor people. Now, be good enough to refund these ladies' money and have Grossby drive them to the station so they can catch a train to some place suitable for . . . some place where tourists are easily accommodated."

Sue-Ellen pursed her lips before she said, "What's happened here?"

Mabel turned her back on the women, and malevolence oozed from her pinched face. "What would possess you to arrange for screams in the night?"

"Screams? I don't understand you." The Little Prince's Room had been the one allotted to the King sisters. Sue-Ellen couldn't imagine what had gone wrong there.

"Screams that woke these ladies up and brought them out of their room to find two crumpled little bodies at their feet." Mabel's grin revealed stained teeth.

"Don't be ridiculous," Sue-Ellen said. "That's not possible."

"Oh, they weren't real bodies," Mabel said, leaning heavily on her ebony cane. "Just very real-looking effigies but hardly conducive to a good night's sleep."

Sue-Ellen's last thought as she saw the two unhappy customers out of the house, was that she wondered how much

Mabel Ormsby-Jones needed that silver-handled ebony cane.

"I DIDN'T WANT to bother you with this," Bea said to Edward, "but I thought you ought to know. We had quite a night. Today Sue-Ellen and I arranged a system for checking rooms right before guests retire, but I've got grave doubts about all this now."

Edward, still dressed in the suit he'd worn to the office, took up his favorite position, looking out at dripping trees beyond his sitting-room window. Bea had been talking steadily behind him for half an hour, and the gist of all she said was that she thought the hotel had already cost too much and that perhaps it was time to close its doors. In other words, she was suggesting he make a decision to send Sue-Ellen on her way.

Swallowing was painful. Sending Sue-Ellen away was something he didn't think he could do. He missed her more with every day of their estrangement.

"I've asked Michael to join us. He'll be here shortly, right after evensong. I'd like his opinion on all this." He didn't say he'd also asked Sue-Ellen to come, but not until nine when he intended them to be alone. He swallowed again. For once, let him say the right things to her, the things he really thought.

"I'm sure Michael will agree with me," Bea said, sounding regretful. "He came over this morning and he was a rock for Sue-Ellen. She was so upset. Colin came, too, not that I think his idea of, er, humor is helpful. Anyone would think he enjoyed the whole thing."

Edward grunted. Colin probably was enjoying the debacle. Colin probably hoped everything would fold....

"Helen helped us look around. Funny, really. I'm never sure she likes me, and I could have sworn she didn't like Sue-Ellen. Can't imagine why."

Neither could Edward and he didn't care.

The front door slammed and Michael came in. "Evening, all." His hat hung from one hand while he undid his coat.

Edward outlined Bea's comments and asked Michael for his opinion.

The man was silent for a long uncomfortable time. He joined Edward to stare out into the damp night.

"There's only one thing I'm worried about," he said when Edward was at breaking point with expectancy. "Sue-Ellen's safety. I think it's time you called in the police."

"Absolutely not." Bea's voice rose sharply, and Edward faced her.

She glared at Michael. "How can you suggest a thing like that? What would we say if we did call in that old gossip, Merryfield? That we can't control our own affairs here?"

"They're Edward's affairs," Michael said, his tone mild.

Bea became as puce as her blouse. "I don't need to be reminded of my position here, Michael," she said. "*I* at least have nothing but the best interests of Sir Arthur and Edward, and Airstone Hall, in mind. I know that if we simply stop this hotel thing everything will go back to normal."

"How do you know?" Michael thrust out his chin.

"Please," Edward said, keeping a straight face with difficulty. He'd always suspected that these two didn't especially like each other, that they were, in some obscure manner, in competition. "Let's keep calm and on track. I think the best thing to do is to call a twenty-four-hour moratorium while I think. Then we'll all get together, Sue-Ellen included, and decide what to do. I do lean toward an official investigation of all this mischief."

"Really, Edward—"

"No, Bea. No more talk now. Thank you both for coming. We'll meet here at the same time tomorrow, if that's all right with you."

They left almost immediately to be replaced within half an hour by Sue-Ellen. Rather than use the key he'd urged her to regard as her own, she knocked lightly. He opened the door almost before she could withdraw her hand, and she took a step backward.

"You asked to see me."

Wordlessly he pulled her inside and waited for her to give him her raincoat. Her straight hair fell softly forward. In a magenta wool dress and matching pumps she managed an effect that was professional yet feminine . . . and he wanted to take her in his arms and forget there'd ever been a harsh word between them."

She refused a drink and stood in the middle of the room, her back ramrod straight.

"You should have called me last night," he said when it became evident she wouldn't initiate conversation. "I would have liked to be with you."

Her chin came up. "I coped. Troubleshooting comes with the territory."

"Would you call what happened the usual type of trouble in your business?" There was a shimmer in her eyes. Damn, he was already doing it all wrong.

"No, it wasn't usual. Very little has been usual since I came here, but neither has it been all bad." Now tears showed clearly. "I'll take some wonderful memories away with me. Some of the best of my life."

His hand felt too big, his body awkward. There had been so little opportunity to learn how to deal with deep emotion, his own or someone else's. He'd come to realize that even with Lenore there'd never been quite this sense of being joined.

"Sue-Ellen, I know I managed some sort of apology for that quip of mine at the Arms. It didn't come close to covering what a heel I felt about it."

"It's not important. You were right. There's no reason you should care what happens to someone who works for you, as long as they do their job. And that isn't an issue anymore, is it?"

Her meaning dawned slowly. She thought he was going to fire her. "Listen—"

"It'll take a week or two to gear down. I do think I should be here until the two parties of guests we've still got leave, and I also want to contact the travel agents who've got our listings."

She left him speechless. Even now, when she thought she was to be sent packing, she was still thinking of what would be best for him.

Enough words. When he laced his fingers around her neck she didn't move. But her eyes widened and her lips parted. Tears started coursing down her cheeks, taking mascara with them, and he pressed his brow to hers, closing his eyes.

They stood like that for what felt an age. "I don't want you to go," he told her in a voice that didn't sound like his own. "I don't ever want you to go. I'm lousy at expressing myself. I've been out of my mind worrying about you, but I couldn't seem to let go and explain that very well."

She sniffed and he looked at her. He brushed tears away with his thumbs, scrabbled in his pocket for a handkerchief and wiped her eyes. She took the handkerchief from him, smiled a watery smile and blew her nose loudly.

"I must look terrible."

"You look wonderful. You always do." He kissed her trembling lips, opening them gently beneath his own to touch his tongue to the soft places inside. Gradually she relaxed and brought her body against him, wound her arms about his neck and pushed her fingers into his hair.

As one, they turned their faces to rest against one another's necks. "You are going to close the hotel, aren't you?" Sue-Ellen asked. "I know you think I'm a nut to care so much, but it could be so good."

"I don't think I'm going to close it," he said into her ear and blew gently until she shuddered. "But I do think I've got to take a firm hand now, and who knows what, or should I say who, is going to turn out a casualty."

"I've thought of that," she said. "But I don't know how we can avoid a real mess."

"Bea's determined to keep it among ourselves, but I don't know if we can." He wouldn't say that Bea would prefer the hotel to be abandoned. "But I've given myself twenty-four hours to deal with that. Tonight I want to make things right between you and me."

She arched her neck to see him. Her eyes were on his mouth, and her own soft lips parted again. He answered the invitation with a deep kiss and felt heat flare within him. A small seductive smile only increased his desire.

If he didn't say it all quickly he might not get to it tonight, and he didn't want to go on without letting her know how he felt. "The reason I was such a bastard the other day is because you've become very important to me."

"Edward." Her lips and tongue outlined his jaw and the sensitive spot beneath his ear. "You are so important to me, too."

"I'm sorry I'm not good at saying what I mean," he told her. "I've been terrified something would happen to you, that's all, and it's made me the monster I'm capable of being."

She laughed, rolling against him with unbearable languor, which let him feel her soft breasts pressed to his chest.

"This isn't funny," he said. Soon he would lose control, or at least reason. "You need to know what a bad-tempered devil I can be."

She laughed again, but she was unbuttoning his shirt and slipping her hands inside. "I'll remember that," she said, kissing the skin she'd bared. "Is it okay if I remember some other time?"

"If you say so— No, I don't believe it." The phone in the hall jangled raucously. "Interrupted. Like some bloody awful movie."

"Ignore it," she said, disposing of his tie with his jacket and pulling free his shirttails.

"Wise woman." He reached for the tiny buttons that ran from the V-neck of her dress to its waist.

The jangling didn't stop. "Who do you suppose it is?" Sue-Ellen spread her fingers over her shoulders, stroked, but she looked toward the ringing. ''There could be an emergency at the house.''

''Oh, hell.'' Edward hung his head, frustrated. ''I'd better get it.''

In seconds he returned, blood pounding in his head. He grabbed his shirt, put it on and tucked it in. ''Come on.'' With Sue-Ellen's hand in his, he dashed into the hallway, grabbing their coats as he went.

They covered the distance to the Hall so fast that they arrived panting. Sue-Ellen hadn't asked what was going on. She knew that something was seriously wrong and that talk wouldn't help.

''Kitchen,'' he told her and they raced on, through the scullery and into the big functional room.

Miles Grossby blocked their path. His face bore a sickly greenish tinge. ''I don't think it's such a good idea for Sue-Ellen to see—''

''I'll see whatever there is to see,'' she said, and Edward didn't bother to argue.

On one side of the room he could see Mary Leaming slumped in a chair, sobbing quietly. Connie leaned over her, apparently composed. Massing, strangely out of place, appeared, for the first time Edward remembered, disconcerted. Only Pitts, standing for a change, wore a serene expression.

''We'd better take a look.''

''If you're sure,'' Grossby said with a significant glance at Sue-Ellen. ''We've called the Reverend Bastible.''

Edward lost patience. ''Nothing can be that bad, man. What's all the flap about?''

Grossby shrugged and moved aside. ''That,'' he said, indicating the far side of the kitchen.

What he felt was like nothing he'd ever experienced before. Edward walked on boneless legs to the place where the door to the old dumbwaiter had always been kept shut. It stood open now. Until a few days ago he'd never even considered where the thing came from or went to. It was just there.

Standing beside him, Sue-Ellen made a noise that was half scream, half sob and he suppressed his own urge to cry out.

Bundled into the space, crushed beneath the central shelf, was a woman. Her arms, at an unnatural angle, were bent behind her back and her wrists tied.

Another thin rope still clung to swollen flesh of her neck.

Sylvia's blue eyes, the whites bloodred, stared out of a blackened face. She was very dead.

Chapter Eighteen

Edward had shielded her while she slipped from the kitchen. He'd scowled and tried to question her in whispers, but she'd gotten her message across, and he'd moved so that she could leave unobserved. Constable Merryfield had arrived and, to Sue-Ellen's amazement, proceeded to conduct inquiries in front of poor Sylvia's abused body and without separating the group.

Merryfield was every American's vision of the British bobby. In navy serge and silver buttons from neck to feet, his tall helmet under one arm, he'd had started writing furiously the minute he walked in. But he'd started on one side of the room and made it plain that he'd work in a clockwise rotation. From the time it took him to word whatever he decided to ask, Sue-Ellen figured she had more than enough time to accomplish her mission.

She made it through and up to Sylvia's room in minutes. That was empty, she already knew, but there was one thing the . . . murderer had probably missed. The journal. A man in a hurry to cover his tracks by making it seem that his victim had walked out was unlikely to be careful enough to check under a mattress. Sue-Ellen hoped he hadn't been that careful, because now she was certain the book held the answers she needed. Sylvia had accepted the journal and hidden it. Notations of Esther's vengeance had been made in it, and the death of the girl. Sue-Ellen was certain that girl had been Lettie, and Sylvia had reacted to the mention of

Lettie as if guilty of something...or afraid? Now Sylvia was dead.

Except for the absence of the pile of books and the baby buggy, the room looked exactly as it had the last time Sue-Ellen was there. Clean, almost untouched. And the bed was still made up with its impeccable white chenille spread.

Her palms sweated, and she ran them down her hips. Undoubtedly the journal should go to that bumbling policeman and the other officials he said would soon arrive from London, but she wanted to take another look first.

She flipped up the spread, lifted the mattress, and closed her eyes. He had been careful. The journal was gone.

One more disappointment. But also one more piece of evidence that pointed toward her sketchy but growing theory. Too bad the biggest hole in her theory was motive. Who was violently mourning a death that happened in 1923, the death of an obscure maid? Who feared that if Airstone became a hotel that story might become public knowledge, while at the same time, they risked using its trappings as a means to stop the project? And who would kill to keep the secret and why?

She should be frightened. She was, and frustrated. On the way back across the house she considered what might happen next. The first thing was obvious. No one would be allowed to leave the immediate area, and they would not be able to take in more guests until the crime was cleared up...if it was, and if Edward ever allowed her to resume business.

As she emerged from the passageway behind the family living quarters, Sue-Ellen saw the hurrying form of Michael Bastible on his way toward the kitchen. She opened her mouth to call out, but shouting didn't seem appropriate, so she walked rapidly after him, arriving in the kitchen doorway the instant after he passed Edward. Sue-Ellen quietly took up her former position and touched Edward, who glanced back and raised his brows. She shook her head, indicating she'd explain later.

Michael was repeating Sue-Ellen's name loudly, but he wasn't looking at her.

"Pull yourself together, Michael." Bea's expression was one of confusion.

Michael Bastible took no notice of the housekeeper. "She didn't deserve this. No one deserves this. She came here to do a job. She only wanted a chance to do what she was trained to do. And she was damn good at it. Oh, her poor family. So far from home."

Edward's "Good Lord" preceded Sue-Ellen's understanding by an instant. He said gently, "Michael, it's not Sue-Ellen, it's Sylvia."

Sue-Ellen's legs threatened to crumple. She took a deep calming breath that didn't make her feel any better.

"Calm down, Reverend," Bea said, moving to stand in front of Michael.

"Sylvia," Michael said, sounding dazed. "Why?"

"Maybe you should go home, Michael," Bea said.

"Michael, Bea probably has a point," Edward said. "You don't need to be here for this session. Why not wait in the parlor? Have a brandy, and I'll join you when I can." Edward patted his friend on the back.

Michael went, his face gray. Merryfield continued his plodding investigation and finished by informing them that they should all be prepared for the arrival of an inspector from Scotland Yard and that the body was not to be touched until this man and his team were finished.

The staff dispersed. Edward looped an arm around Sue-Ellen as they went to the parlor, where Michael, looking considerably recovered, sat sipping a large brandy.

When they entered the austere room he got jerkily to his feet. "Hate that fireplace," he said, indicating Sue-Ellen's own personal peeve, the white monster with the inlaid bust. "Don't like this room much at all, in fact. Never could understand why Arthur and Louise didn't change it."

Edward's smile was indulgent. "They spent very little time here, if you remember. Your beloved conservatory and that side of the house was where they liked to be."

"Mmm. Bad business, this, Edward."

Sue-Ellen looked from one man to the other. One thing she was becoming convinced of was that Michael Bastible might be the only person able to reveal the key to the past, the past that was steadily encroaching on the present.

"Sit down," Edward said to Michael. "Sue-Ellen and I will join you in that brandy." He glanced at her and she wanted to hug him, to tell him everything was going to be all right.

"Got to be off," Michael said predictably. He put down his glass. "The Lettie Tinker thing was wrong," he said and crammed on his hat.

Waiting for him to continue, Sue-Ellen could hardly breathe.

Edward stiffened at her side.

"If she'd lived she'd have gone north to your grandfather's Yorkshire estate," Michael said. He pulled absently at his mustache. "It wasn't sold then, of course. I heard all about it. My father... he talked, and I heard. There was a baby, he went anyway, and your grandparents made sure he was adopted by a tenant farm couple on the estate. Your grandparents did the best they could. They sent him to good people. Remember that. They took care of the boy."

He shambled out, and neither Edward nor Sue-Ellen made any attempt to stop him.

Sue-Ellen thought back to the journal. *The couple are good people. The boy will do well up North....* Possibly Lettie's baby?

"Edward, I've got to tell you something... quickly and in private."

He closed the door and she told him everything, about the meeting between Colin and Sylvia, the passing of the journal to the maid, seeing it in Sylvia's room and reading the entries, and that now it was missing.

Edward slumped into a chair. "So it seems we do have a family skeleton, eh?"

"It seems there's a very evil element creeping out of the past, and you'd better be prepared for it to be splashed all over the papers before long."

He ran a hand through his hair. "Do you think Michael knows more than he's saying?"

"Yes."

"Do we confront him?"

"I think so. The final decision's yours. I wish we had that journal."

"Where is it? I wonder. Burned, do you suppose?"

"I don't know," Sue-Ellen said. "Our killer must have been pretty rushed. So rushed he didn't quite make it back to dispose of poor Sylvia."

"If I were the killer and I wanted to get rid of that journal I'd put it back where it came from. As far as he's concerned no one else knows it left the library. Those journals have always been there, in order, and one missing could be noticed. He might not want that. Come on." Edward was already in motion and pulling her with him. "The library, then we talk to Michael."

Sue-Ellen couldn't give the library the inspection it deserved. Walls of beautiful books, heavy oak antique desk, brass studded dark leather chairs and a leather padded window seat deep enough to enfold a reader for long and comfortable hours.

"It's here." Edward was on his knees, a journal open on the floor. In front of him was a row of apparently identical volumes. Sue-Ellen knelt beside him and saw the familiar inscription on the flyleaf.

"Go to the end," she told him. "The last page."

"'Met the master—'" he began.

"No, no. The last page."

"This is the last page."

She snatched up the book and sat on the floor with a thump. "That's it," she said. "If there was ever any doubt that the key was here there isn't any more. The page is gone. Look."

He did and nodded as he saw what she had seen, the careful close trimming of the paper to try to conceal that a page was missing.

IT WAS COLIN who answered the vicarage door. He didn't invite them in. "Father isn't here," he said, and Sue-Ellen saw wariness in his blue eyes. He would have heard about Sylvia by now and no doubt must fear implication. She swallowed. Colin had to be suspect. The pressure of Edward's hand at her waist told her he was thinking the same thing and warning that they should keep silent on the subject.

"Where is Michael?" Edward asked, when Colin did nothing but stand, his chin belligerently thrust forward.

"At the bloody church, I suppose. Isn't that where people go to pray? He was hardly through the door with his charming little story when the phone rang, and then he said he had to go and pray." He laughed, and Sue-Ellen heard more confusion than derision in the sound. "Never could understand praying myself. Who listens d'you suppose? All those nasty stone gargoyles with their gaping mouths?"

Neither of them attempted an answer, and the door shut before they'd completely turned their backs.

"There's a rattled man," Edward said. "Colin never did quite get his act together. Not a bad chap under it all, but weak in some ways."

Without discussing what to do next they set out, side by side, for St. Peter's. The night was dry but heavy, and a distant glow suggested lightning far off. A following rumble of thunder was no more than a menacing growl.

Through the gate they went, making their way by feel and memory. Light did show at the church windows, and Sue-Ellen's spirits lifted a little. Perhaps an answer was in sight.

"How are you doing?" Edward paused unexpectedly and pulled her into his arms. "Everything's going to be all right. We'll come through this, you'll see."

"You bet we will." If only she felt more sure. Here in his powerful arms anything seemed possible, but the shard of doubt was still there.

He kissed her with a slow passion that closed everything out while it lasted. Edward was a master with his mouth and tongue, and he chose this moment, when they were both needy, to put his talent to use. When he'd made a delicate tracing along the outline of her lips and stroked his tongue over the smooth membrane just inside and reached for and found every other tender place, he raised his face from hers in the darkness.

"It's time you and I were together again, my love," he said.

She couldn't speak, only nod and nestle her face into his neck before they reluctantly continued on their way.

"This door needs oiling," Edward remarked as the old hinges groaned under the weight of the church door.

Inside, all the sconces were alight and spreading their fragile umber glow. The air, redolent with the scent of incense and dust, tickled the nose.

"I don't see him," Sue-Ellen said, wincing at the loud clack of her heels.

She walked up the nave as far as the altar, with its silver filigree cross flanked by flowers that must have come from Airstone's conservatory.

"Michael," Edward said, but in a low voice. He laughed, a self-conscious sound. "Funny how one always wants to whisper in church. Do you suppose God gets sick of everybody whispering around him?"

He was trying to ease the mood, but she felt his intensity. "I think God's glad anytime one of us shows we remember him at all ... even Colin," she said.

"Yes." Edward retraced his steps to the center of the church. "Michael isn't here, which is funny because he doesn't leave the lights on all night."

"Is there a sacristy or something?"

"Back there," he said and she checked a room to the left of the altar. Empty.

"Edward." She stared past him. "There's a light on in the belfry."

He spun around. "What would he be doing in there?"

"Returning to the scene of the crime perhaps?" she said, and immediately regretted it. "Forget I said that. It's just that he's strong and agile enough to have pulled off anything that's been done." She stood beside Edward now.

"He thought you'd been murdered, not Sylvia," he said. "That wouldn't fit, would it?"

"It might if he's clever enough to have thought of a way to draw suspicion away from himself."

"I thought of that," Edward said with evident reluctance. "And I'm also wondering if all this could be to cover for his father. If Frederick Bastible had some part in concealing a crime, that is, Lettie's unnatural death if it was murder, then Michael might want to make sure the truth never became public."

"Would he go so far?" Sue-Ellen gritted her teeth, hating it all. "Let's turn off the lights and go home. I've had enough of playing detective for one night. And I expect the Scotland Yard people will be at the Hall by now. We ought to be there, too."

"Right." Edward opened the belfry door and reached inside to turn off the light.

Sue-Ellen saw him grope as if to hold the air, then he gripped the doorjamb and rested his head on his hands.

"What is it?" She rushed to him. "What's wrong with you?"

"No, no, not this."

"Edward!"

He rolled his face toward her. "Don't go in there."

Too late. Beyond him she saw what he had seen.

Her own cry shook her. "Michael!"

He swung gently, the rope that had once rung the bell looped around his throat.

Chapter Nineteen

"Stop it." He shook her and hated doing it. "It's not your fault. How can you even think such a thing? All this started before either of us was born."

She shuddered in spasms, but she'd stopped crying. "You wanted to give up on the project. If we had, Michael wouldn't have killed himself."

He held her shoulders but looked at Michael's legs. God, the world wouldn't be the same without Michael. What would he say to Helen? How would he tell her?

"Edward—"

"Shh. Just a minute." A stool lay toppled near Michael's feet. The side touched his feet. "Something... Sue-Ellen, if Michael hung himself, wouldn't he shorten the rope as much as possible so that when he kicked away the stool the rope action would be almost instant?"

"I don't know what you mean." She was valiant but fading.

"Hold on a bit longer," he told her. "You're doing fine. His feet are barely two or three inches from the floor and that stool must be a foot high. It's also so near his feet... as if it had been put there afterward."

She looked and he saw her narrow her eyes in thought. "You're right. I think someone... Edward, I think someone hung him there."

WITH EDWARD, Sue-Ellen emerged from the Coroner's Court in Dorchester into a morning blessed with thin sunlight. A week of interrogation and total disruption at Airstone had just culminated in an hour's presentation of forensic and pathological reports.

Edward held her arm and steered her across the wide street lined with old but nondescript terraced buildings. "My offices are up there." He inclined his head to the right. "The museum with all the stuff about Thomas Hardy's the other way. Maybe we'll get to go there sometime."

Just words. Conversation. Sue-Ellen murmured agreement, but her mind was still on what they'd heard in court.

"Let's have tea and some food before driving back," Edward suggested. "Horse with the Red Umbrella okay?"

"Fine." Anywhere was fine. This was her first visit to the county town, and she couldn't imagine a time when she might come again.

In the warm tearoom with its bright red-and-white decor, surrounded by the aroma of freshly baked current buns, it was hard to believe that once they left they must return to a place shrouded by death and fear.

"Both murdered," Edward said when the tea and shortbread they'd ordered had been served. "Knocked unconscious by blows to the back of the head with a blunt instrument, then one strangled and one hung. My God."

Sue-Ellen swallowed the warm liquid. "And even wonderful Scotland Yard, Chief Inspector Carruthers included, doesn't seem to have any suspects lined up. Either that or we're all suspects, and they haven't descended on one of us yet."

"Sue-Ellen." Edward held both of her hands but didn't look at her. "I know the theory is that some workman or vagrant may be responsible, but I don't believe it. Will you promise me something?"

Her throat tightened. "You know I will."

"Be with me as much of the time as possible when I don't have to be at the office. And when I'm not at Airstone, please don't take any chances. I can't lose you now."

It was the closest he'd come to a declaration about their future, and she scarcely knew how to answer. "We won't lose each other," was as much as she could trust herself to say.

A WHOLE WEEK of waiting, watching, and nothing had happened—except for the blanketing of Airstone in a mantle of melancholy jumpiness. In the growing gloom of late afternoon, Sue-Ellen walked the corridors in the now empty conservatory wing. At least the police had allowed the last two parties of guests to leave, and she was grateful not to have to worry about them.

She thought of Edward and smiled. With the smile tears came prickling into her eyes. Did they have a future? Everything seemed to suggest they did, if and when this nightmare was over.

Last night they'd been together again. Each time they made love they grew closer, as much in mind as in body, and the one truth she knew for sure was that she could never feel with another man what she felt with him.

He was due back from Dorchester again. She'd promised to meet him, and her heart pumped faster at the thought.

The questions that were never far away came yet again. She and Edward had thought that Michael Bastible might be behind everything, even Sylvia's killing. It would have been possible for him to incite the aunts into trying to undermine Sue-Ellen. Michael was trusted by everyone. But now Michael was dead and he hadn't committed suicide. Could Michael have had an accomplice who turned on him?

Sue-Ellen stood in the oval sun room with its glass walls and roof heavily encrusted with blood-purple grapes and jewel-green leaves. No wonder Edward's parents had liked being together here, looking out at the conservatory and the plantings in the courtyard around it. She sat in a rickety bentwood chair and stretched out her legs. Only four o'clock, yet the conservatory was scarcely visible in the dusk.

The parquet floor needed waxing. A bright glimmer beneath another chair caught her eye and she got up to look. A locket, small, and a broken chain. Sue-Ellen turned it over, recognizing it as Bea's and noticing that it was open.

Bea must be frantic looking for this. She never spoke of family or friends. Curiosity took over, and Sue-Ellen glanced inside. No photos, only faded writing on the yellowing disks behind each circle. She looked more closely...

"Sue-Ellen!"

She jumped so hard she felt weak. Bea. Sue-Ellen folded the locket into her palm and put her hands behind her back. The coincidence was too great to ignore. She needed time to find out if the connection she'd begun to make was real. "Here, Bea."

Bea strode in, dressed in tweeds and heavy brogues, a raincoat over her arm. "I've got to get out for an hour or so," she said. "You understand, I'm sure. I'm going to have tea with some friends in the village. If anyone wants to know where I am, say I'm running errands."

"Where can we reach you if something comes up?" Sue-Ellen asked.

"You can't. I mean, I don't want to be... Look, you can cope, I know you can. All I want is an hour or so to myself."

Sue-Ellen waited long enough for Bea to reach the family wing before racing to the closest room with a phone and a view of the stable yard where Bea kept her seldom-used and elderly white Hillman Minx. While she watched through the window, Sue-Ellen dialed Edward's number. To visit friends, Bea had said, yet she'd never mentioned friends before or visited anyone.

"Hello—"

"Edward. I was afraid you wouldn't be there yet." Bea had appeared in the yard, a large box in her arms. "I want you to start the Jeep's engine, then wait for me inside the gate house. I'm leaving now."

"What—"

"Do as I ask. Something's happened."

Bea struggled to get the box into the trunk, tied the lid down and returned to the house. Sue-Ellen couldn't wait to see what else she would do. This could be a crazy path to nothing, but something had to break soon or she *would* be crazy.

She went as she was, in jeans, sweater and sneakers, with no coat. Every step of the way to the gate house she expected to hear the engine of Bea's car and know it was too late. The sound didn't come and she made it past the Jeep, its engine running, and inside Edward's front door.

He grabbed her against him. "Are you all right? What's happened?"

"Put on your skins," she said. "Let me have one of your parkas. Quick." She reached around him, waited until he'd done as she asked and switched off the hall light.

He stood behind her as she peered through the barely opened door. The Hillman passed, traveling fast. Sue-Ellen counted to five. "Now!"

Edward moved even faster then she. By the time she'd jumped into the Jeep he'd put it in gear. "Now what?"

"We're following Bea. I'll explain as we go. She's gone to the left, toward the village. I don't want her to know we're following her."

"This had better be good." The Jeep jolted and bumped over deep ruts in the lane. The white car was far ahead, and in Bea's rearview mirror they should be no more than one of the many similar vehicles around here. Particularly since the Jeep was a dark color and the light had almost totally failed.

By the time Sue-Ellen had explained about the locket, Edward's face, in the light of the dash, was a study in grim lines. "Bea? Good God, what irony. The last person I'd ever have suspected of being involved."

"We can't be sure she's done anything," Sue-Ellen reminded him. "There just seems a connection, that's all. Pull over. She's going down that track."

Edward reacted reflexively, driving the Jeep off the road, and through a gap in the hedgerow. Rapidly he backed across the opening until they were all but hidden, but still had a view of the track Bea had taken.

"There's nothing down there," he said. "Just fields lying fallow and a barn that should be taken completely down. Belongs to us, but we haven't been able to work it for years."

An hour passed before Sue-Ellen heard the rumble of an engine. She started to sit straighter, but Edward held her down and scrunched beside her. "Pray she doesn't see light on the windshield," he said.

Edward also thought they were on to something. Sue-Ellen didn't know if she was glad.

Minutes later they were at the end of the overgrown trail, with Edward shining a flashlight on the spot where Bea must have parked—only yards from the barn he'd mentioned.

The leaning structure appeared nothing more than a place for the rodents that skittered from sight at the approach of Edward, Sue-Ellen and the flashlight.

"Why would she come here?" Inside, Edward scanned every corner.

"I don't know, unless that box I told you about had something in it she wanted to hide." She began her own cautious search and found nothing . . . until her shoe caught between two boards on the warped floor. "Flashlight," she called.

Some of the boards had been pulled free of their nails. They lifted easily to reveal a space beneath. Edward lay flat to lean into the hole. She saw his shoulders flex as he braced himself. The box came first, then a long burlap-covered bundle tied with string.

"Bingo," Sue-Ellen said. Then, "Why don't I feel we've won something?"

She caught the downward turn of his mouth. "We seem to have been short of winners lately." He opened the box and rested his chin on his chest. "Oh, my God. I think I remember seeing this."

Sue-Ellen peered inside and had to sit down. On its side rested Sylvia's child-sized baby buggy. "She had so little."

Sue-Ellen covered her face. "I guess this was the one thing that wasn't easy to burn or hide without risking its being found."

Edward unwound the burlap to reveal a shovel.

"I suppose she thought she might have to bury the box," Sue-Ellen said. "Doesn't she expect to get caught?"

"She hasn't been caught yet," Edward said, a menacing hardness to his voice. "And we'd better be sure we've got everything we need to make certain she is before we try to close in. Bea Smallman's no fool, and if I say she's dangerous I haven't even scratched the surface of what she really is. My father must have known all that happened in Grandfather's time. We may have to try to question him."

Taking their precious cargo they headed for Airstone, and were met there by a figure with arms flailing. The headlights picked up Colin Bastible's stark face before he dashed aside to let them pass.

He started talking before they could close the gate-house door behind them all. "I had to come," he said and his eyes shot wildly from Edward's face to Sue-Ellen's. "They're going to come after me. They'll find out I knew her and accuse me of killing her."

Helen and Colin had taken Michael's death more violently than Sue-Ellen could ever have imagined. She'd gone with Edward to break the news, and when they left the brother and sister were exhausted in their grief and rage. This was the first time she'd seen either of them since.

"Be calm, Colin," Edward said. "You're talking about Sylvia, I take it."

Colin stared. "You know? My God, everyone must know."

"I saw you with her," Sue-Ellen said quietly. "The night you gave her the journal.

Amazingly he became even paler. "Do the police know about that yet?"

"No. But they'll have to." She felt sorry for him.

"I'm sorry, Edward," Colin said, wringing his hands. His brown woolen coat was wrongly buttoned. "I've been such an ass. It was years ago when I first saw that journal. I was with... My father took me with him to the library at Airstone sometimes. He loved it there. And I loved...I did love to be with him, unlikely as that sounds. Anyway, I found some entries in a journal, the one I took, that didn't make any sense, and I pestered Father about them until he told me about a girl named Lettie Tinker. *The* Lettie Tinker, of course."

Sue-Ellen met Edward's eyes but didn't comment.

Colin clutched a handful of his hair. "I never forgot that story, and years later I...hell, I couldn't get over Lenore leaving me for you the way she did. I hated you for that. When Father got upset about the Hall being turned into a hotel I didn't understand it. But I didn't want it to happen, either, because I was sick of seeing you get what you wanted."

Edward sat down and rested his chin on a fist.

"I've got to go on with this," Colin said. "I finally got it out of Father that he was afraid of what Bea Smallman might do to the person you hired for the hotel project. He thought Bea would see her as competition. Evidently Bea thinks she's the lady of the house...and will make sure no one else takes her place!"

Now Sue-Ellen sat.

"I gave the journal to Sylvia to keep," Colin continued. "Taking it back to the vicarage seemed too dangerous. I couldn't risk Father finding out what I'd done. But Sylvia was sly. I had to tell her some of the background and promise her that she'd benefit in the end, only she didn't wait. She couldn't have. Bea had already used her to splash nail polish around or something—I never knew what all that was about. Supposedly Bea only wanted to help the staff by making sure there was no hotel. But that aside, all I can think is that Sylvia went to Bea with the journal and threatened blackmail...and Bea killed her!"

"Why did you take the journal?" Edward asked in a flat voice.

"I was going to wait for the right moment to take you down a peg or two." Colin was crying now. "I wanted to show you that you weren't better than me, not as good in some ways. My father's death was my fault, wasn't it? Because of me Bea felt pushed to get rid of anyone who knew about her past."

Edward didn't answer. He kicked at the shovel in its burlap wrapper that lay at his feet. Then he bent over and moved the coarse fabric aside. "We'd better get these to the police."

He picked up the handle and turned it. "Ernie Butters. His name's scratched on this. Where would Bea get Ernie's shovel?"

A steady trembling started in Sue-Ellen's legs. "You do know Ernie's missing?"

Edward frowned. "No, I don't think anyone mentioned it."

"He's been gone since...since the night you had that near miss in the belfry."

Edward stood, his knuckles whitening around the shovel handle. "My, God, we've got to go. Now. She's mad. I saw Ernie that night. In the churchyard."

"Yes," Sue-Ellen said. "He worked overtime to bury—"

"Mrs. Hawker. Close to the belfry. Right where he might have seen Bea climbing down the tree. She probably killed him. With this shovel, for all we know. One more piece of evidence to hide. And she'll keep on killing until she thinks there's no one left who can threaten her."

Chapter Twenty

"A man's body has been found under a couple of feet of dirt in a Mrs. Adeline Hawker's grave. The description matches this Ernie Butters." Inspector Carruthers, tall, stooped, sandy and weary-looking, dropped the parlor phone back into its cradle.

"Poor Connie," Sue-Ellen said.

Edward stood beside her in front of the fireplace. "Connie will be fine. I'll see to that. What about the call to Yorkshire, Inspector?"

Carruthers ran a hand over thinning hair. "Podsbury's a small town. Not far from what used to be your estate. It's late to get much out of anyone, but Bea Smallman did work in the county offices there, as did her father before her. Tomorrow we'll make more inquiries."

"And her father's name?" Edward asked. He held the back of Sue-Ellen's neck in tightening fingers.

"George Smallman."

Sue-Ellen let out the breath she'd been holding. "That's it then. We've got to find her. I can't understand why she didn't come back here." When they'd arrived at the Hall with Colin, hours ago now, there had been no sign of either Bea or her car.

Carruthers didn't respond. Official caution, Sue-Ellen supposed. He gathered his notebook and pen from beside the phone.

"Sir," Carruthers said to Edward, "I don't think Miss Smallman will come back as long as I'm here. Probably not with you and Mr. Bastible here, either."

"How will she know who . . . ?"

"I would suggest we assume that she's in a place where she can see who comes and goes here. I'd guess that she may already have approached, seen my car and left. It's also fair to assume she may have reached some emotional crisis and be unwilling to face me. In fact, it could be that what she's waiting for is a chance to be alone with Miss Hill."

"She won't get it." Edward clamped his arm around Sue-Ellen's shoulders. "Track her down."

"You'd think you'd have the woman by now," Colin said.

"We're doing our best, sir," Carruthers said, unmoved. "I suggest we leave. You and Mr. Ormsby-Jones and myself. We will, of course, keep the premises under surveillance. I've got a team out there now."

"No," Edward said. "Sue-Ellen doesn't stay here alone."

She stepped away from him and smiled what she hoped was a reassuring smile. "The inspector's right. I'll be fine. Please, let's try to get this over with."

When Edward didn't move, Colin got up and went to the door. "Sue-Ellen's right," he said. "Seeing the inspector's car must have frightened Bea off. Once it's gone and she sees us leaving, too, she'll decide she doesn't have anything to worry about, after all, and come home."

Edward argued on but eventually said, "Okay. But I'm going to be where I can watch that driveway, because I don't want Sue-Ellen alone in this house with that madwoman."

He kissed her before he left, and the warmth of his arms remained afterward, but not long enough. She wasn't as brave as her words.

A clock, a small gold-and-china masterpiece Bea had said was sixteenth-century French, ticked, softly, with the timbre of a glass wind chime.

Edward was outside, Colin, and a hoard of policemen. And so was Bea.

Sue-Ellen sat where she could watch the door.

The servants were all in their quarters, except Connie, who still stayed in a room near the aunts.

How long would it be?

At midnight, cold and cramped, she got up and went into the entry hall. The great house loomed around her, more silent than it had ever seemed.

With a heart that felt bent on escaping her chest, she climbed the stairs slowly and walked the corridors toward her room.

Bea's door stood open. Earlier they'd searched the house and gone into the housekeeper's rooms. There had been no evidence of her having returned.

Sue-Ellen went in and turned on the light. So Bea had somehow contrived to live in the suite that had belonged to Lady Esther, the woman supposedly responsible for Lettie's imprisonment. Why?

She wandered farther, to the gun cabinet Bea treasured. One new addition there, a photograph beside George Smallman's last acquisition. Sue-Ellen knelt to look at it—and gripped the ledge under the glass. The photo was of a young woman in riding habit; dark-haired, slender, smiling into the sun.

The cabinet wasn't locked. Sue-Ellen opened it and lifted the silver-framed picture. It was signed: *To My darling Edward, Love always, Lenore.*

Sue-Ellen's body became weak. She picked up the gun that supposedly went with the picture and turned it over and over.

The gun and photo must have some significance. Carrying them, she went across the corridor to her own sitting room . . . and immediately saw the note propped against the lamp. The folded sheet bore few words:

Sue-Ellen,
I regret my life and what I've done wrong. I'm going to die where my grandmother, Lettie Tinker, died. Forgive me.

Bea.

Bea knew she'd been found out. And she'd decided to kill herself in that dark cellar room. She'd been in the house all the time!

The tiny hairs on Sue-Ellen's spine prickled. Then she moved, ran, tearing to the stairs and leaping down two, three at a time, and dashing across the Great Hall to the tapestry. Bea was sick and needed help. There might still be time.

As she'd expected, the door was open, and the instant she stepped through her courage fled. The erratic beating of blood started in her ears. Moving as if through deep water, she went where she must, put foot in front of foot in the yellow gloom until she stood on the threshold of the room.

Bea lay on the floor facing the wall. Her knees were drawn up and a lax hand trailed behind her . . . on top of a crimson stain that spread in a puddle from the wrist over the rough stone floor.

"Bea?" Holding her stomach, Sue-Ellen crept closer. The figure didn't move. Hair, normally so carefully arranged, had fallen in matted clumps around the white still face.

It was over.

Sue-Ellen turned away. So much death. She wanted Edward.

"Sue-Ellen."

The voice ripped through her, searing nerve and muscle. "Bea?" She turned slowly, barely able to breathe.

Fluidly the woman rose, her torso held rigid, her arms at her sides. And just as gracefully she approached Sue-Ellen.

"You're hurt. You need a doctor." Sue-Ellen's voice was a pant. She mustn't panic. "Come with me and we'll go get help."

"That old fool Michael ruined everything. He wanted me to tell what I'd done. He figured out who I was from the name Smallman. No one was supposed to have known the name of the people they sent my father, George, to, but Michael did. The Reverend worried that people would find out that *his* father helped *them*—helped my grandmother

Lettie's killers." Bea's laugh echoed off the stone. "But then he got cold feet and said it wasn't right. I was supposed to confess. He said God would pardon me. That the world would pardon me because I was sick. Only I'm not sick. He was heavy. It was hard to get him off the ground. But I did it!"

If she ran, Bea would overtake her. "Of course you're not sick. Let me see your wrists."

Again the screeching laugh. "My wrists? The catsup, you mean? Did you really think I would die the way Edward's grandmother killed mine? Oh, Lettie, cut her own wrists, but Lady Esther gave her the weapon. Then the *lady's* maid took my father—Lettie's illegitimate son—to Yorkshire, and she told the Smallmans all about what happened in *this* cell. Then they told me the story, and I knew what I must do...."

A glint. Close to Bea's skirt had come a brilliant flash. Sue-Ellen stepped backward, but Bea was faster. Her arm shot out, and in her hand she held a knife—long, pointed, ground fine. And the hand that gripped the knife was between Sue-Ellen and the door.

Bea slid around until Sue-Ellen's retreat was blocked. "Over there." She waved toward a far corner.

Sue-Ellen didn't move, couldn't move.

"Go." The word was a scream underscored by a sharp jab of pain as the point of the knife met Sue-Ellen's neck. "Move, you fool, move. I'm going to kill you, you know. But you'll hope. Right until the last second you'll hope. They don't know I'm in here. I heard them say that. While they're out there waiting for me, I'm in here killing you."

Sue-Ellen walked backward. Wild things happened inside her: pulsings, shrinkings, tapping pain in her head. "Edward!"

"Edward." Bea mimicked. "I killed Michael. And I killed that fool Ernie Butters. He saw me climbing down the tree by the belfry. 'What you be up to, miss?' Fool. Before the night was out he'd have been at the Arms telling all about it. But I asked to see his shovel, and he gave it to me. I told him to look at an animal in the grave, and he looked. Then he was down there, and there was hardly any more earth to move.''

"Bea, please—"

"Sylvia wanted to be my friend, y'know. *My friend*. That little fool with her help. She was the one who wrote that note to get you down here. I was supposed to be so grateful I'd pay her. When I didn't, she blackmailed me! She had...she had nothing and I killed her!''

"She had the journal," Sue-Ellen said and shrank away, covering her mouth.

"How do you know?" Now Bea's voice was soft. "Did she come to you? Were you planning to try to get rid of me and have Sylvia help you?''

"No." Her back hit the wall, and her skull. She felt a trickle of warm blood on her neck where the knife had pressed.

"Do you want to know how you're going to die?''

"We can talk about this. I'm sure you can get help if—"

"Shut up! Did you think you could take my place? Lenore thought she could, and even that Jennifer. I drowned her, y'know. Verdict was accidental death. Cardiac arrest due to too much alcohol and the shock of the cold water. It was easy. Lenore wasn't so easy. I got the horse's neck with the pellet and he threw her. She fought and she was strong, but I was stronger and I wasn't stunned. A perfect killing!''

Sue-Ellen's brain felt too big. The edges were fuzzy. She blinked and widened her eyes, stood straighter. "They'll get you if you hurt me. I signaled when I found your note, and they're coming in now." Why hadn't she gone for help rather than coming here alone?

"This should have been my father George's house—my house! No other woman will take my place. I've promised my grandmother that. Lettie knows I'll keep Airstone for her.''

Bea raised the knife, her eyes fixed, and Sue-Ellen dropped and thrust herself headfirst into the woman's belly.

"I'll take that." Edward's voice, deadly low, barely punctured Sue-Ellen's desperation. She looked up—in time to see Bea's wrist squeezed in his fist while he twisted the knife loose.

Inspector Carruthers panted in behind him, with Colin amid a sea of navy-blue serge, silver buttons and helmets.

Sue-Ellen staggered to her feet, in time to walk into Edward's arms. "She admitted everything."

"We heard most of it." He shepherded her past the policemen who held Bea—silent, now, seeming to stare at nothing—upstairs and out into the night.

"Why did you come into the house?" Sue-Ellen asked.

Edward rubbed her back. "Fluke. I remembered that big tack room to the right in the yard. It isn't one of the ones to be used for a tearoom."

"I know which one you mean."

"The thing's big enough to put a car in—it's just that no one ever had. But I checked, and there was Bea's Hillman where she must have deliberately hidden it. We went into the house as quickly and quietly as we could, and when you weren't in the parlor I went to your room and found the note—the photo of Lenore and the pellet gun." He fell silent.

"I'm sorry." There was nothing more to say.

"So am I. I'll always feel responsible, but I can't change it. Smell this air, will you? Feel that marvelous English wet stuff."

"This country is wonderful," Sue-Ellen said. "I never thought I'd say I was crazy about rain, but I am." It fell, cool and clean, and she raised her face, closed her eyes.

Edward took her hand, opened it and kissed the palm. "This *is* a wonderful country . . . now."

She looked at him and he brought his face close.

"Now, it's all over, you mean?" she said. "All the horror?"

"That and other things. I'd like to tell you something."

"Okay." Not that she could stop him. He'd say as much as he wanted to say and it might not all be what she wanted to hear.

"Sue-Ellen, I love you. I'll always love you."

At the Trial of Beatrice Smallman

The following, to be read by the clerk to this court, will be admissible evidence in the trial of Beatrice Smallman for the crimes already placed before the members of the jury and this court.

The Misses Mabel and Alice Ormsby-Jones, being unfit to make the journey to this proceeding, wished to submit details at their disposal by letter. These details have been substantiated.

To Whom It May Concern:

First we must make clear that any attempt to sully the reputations of our parents, Sir Charles and Lady Esther Ormsby-Jones, would be unjust. At the time of the problem, our mother was not well and our father was beside himself with worry.

Lettie Tinker was seventeen when she came to us as a scullery maid. Good help was becoming hard to secure or she would never have been employed. She was voluptuous, a common girl, but bright, and she capitalized on Mama's indisposition by tempting Papa at a time when he wasn't himself.

The girl became pregnant but who knows for sure by whom. Mama told her, and she was quite correct, that if Lettie suggested our father was responsible for the child, then Lettie's reputation, not our father's, would be ruined.

Mama hid Lettie from all the eyes that would have condemned. The Tinkers would have shunned her. Only Mama was kind and shielded her from the world.

Papa arranged for Lettie and her baby to go to what was then our estate in Yorkshire. But Mama didn't feel Lettie recovered quickly enough, so the baby, George, was sent ahead with a trusted maid to a childless couple who were tenant farmers on the estate. Their name, as you now know, was Smallman.

Lettie didn't get well. She languished and, as Mama told us, began to lose her mind. The poor girl killed herself a month after childbirth, cut her wrists with a piece of broken china.

Here we must apologize for a deception. For the sake of Lettie's memory, the Tinkers were never told either about the baby or the way their daughter died. They accepted that she died of a raging fever. Dear Reverend Frederick Bastible, and our family doctor of the time, were very understanding. Without their cooperation Lettie's name would have been smeared forever.

Yours truly,
Mabel Ormsby-Jones
Alice Ormsby-Jones

On behalf of Beatrice Smallman, the following deposition is to be entered into evidence:

Lady Esther Ormsby-Jones's maid remained in communication with Will and Tess Smallman, my grandparents by adoption. My father, George, was explained to neighbors by the Smallmans as their orphaned nephew. Later they adopted him.

The Smallmans were good people. They loved my father, and through the guilt-money paid by Sir Charles Ormsby-Jones, were able to give him a comfortable life. My father married my mother when he was eighteen, and I was their only child. He did well in school and became a respected clerk in Podsbury's county council offices, where I eventually worked.

Throughout the years Will and Tess Smallman guarded the story Lady Esther's maid told them, the true story of my father's parentage and birth. It wasn't until after Will's death that Grandma Tess, as I called her, felt it was time for me to know all. My father would never listen to the story—no doubt the frustration was too much for him—so Grandma Tess told it to me. Tess has been dead for many years. My father and mother are also deceased.

I have read the letter written by Mabel and Alice Ormsby-Jones. What they do not write is that Esther Ormsby-Jones decided to keep Lettie captive at Airstone, not because she was sick, but because Lady Esther wanted to torture her more for trying to ease Sir Charles's misery. Sir Charles dared not go against his wife for fear of his own exposure and bringing disgrace upon the rest of his family. Only three days passed after the baby's birth before he was sent to Yorkshire and Lady Esther embarked on her plan to drive Lettie to her death. As already presented, this took a month.

The gold locket I know you have as evidence was given to Lettie by Sir Charles Ormsby-Jones. She sent it to Yorkshire with my father and it has been my talisman, the proof of my heritage.

I was twenty-five when I made my first visit to East Puddle. There I met the cook at Airstone and subsequently made the acquaintance of the family. Sir Charles and Lady Esther were long dead. Their daughters, Mabel and Alice, lived at the house and were expected to remain spinsters. A son, Arthur, had married and had his own young son, Edward.

When I was forty, nine years ago, Sir Arthur's wife, Lady Louise, died. I had been spending my yearly vacations in East Puddle, watching and waiting as was the right thing to do. I then took my rightful place in the house that should have been my father's home.

The two old women had to be dealt with, but that was easy. Once they knew who I was and that their precious reputations were at stake, they gladly stepped into the shadows where they belong. Michael Bastible was not as intelligent, but I did what had to be done there.

My grandmother Lettie was wronged, as was my father. Even now, I am wronged. I sought only to keep what was mine. Edward would have been allowed to remain at Airstone. What happened long ago wasn't his fault. But for him to put another woman in my place was out of the question, and I have acted accordingly over the years.

I regret nothing, apologize for nothing.

Respectfully,
Beatrice Smallman

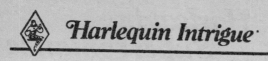

Harlequin Intrigue

COMING NEXT MONTH

#109 EXPIRATION DATE by Aimée Thurlo
Andy O'Reilly was dead . . . and no one knew why.
His partner, private investigator Melanie Cardenas,
was desperate for answers. His estranged son,
Patrick, was out for revenge. They had a common
quarry—Andy's killer—and working together was
their only hope for success, for justice, for love.

#110 STRANGER THAN FICTION by M. L. Gamble
Claire Kennedy couldn't believe her bestselling
writer's latest mystery was plagiarized. Was the
accusing Tony Nichols just masterminding a vicious
hoax? But then evidence disappeared, people
vanished—and a corpse appeared. Now more than
just Claire's reputation was threatened—her life was
at stake.

Harlequin Superromance

MORE THAN A FEELING

A powerful new Superromance from
ELAINE K. STIRLING

Andonis Sotera was the kind of man a woman might encounter in
a Moroccan café after dark, or on the deck of a luxury cruise ship.
In short, Andonis was the kind of man a woman like Karen Miller
would never meet.

And yet they fell in love. Suddenly the civil servant from a small Ca-
nadian city was swept into the drama of Andonis's life. For he was
not only her passionate, caring lover, he was *The Deliverer*, the one
man who could save a small Mediterranean country from the terror
of a ruthless dictator.

But Andonis needed Karen's help. And she was willing to risk her
life to save their love....

MORE THAN A FEELING...
Coming in February from Harlequin Superromance

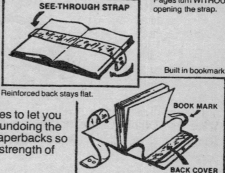

Harlequin Temptation dares to be different!

Once in a while, we Temptation editors spot a romance that's truly innovative. To make sure *you* don't miss any one of these outstanding selections, we'll mark them for you.

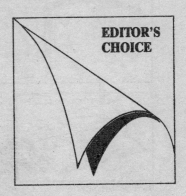

EDITOR'S CHOICE

When the "Editors' Choice" fold-back appears on a Temptation cover, you'll know we've found that extra-special page-turner!

THE *Temptation* EDITORS

Spot-1B

Fred Saberhagen

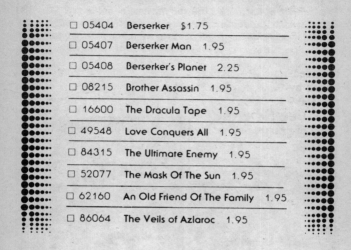
146